I0819668

Wolvers

ALSO BY TAYLOR BROWN

Rednecks

Wingwalkers

Pride of Eden

Gods of Howl Mountain

The River of Kings

Fallen Land

In the Season of Blood and Gold

Wolvers

TAYLOR BROWN

ST. MARTIN'S PRESS
NEW YORK

This is a work of fiction. All of the names, characters, organizations, places, and events portrayed in this work are either products of the author's imagination or are used fictitiously.

First published in the United States by St. Martin's Press, an imprint of St. Martin's Publishing Group

EU Representative: Macmillan Publishers Ireland Ltd, 1st Floor, The Liffey Trust Centre, 117–126 Sheriff Street Upper, Dublin 1, D01 YC43

www.stmartins.com

Designed by Omar Chapa

Map by Taylor Brown

The Library of Congress Cataloging-in-Publication Data
is available upon request.

ISBN 978-1-250-40137-3 (hardcover)
ISBN 978-1-250-40138-0 (ebook)

First Edition: 2026

10 9 8 7 6 5 4 3 2 1

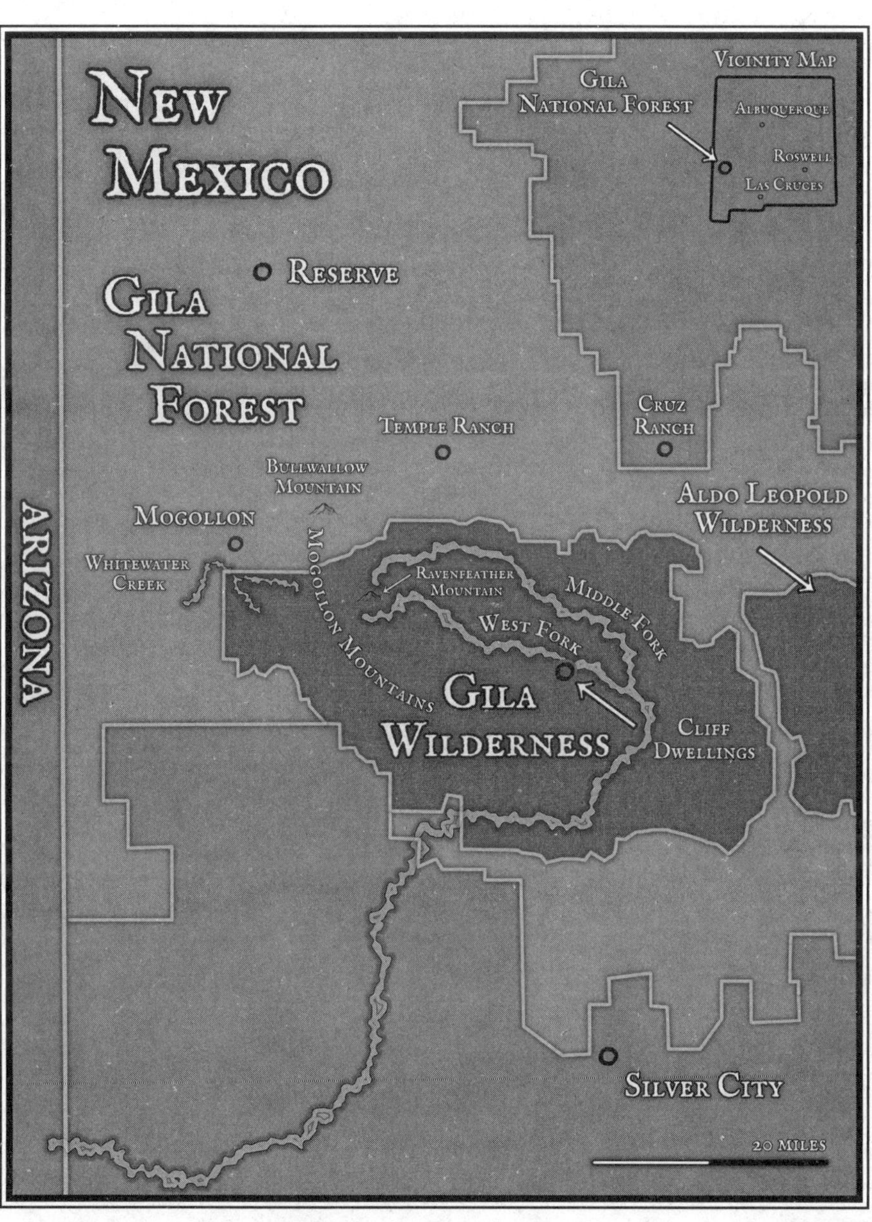
New Mexico
Gila National Forest
Vicinity Map
Gila National Forest
Albuquerque
Roswell
Las Cruces
Reserve
Temple Ranch
Cruz Ranch
Bullwallow Mountain
Mogollon
Aldo Leopold Wilderness
Whitewater Creek
Ravenfeather Mountain
Middle Fork
West Fork
Mogollon Mountains
Arizona
Gila Wilderness
Cliff Dwellings
Silver City
20 miles

What but the wolf's tooth whittled so fine
The fleet limbs of the antelope?

—ROBINSON JEFFERS, "THE BLOODY SIRE"

Wolver

Earliest known use: late 1500s

1: One who behaves like a wolf

2: One who searches or hunts for wolves

Preface

Wolves were once the most widely distributed land mammal on earth. When Europeans began arriving in North America in the 1500s, around two million wolves existed on this continent.

Due to campaigns of eradication, both public and private, the wolf was driven to the brink of extinction in the contiguous United States by the early 1900s.

In the 1970s, the gray wolf was placed under the protection of the Endangered Species Act. In order to restore the species to fragments of their former range, small packs of gray wolves have been reintroduced into areas such as Yellowstone National Park, rural Idaho, remote sections of Arizona and New Mexico (as the Mexican gray wolf subspecies), and the Western Slope of Colorado.

Today, the gray wolf remains endangered in most of the United States.

Prologue

Fields black beneath a starless sky. A land feathered riders once rode on painted horses, following inland seas of bison as the bones of the mastodon and dire wolf slept beneath their hooves.

A van takes the next highway exit. A snub-nosed machine with meaty tires and a throaty motor. The small tin hat of a stovepipe protrudes from the roof. The driver pulls up to the outermost pump and steps out.

A small man but hard-made. A face like a flint hatchet, chipped and sharp. Words visible on his skin, tattooed beneath a tattered tank top. They scroll down his arms and across his back, racing like animals across his skin. A line is draped across his chest like a necklace:

THOU WOLF IN SHEEP'S ARRAY

He walks into the truck stop, limping slightly, weaving his way through the aisles to the restroom. A television hangs over the long metal trough of the urinals, tuned to the news. A tickertape of headlines runs along the bottom of the screen, announcing wildfires and floods and crop losses. Meanwhile, a reporter is speaking from the Apache National Forest in New Mexico, where the body of a wolf from a federal reintroduction program has been recovered.

"This is the second Mexican wolf from the program found dead in recent months. Illegally shot. Officials say the animals' deaths could be linked, but they're short on leads. Many ranchers, outfitters, and militia groups have remained vehemently opposed to the reintroduction program since its inception."

Two men are standing down the trough. Big men with camouflage ballcaps and rubber boots. Perhaps father and son. The older one shakes his head, one fist perched on his hip. "Can you imagine it, being a cattleman and the feds decide to reintroduce wolves into your backyard? Wolves? Animals born to take down heifers. What a country we live in."

The younger one shakes his head. "Time was, government couldn't dictate what we allowed on our own property. Country's gone to hell in a handbasket. Time somebody did something about it."

The older man growls. "Amen to that. High time to free the West."

"Then we'll open up hunting season on the beasts."

The older man chuckles. "Smoke a pack a day."

The tattooed driver flushes his side of the trough. "You shouldn't call it hunting."

The older man yanks up his fly and looks over. "Excuse me?"

"You shouldn't call it hunting."

"Yeah, and why the hell not?"

"Nobody eats wolves."

The older man's face reddens. "You got a smart mouth."

The driver takes a step back and the two bigger men can't help themselves—they advance on him, their ire fueling them. They close the distance quickly, driving him toward the door. They expect the smaller man to run.

He stops.

His hands hang low at his sides. The knuckles monstrous and outsize, hardened against fence posts and cell walls until calcified. Bone-bossed like knuckledusters that never come off. They crackle into fists.

The older man lifts his shirttail, revealing a pistol clipped inside his waistband. "The hell you gonna do with them sluggers, Wolf Boy?"

The driver grins, his top teeth perched on his bottom lip. His canines long and sharp, as if honed. "You boys don't know the 21-Foot Rule."

Their eyes dart to the distance between them. Ten feet. Surprise in their faces, as if they've been caught in a trap.

"The what?"

The driver walks out of the truck stop. Hands in his pockets, scrubbed clean, a black watch cap pulled low over his brow. The men will wake and slobber and moan. He'll change his license plate at the next town, again.

He is merging back onto the highway when the black sky blazes white. A crooked fork of lightning splinters the horizon, a wild fortress of thunderclouds thrust pale from the night. He flicks his eyes to the rearview, making sure he hasn't been followed. Then he presses on toward the storm, heading for the vast badlands of old Apacheria, where he's been called.

BOOK I

CHAPTER 1

One-Eleven and her mate came trotting down a narrow chute in the canyon dusk. They moved in echelon, breath pouring from their open jaws. A fine flurry of ash was falling around them, dusting their backs and the craggy spires of moonstone along the canyon's rim. A dark wind that blew off the old burn scar on the western slope of the mountain.

The pair were following a black jag of creek, the boulders and scree polished smooth from spring freshets that roared through the steep walls of the canyon like liquid jade, swelled with storms and snowmelt. Over eons, the river had carved down through caves in the earth, leaving hollows high in the canyon walls. Here lay the ruins of ancient cliff dwellers, abandoned even in the days of the Apache.

Below, the wolves moved light-footed through the canyon, heads low, shoulder blades slicing over springy legs. With their slender chests and long limbs, the wolves each cut a narrow trail, left and right paws striking nearly in line with one another. The slightest weave when tracked.

The she-wolf led. One-Eleven, queen of the Gila. A gray-furred loba with a pale ruff around her neck, almost a mane, and patches of buff and rust in her coat. She looked made of the very stuff of the land—a creature of stone and dust and clay. A sliver chipped from the canyon, made animate, loosed to keep the deer in trim.

Her mate was older, darker, moving like a shadow at her shoulder. Graynose, an old battler. A heavy leather radio collar encircled his throat. A string of four wolves followed close behind the alpha pair. An oversize yearling, also collared, and three smaller pups.

One-Eleven had whelped in the spring, as she did every year, in a den on the mountain. Three tiny ones, blind at first, already hungry. Graynose brought food to the den for them, often the regurgitated meat of a kill too big to carry. Deer, elk, antelope, javelina. The pups would whine and dance and lick his mouth, begging to eat. His snout was frosty, his teeth blunted against old foes, but he had wise blood, a game heart.

Over the summer, they moved the pups to high meadows to chase mice and pounce on grasshoppers, wrestle their siblings and stalk their parents—rudiments of the hunt. Then they began bringing them along to their kills. The pups gnawed on the overlarge bones, their milk teeth threaded with blood.

Now it was fall. Rifle shots caromed through the canyons and mesas, streaking through thick stands of ponderosa and Chihuahuan pine, down slopes of pinyon and juniper, across the rubble-strewn moonscapes of the tablelands. Elk and mule deer and antelope staggered gutshot through the trees and boulders, ripe for the taking.

Now the pups' real teeth had come in, and the pack was on the hunt.

CHAPTER 2

The wolver lowered his binoculars and made a note on his map. He wore a camouflage suit in a high desert pattern, and he'd positioned himself against the descending sun so the lenses of the field glasses wouldn't catch the light. Beside him lay a folding topographic map and a small tablet showing the same section of wilderness in digital format, the terrain contours overlaid with labels and numbers denoting the past locations of collared animals. Next to that, a radio receiver tuned to the wolves' VHF frequency, an H-bar antenna folded beside it.

He was tracking Mexican wolves—*lobos*—the rarest of all gray wolves. A hunter had to know his quarry, and he'd made himself a student of the species. *Canis lupus baileyi*, native to Northern Mexico and the American Southwest. This was the original American wolf, some said, descended from the first wolves to cross the land bridge from Siberia during the last ice age. Lobos had roved the lands of Aridoamerica in small bands, hunting elk and deer and antelope, rabbit and javelina and fox, pouring into the dreams of early civilizations. The Mayans wrote of the lightning-dog, which leapt from the bellies of thunderclouds, and the Aztec god of death and lightning, Xolotl, bore the head of a lobo, guarding the sun as it traversed the underworld each night. Apache war parties, before battle, would sing the wolf song.

At the turn of the twenty-first century, the federal government began reintroducing wolves into the wild, releasing them into rugged, isolated areas of Arizona and New Mexico. Since then, the species had lived on the knife's edge of survival, rarely numbering more than two hundred animals.

Too many, thought some.

The wolver shifted on the rocks to get comfortable. Below him the wolves lowered their heads to the creek, six in a line, lapping their reflections from the water. The she-wolf kept her yellow eyes on an invisible boundary around the pack, a fluid perimeter that expanded and contracted with season, strength, hunger.

They were deep in the Gila Wilderness—the world's oldest designated wilderness area—where nothing mechanized was allowed. No trucks or ATVs, not even bicycles. An isolated warren, not far from the headwaters of the Gila River, birthplace of Geronimo. The wolver had tracked the wolves here using physical sign, telemetry data, and the radio receiver, whose tone rose in the wolves' proximity.

Now he was breathing hard, his heart slapping the earth beneath him. He set down the binoculars and reached for the long rifle lying beside him on its bipod. The weapon was tiger-striped coyote-tan and sage, chambered in .308 Winchester and tipped with the bulbous muzzle of a suppressor. The oversize lens of a low-light scope concentrated the dusk, making the wolves glow slightly before him, like creatures beneath an approaching storm.

The barrel rocked with the pump of his blood. He willed his heart to slow, picturing a cold stone in the hollow of his chest, a hundred years untouched. A pebble. A speck. He floated the crosshairs over the shoulder of the alpha female. One-Eleven, the heart of the Dark Canyon pack. A storied she-wolf who'd never been collared. She seemed to vanish each time the helicopters of the wolf recovery program appeared, their door-gunners armed with tranquilizer darts, and she'd birthed the alphas of two new packs, as if on a mission to revive her species. People called her One-Eleven after the F-111, the low-level supersonic bomber once stationed out of Clovis, New Mexico, seen streaking across the deserts and badlands of the state.

She'd become an internet sensation after a line of motorists, who happened to be stopped for roadwork, filmed her chase down an elk off the side of the highway. A wolf streaking so fast across the earth she appeared to be flying, ears folded back, legs invisible with speed, like a swept-wing attack aircraft booming across the dusty plain. She struck the elk so hard it lost its footing—an animal ten times her size, brought down in a tumult of dust and hooves.

The footage made her a darling of wolf-lovers and environmentalists—and public enemy number one for many sportsmen and ranchers, who blamed fewer elk and cattle losses on the presence of wolves and the government that protected them. A firestorm erupted on social media as people exalted or condemned the animal. Surely the she-wolf had no idea she'd become a flashpoint for a culture as riven as the land itself.

The wolver set his finger on the trigger.

He had his own reasons for wanting her dead.

The crosshairs stilled, alighting just behind the pale ruff of her neck. He could feel his pulse in the pink tip of his finger. The trigger's draw was three pounds. He reached the bottom of his breath and held still, ready to squeeze. The she-wolf looked right in his direction, fast, her yellow eyes sparking gold in his scope, ears erect. She'd heard something, a crackle in the brush behind him—something he'd disregarded, but she hadn't.

He turned to look over his shoulder and saw nothing out of place, a terrain of sagebrush and pinyon pine moving ever so slightly in the breeze. A white-nosed coati, perhaps, or a rock squirrel or jackrabbit passing on its errand, darting through the grama grass. No threat.

When he returned to the scope, the wolves were on the move, fleeing up the creek at speed, their haunches whisking over the rough ground.

He let off a shot—a single hard chuff from the long canister of the suppressor. The round snapped through the canyon, kicking up dust in the wake of the wolves. He cursed under his breath. That shot, sure as any word, would tell One-Eleven that she and her pack were being hunted. She would be that much harder to take, to kill.

The wolver lifted himself from his prone position and began to break down the rifle for the hike out. A dark angel of sweat lay in the dust beneath his boots.

CHAPTER 3

One-Eleven led her pack hard-pawed through the canyons, moving at speed, gaining distance from the crash of shots. The Dark Canyons were strung behind her in a line, breathing hard through their mouths. She kept to cover when she could, crossing and recrossing streams, leaving no scent marks or scratches as she normally would.

Men were most common this time of year, when the scent of elk urine and gun oil and horses drifted through the forest. Boots crackling through dry brush, the clop of iron-shod hooves. At night, cackles and belches from the camps, wheezes and snores. At morning, rifles.

One-Eleven knew to remain invisible, unseen. For men had powerful magic. They could kill from a distance, dropping prey with a single thundercrack, and they collared the predators of the land. The wolf, the bear, the lion. Sweeping down in a cyclone of thunder and shrieking grit, sending the dart that slowed an animal's blood to a crawl, turning their mind dreamy. Tongues falling out, legs buckling. Eyes open, seeing everything, yet unable to move.

One-Eleven was just a yearling when she'd first heard the sound of a Thunderbird, that rhythmic terror. Her mother, a rare white loba, had steered the pack for a narrow canyon in the tablelands. They were strung out in a line, bodies elongating, stretching for speed, and One-Eleven could feel the violence crazing down upon them, the wind and grit whipping her flanks. A fury of dust in which she watched the pale shape of her mother fall before her, tumbling right over the edge of the ravine.

They found her at the bottom, a feathered thorn in her side. Blood everywhere on the rocks. When green-clad men appeared on the canyon rim, the young wolves fled.

For days they howled.

One-Eleven had never been collared. She knew to run hard and fast as soon as she sensed the first pulse of the Thunderbird in the earth or atmosphere, to descend into the narrow canyons and ravines where the cyclone couldn't reach.

Now she looked over her shoulder. She was pulling the pack hard, at the ragged edge of what they could sustain, making distance from the shots. For days, she'd sensed a new enemy in their territory. The shot made it clear, the stones exploding at their flanks. She looked at Graynose. The old battle-wolf, black and silver. His bone-house broad and irregular, once-broken ribs and limbs healed knobby and untrue. His muzzle and coat blazed gray, streaked with age. An old nomad, ear-nocked and scarred.

One-Eleven first encountered him two springs ago. She was a lone mother then, her new litter rambling around her legs. In the days before she'd whelped, her first mate had gone looking for food in the ranchlands beyond their territory and never returned. Killed. One-Eleven had heard the shot carry across the land, felt it in her bones and meat. She'd given birth that night, alone. Four pups in that year's litter, blind and pink, mewling for milk. When she ran dry, she rose bloodied and sore to hunt. Without meat, her body would not make milk. Twice she returned to find a pup dead or disappeared. Two of four survived.

The pups were just out of the den when Graynose appeared. One-Eleven saw a lone wolf trotting along the canyon rim, an outsider. Her hackles rose at his presence, stiff as quills. She tasted the length and sharpness of her teeth. When he emerged at the edge of the meadow, she charged. The lone wolf stood unmoved. They tied shoulders and One-Eleven pinned him to the ground. The old battler's eyes rounded up at her, as if seeing a creature new to him. He stuck his tongue out and pawed at her chest. She sprang away from him and they leapt and sparred around the meadow, clicking their teeth.

They were never apart after that. Graynose no longer wandered.

Now the old wolf had his head low and ears back, his hackles fanned flat from his radio collar. He held his tail stiff from his flanks. Spooked. Never had a man surprised them inside their own territory. They had to be vigilant now.

They were being hunted.

CHAPTER 4

The wolver lived out of his pickup truck—a 4x4 camper outfitted like a covered wagon. Tube bumpers and oversize tires and winches at both ends, axes and shovels and fuel cans mounted along the sides. The camper shell windows had glowed in national parks and campgrounds and the dark corners of parking lots around the Southwest for the last two years—ever since his family had lost their ranch.

His name was Trace. For the past several weeks, he'd spent his nights deep in the Apache and Gila National Forests, tracking wolves. He'd taken two members of the Hoodoo pack on the Arizona side—known stock-killers—then moved on before the rangers could catch his trail. As long as he kept switching which pack he targeted, it would be nearly impossible for them to catch him. After all, the lobos covered an area of more than three million acres.

To avoid attention, he never stayed in the same place more than three nights in a row. At campgrounds he kept his fires small and music low, going to bed before anyone could stumble over from one of the surrounding campsites, friendly with booze. Once a week, he went out for a drink and a meal.

Tonight he drove down to Silver City, the nearest town. For generations, it had been the site of an Apache camping ground. Then vast deposits of copper and silver were discovered and it became a boomtown overnight. Miners, prospectors, speculators, outlaws. Billy the Kid had been arrested here for the first time, at fifteen years old, and made his first escape here, too, climbing out through the prison chimney. Butch Cassidy and his Wild Bunch had worked a ranch outside town between robberies, frequenting the saloons and brothels. The surrounding copper mines were still a main part of the economy.

The moon was up when Trace pulled into the gravel lot of the Dead Dove Saloon, a honky-tonk on the outskirts of town. Neon beer signs sizzled behind the barred windows of the concrete block structure and the parking lot was full, mostly with American-made trucks and compacts. A layer of silver dust coated their dents and scratches, run-ins with guardrails and mailboxes and ex's keys. Trace stepped out, stretched, and headed toward the door, nodding to a giant bearded bouncer in a black leather biker's vest that read FLACO—"thin one."

Inside, the heads of trophy animals jutted from the wood-paneled walls, elk and mule deer and tusked javelina watching over the pool tables and mismatched furniture—even an exotic oryx killed on the White Sands Missile Range. The armchairs were dusty wingbacks from the houses of dead grandmothers, bought secondhand from thrift stores because they were too ungainly for use in brawls. He took a barstool bolted to the floor and the bartender wiped his spot clean with a dirty rag.

"Hungry or just thirsty?"

"Both."

"Need a menu?"

"No, ma'am. A shot of mezcal, a Coors, and a cheeseburger, please."

"Onions and mayo on your burger?"

"Onions, no mayo."

"You got it."

Trace shot the mezcal and chased it with a cold slug of beer. From the pool tables, the hard crack of a break. He looked over his shoulder. Imogen Cruz stood up from the rail, cue in hand, eyeing the stripes and solids still rolling around the green felt. She circled the table in her black gambler hat, the tattoo of a cow skull adorning one muscled shoulder. Trace's heart turned in his chest and he looked away before she could see him.

They'd gone to kindergarten, grade school, and junior high together, where Imogen went steady with his best friend, Garrison. The pair seemed meant for each other, bold and dark and magnetic, experimenting with drugs and sex before Trace had hardly even kissed a girl. Then Garrison started getting into harder drugs, and trouble with the law, and soon Imogen's parents were looking for any excuse to get her away from the wayward son of a drunk ex–rodeo star. They sent her away for high school, a boarding school in California somewhere. Trace heard she'd lived in all kinds of places after that—Buenos Aires, New York, Los Angeles—pursuing an art career before coming home to help with the ranch when her father got sick.

After the old man passed, she'd stayed on to run the Cruz Ranch—one of the oldest in the state. Trace saw her every once in a while at the feedstore or auction house or here at the Dead Dove, where she drank seltzer water and shot pool and men followed her around like begging dogs. She'd been featured in magazines like *Western Horseman* and *Cowboys & Indians*, pissing off some of the old cowhands who just couldn't imagine a woman who looked like she did running a ranch.

Two old hands were sitting just down the bar from him, a pair of drunks who'd worked half the ranches in this part of the state and been fired from just as many. One of them hugged his drink in the crook of his arm, forty years of Marlboros in his voice: "Old Man Cruz'd shit a brick he knew his daughter was using solar feeders or raising *predator-friendly* beef."

The other hand shook his head as if he'd tasted something awful. "Or drinking sparkle water in a honky-tonk, Jesus God."

"If she don't come here to drink, what's she come for?"

"Not for us, amigo. I hear she screws all her hands."

"And you ain't hired on yet?"

Trace white-knuckled his beer. He imagined lifting the hat off the nearest cowboy and bringing down the heel of the bottle on the man's head, then kicking the stool out from under the second one. He was seeing it all in his mind, planning it. What he would do to them, as if it would somehow right his world.

The cheeseburger saved them. It arrived in a red plastic basket with wax paper, the brown skin of the sesame bun gleaming. Trace hadn't had a burger in weeks. He'd been eating from cans and boxes and pouches on the trail. *Goo food*, his grandfather used to call it. Soon he had the burger held both-handed before him, a bite already gone. He leaned back and chewed and squinted at the mounted head of a Mexican wolf over the bar. The lobo was snarling, ears back and fangs bared.

A man took the barstool beside him and ordered a shot of mezcal. He had a jagged nose and long dark beard, stiff and straight as a wire brush. Dark skullcap and dusty jumpsuit. A miner, most likely. He shot the mezcal and set the glass back on the bar, then looked up at the loba on the wall. "The rest of her gets through that wall, reckon we're fucked."

Trace thumbed a crumb from his lip. "Lobos don't attack people, actually. Real rare. Now if we was a herd of cattle, different story. We'd have a slaughterhouse up in here."

The miner kept eyeing the wolf on the wall. He held his hands in his lap, under the bar. "They kill a lot of cattle these days?"

Trace snorted. "They shouldn't kill a damn one. The wolf was all but eradicated in these parts till the government brought them back. *Reintroduced* them as they call it. Since then it's been a fight."

"I heard numbers been on the rise lately."

Trace nodded. "Nearing three hundred now. Our ancestors fought to kill off the last lobos in this country so the livestock would be safe. Now it's on again. There's ranchers up here patrol their grazing grounds with ATVs and rifles."

"They're allowed to shoot them?"

"If the wolves are attacking livestock, they can. Otherwise you could be looking at a fine of up to $50,000 and one year in prison. Per animal. Kill a pack and they could put you down a hole you won't soon see the outside of."

The bearded man nodded, lifting one hand to twist his shot glass on the bar top. His knuckles looked oversize, perhaps swollen. A tattoo ran across the finger joints that read: SONG. Trace couldn't see the four-letter word on his other hand.

The man looked at him. Eyes close-set, forward and alert, like those of a predator.

"Still, it's a wonder the ranchers or somebody don't do something."

Trace clenched his teeth. "Ain't it?"

CHAPTER 5

They'd approached him outside the Dead Dove several months ago. Three upright men in silverbelly Stetsons and fancy boots, carrying custom 1911 automatics on the outside of their belts. Like lawmen but not. No government employee could afford those hats, boots, and guns.

The lead man tapped his wedding ring on the butt of his pistol. "You Trace Temple?"

"Last time I checked."

"Your grandfather was 'Old' Jeremiah Temple?"

Trace looked from one man to the next. "Still is, I reckon, even dead."

The lead man nodded and squinted across the moon-dusted cars in the lot. A log truck rattled past. He thumbed up his silverbelly hat—a color named for the pale underbellies of furbearers skinned for felt. Beaver, hare, chinchilla. These looked like true silverbellies, undyed to create the silvery warm color. The man looked back at Trace.

"How'd you like a job would make Old Temple proud?"

Trace had been working at the open-pit copper mine outside town since they lost the ranch. The Chino mine, one of the largest in the world. So big astronauts could see it from space. Terraced walls hewn more than a thousand feet down into the earth, three-hundred-ton haul trucks winding their way to the surface day and night, small as Tonka toys against the terrain. Trace was employed as a mine production technician, a fancy name for an entry-level miner.

"You don't think he'd be proud of me working the Chino?"

The man cocked his head. "You know when that mine opened, back around 1800, the Spaniard that owned it was employing convict labor, housing them in a presidio he'd built to protect against the Apache. Sending mule-trains down to Chihuahua loaded with copper. Well, what the Apache did was they killed all the trappers in the whole area, cutting the fort off from resupply. So the miners and everybody fled south, some three or four hundred of them, most on foot. Overland, 150 miles through Apache country. And hardly any of them survived."

The man tapped his wedding ring on the butt of his pistol again. A fancy piece, like strapping several thousand dollars to your belt. The plated leather of his boots suggested something exotic, perhaps illegal. Pangolin, arapaima, even sea turtle.

"Your granddaddy was one of the most respected ranchers in this state. My own father sent me to work for him the summer I turned fifteen, just to learn. No, I don't think Old Temple would be proud of his only grandson, one of the most gifted hunters and trackers in the Gila, working the same goddamn mine as a bunch of scalped Mexican convicts two hundred years ago. I think he'd hope his bloodline had risen a little since that time, cut themselves off a better piece of the world."

Trace cocked his head. He didn't much like these men with their fancy double-stack 1911s and expensive boots and matching Stetsons. *The men in the pale hats.* He'd heard whispers of them. Militia, maybe, but well funded, highly organized. Or some secret landowners' coalition. Regular John Waynes, dangerous as a cowboy cartel. The kind that once you got in with them, you might not get out. But he was living hand-to-mouth at the mine, sleeping in the back corners of Walmart parking lots in his truck. Then there was his mama, who'd relapsed after his old man died. Treatment didn't come cheap.

"What's the job?" he asked.

Dawn found him back in the canyons. The high forest swayed in cold slumber around him, heavy spears of ponderosa pine groaning and shifting in the dull blue glow. Trace held the H-bar antenna aloft, his earpiece emitting a high tone, telling him the wolves were close. He'd cut the track of a gutshot bull elk, the dark blood stamped with each print of the large hind hooves. The sloppy work of some fly-in hunter with more rifle than skill. If the Dark Canyons were in the vicinity, they'd soon home in on the wounded animal.

When the men in the pale hats hired him on for this job, poison was brought up. After all, it had been a primary weapon against the wolf during the eradication campaigns of the early 1900s, when thousands of the animals were shot, trapped, or poisoned, the pups dug out from their dens. Ranchers and drovers and government wolvers would lace animal carcasses with strychnine, cyanide, or compound 1080. Whole wolfpacks could be found scattered around a poisoned elk or mule deer like victims of some ritual sacrifice. Their slaver would dry in the grass, still poisonous, killing wild horses and antelope and elk for years to come.

A hunter, on the other hand, had to find and pursue the wolf through its own rugged country, learning its habits and mind. A hunter had to think like the wolf, placing himself in close company to the animal, achieving a clear line of sight on one of the most cunning predators ever to roam the earth. One of the rarest. Then he had to kill it.

The government and the cattlemen of the previous century had been trying to kill a whole nation of wolves, ridding the West of a menace not unlike the Apache or Comanche in their eyes. A force of depredation, barbarity. Wildness. A primeval force, which kept the frontier uncivilized. The West was a new addition to their realm, and they wanted it clean, free of predators.

Trace faced a different mission from the trappers of a century ago. His mission was not just to kill, but to prove a point. The men in the pale hats wanted to show that man was still superior, and the ways of nature had played their part in the West. The time of the wolf was gone. Man reigned out here, and the wolf got what it deserved.

The tone of the radio transmitter warbled, but Trace paid no mind. The terrain here jounced the signal; the radio waves ricocheted through the canyons. So he kept to the trail the wolves would use: the blood and sign of the wounded elk, which showed the animal moving through the forest in short, straight bursts. It would bound through the trees, threading their trunks and leaving high brushes of blood on the branches and understory. Then pause to gather strength, adjust direction, and start again. He wondered at the fear and agony of the wounded animal. A thing driven by the purest of sensations, burning up with them, like a creature set on fire.

Soon the prints of the Dark Canyon pack came crashing down from a higher ridge, cascading down a wash, and he watched as their tracks wove around those of the elk, flowing and mingling, plaiting the animal's wake. And so the valley became darker still for the bull. They'd caught his scent and attached themselves to him, their minds locked like iron traps on his long limbs and wide antlers, seeking the muscle and blood beneath his hide. The stories of these creatures had intertwined.

Trace was watching it happen, a weaving of fates.

Without stopping, he folded down the radio antenna, stowed it in the side netting of his pack, and unclipped his rifle from the opposite side, lifting the sling over his neck and left arm, cinching the weapon high to his chest. He sped up slightly, moving just below a jog. The trails of the wolves threaded through the high forest, the alphas sidetracking here and there for a broader scent picture and then striking back to the elk's track, their prints crisscrossing, coiling and uncoiling. By the heavy gum of the elk's spent blood, he was some twenty to thirty minutes behind the animal, the wolves maybe half that. Soon they would all converge.

The dawn sun came lancing down from the eastern ridges, filtering into the treetops, a golden riot over the cold twilight of the forest floor. The tracks veered downhill, the wounded bull trading altitude for speed and darkness, trying to keep ahead of his pursuers. The trail was hot. Sign everywhere, blood and prints and mangled understory. He could almost sense the body heat of the animals that had passed just before him. Soon the trail broke into the canyon bottom, a black raft of creek crawling through the stones.

Not long now.

He was breathing hard but steady, picking his way quickly along the creek, the long rifle clutched across his chest. He thought of his grandfather, Old Temple, who'd first taught him fieldcraft and the language of animal sign. The man had been a Marine Corps rifleman in the Pacific, a Depression-raised cowhand who'd fought soldiers descended from the samurai. He'd come home and never spoken again of that experience, too busy running a ranch that would grow to ten thousand acres over his lifetime, his vast herds of cattle grazing on lands leased from the federal government for ten years at a time.

The old man had been in his last days when the wolves returned. A shriveled cowboy sucking oxygen through tubes in his nose, a cattleman's hat slouched like an umbrella over his shrunken shoulders. To him, it was like the government had parachuted Krauts or communists or terrorists into his backyard. He was pulled out of a decade-long twilight, roused upright in his armchair, his heart burning with outrage, even hate.

Trace always knew him to be a kind man, prone to giving away all his cash to homeless vets on his way to the bar. But wolves. It was like someone had dropped an incendiary grenade in his chest. He nearly foamed. *Wolves.* The same government that paid to eradicate the beasts now wanted them back. The fickleness of men. The viciousness of wolves. Old Temple had grown up on the stories of the great cow-killers, true outlaws of the American West, telling his grandboy of terrors like the Custer Wolf.

"Now there was a butcher beast. Some said he wasn't even pure wolf but a monstrosity of nature, a gray wolf crossbred with a mountain lion." The old man clucked. "Unlikely. But we do know he had a pair of coyotes followed him like sentinels, feeding off his kills and alerting him to danger on his flanks. For nine years, he eluded everybody from local ranchers to federal trappers to professional bounty hunters and sportsmen, taking down some $25,000 in livestock—cattle, calves, horses, sheep, you name it."

As a boy, Trace would imagine the monstrous wolf ranging the Black Hills and Badlands of South Dakota, his coyote guards trailing him past craggy pinnacles of stone, making for pasturelands rich with beef.

His grandfather nodded. "Some said his mate and pups had been killed for their bounties and that's what drove him. Revenge. Others said it was the lack of buffalo, he had to turn to cattle to eat. One old boy told me the Custer Wolf was possessed by the spirit of an Indian brave that died at Little Bighorn, pledging everlasting war on old Long Hair and his paleface kin.

"In the end, the government had to send in their top wolver, told him not to come home till the wolf was dead. Now this man was a legend, had over a thousand dead wolves to his name. What he did was he shot them coyote sentinels first. Rocked the old wolf's world, that did. Here was an animal known to see traps like they glowed in the ground. People thought he'd never be caught, that he was God-cursed or Devil-blessed. But soon enough, a tuft of his hair turned up in one of that government man's traps. Then a second one got his arm. The wolf dragged off the trap and broke it against a tree but it was too late. He was mangled, done. The wolver tracked three miles of fresh blood and shot him. Said he expected his rifle to misfire, but it didn't. They say the Custer Wolf was so old his pelt had turned fully white, like the pure ghost of himself."

Old Temple nodded in his armchair, his voice scraping like snakeskin in his throat. "Then you had Old Three Toes of Harding County, most destructive single animal on record anywhere. Lost a toe to a trap as a pup and got hell-bent for revenge. Took down more than fifty thou worth of livestock in the 1920s—hell of a lot of money back then. They sent a whole army after him, 150 men. Guns, traps, poison, hounds. That three-toed wolf used to run circles the size of counties while the trackers switched out mounts again and again, till the hounds laid down to rest and there weren't no horses left to saddle. They say Old Three Toes was more than six feet long and twenty years old when a state trapper caught him in 1925. Man tried to deliver him alive, but Old Three Toes, unwounded, managed to die in the back seat of the man's car. His final escape."

Old Temple lifted his ten-gallon hat, scratched his forehead with his thumb. He was bald, his skull evident beneath the translucent pale of his scalp. "Some say Old Three Toes was demonically possessed, like them swine from the Holy Bible. Once killed him sixty-six sheep in two nights, like he was doing it just for fun." The old man shook his head and replaced his hat. "But it wasn't that. It's that he was a wolf, plain and simple. A killer. It's what they are."

Trace froze midstep, the black creek hissing beside his boots. He'd heard something. His scalp prickled, an eerie sensation at the back of his neck. A sense he was being watched, followed. He turned slowly in place. Nothing. The stone-strewn creek, the tree line, the dawn surging down into the canyon, alighting on yellow-flowered rabbitbrush and alligator juniper. He was tempted to backtrack and cut for sign of pursuers, but he'd lose the Dark Canyons that way. His trigger finger tapped the receiver twice. Then he turned and carried on, following the trail of the bull down the creek.

Spent blood everywhere, haunted with wolf prints. He slowed as the canyon turned east into the rising sun. He was downwind, which made it more difficult for the wolves to scent him, but they had the sun to their advantage. He moved away from the creek, into the cover of the trees, threading quietly through the willows until he reached the other side of the bend. He lowered himself on one knee to surveil the next stretch of the canyon.

There. The Dark Canyon pack. Silhouettes scrawled against the rising sun, lashing themselves around the shoulders of the standing bull. Above them all, a crown of antlers thorny and huge as a pair of bentwood rocking chairs. Trace's heart rioted at the sight; his blood pounded hot behind his ears.

He began to pick his way up the slope, looking for a better vantage; he didn't want to be shooting directly into the sun. The snarling of the pack came through the trees in shreds, sharp and guttural sounds like teeth on bone. A heavy crash as the bull went down. Trace laid himself out on a long jut of sandstone that gave a clear view onto the creek. They'd felled the bull in the shallows, his antlers canted like a wrecked ship. The wolves were feeding now, a red sash running slowly downstream, into the sun.

Trace got his rifle up, steadying the suppressed barrel on its bipod. One arm folded before him, left hand touching right shoulder. He laid his eye to the scope. The world condensed, magnified.

He could see the she-wolf, One-Eleven, snapping red-jawed at the pups. Making them wait their turn, teaching them they couldn't always depend on her for meat. They swept back their ears and dropped their heads, even the big yearling born from the previous spring's litter. He was larger than his parents but soft, almost chubby, like a bear cub. He wore the only active radio collar in the pack, which made him off-limits—taking him would make the Dark Canyons impossible to locate. The GPS location data was published for the public, so ranchers and landowners could know if a pack was close.

The gray-faced alpha male was tearing the guts from the elk, ears swiveling this way and that, eyes sweeping the banks and ridges. One-Eleven did the same. After a moment, she straightened and led the pups to the hindquarters of the animal, blocking Trace's view. Now the only shot was the older male. He wore a radio collar, too, but the batteries had died years ago and the field team had decided not to replace them given his age.

Trace laid the crosshairs over the wolf's shoulder, his finger moving to the trigger. He exhaled slowly, emptying himself, blowing out tension like so much smoke. He imagined his heart shrinking again, cooling, no more than a pebble. A grain. A speck. He was a ghost, about to take down an elder lobo of the West.

Later, he would try to remember if there'd been any sound or warning—anything he'd missed before his face was shoved hard into the ground and the cold blade laid against his neck. He roared through his teeth, unable to breathe. His carotid artery thumped against the steel edge, his life beating on a thin red string.

CHAPTER 6

One-Eleven bolted. She became the point of a spear, nose thrust forward, ears laid flat for speed, running the pack hard through the canyon. She led them from one side of the river to the other, splashing across shoals, bounding over dead-fallen timber and tumbled rockfalls.

There'd been a scuffle in the trees, a fight. *Men.* She and Graynose knew the sound of them, their voices and cries, the swish and clatter of their gear. Now she looked over her shoulder. The Dark Canyons were strung behind her on an invisible line. Breath spooling from their mouths, teeth still red with elk. The pups struggling, no time to digest the meat they'd just gorged.

Little Paw was straining the hardest, barely hanging on to the tail of the pack with his hobbled gait. He was the runt of the litter, born half the size of his siblings with one small club-like hind foot. One-Eleven never expected him to survive his denhood, let alone his first season in the field, but there was something big inside the little pup.

In late spring, she'd returned from a hunt to find a bobcat hissing before the den, crouched low to nab one of the pups. Little Paw stood stiff-legged before the she-cat, snarling from his tiny throat while his littermates squirmed in the darkness behind him. The pup's outsize boldness confused the bobcat, gave her pause. So she never saw One-Eleven hit her with the full fury of a mother wolf.

Little Paw ran slack-jawed, head twisted, tongue out, fighting to stay with the pack. He had to work double hard to keep up, hurting twice as much as the others. It might make him twice the wolf, if he survived.

One-Eleven paused beneath a thick stand of willows, the shadows swaying over them. She walked back through the pack, sniffing and eyeing, checking for blood or injury. Keeping her picture of their states present, fresh in her knowing. She took a moment longer with Little Paw, scenting and probing, making sure nothing was broken or bleeding. He stared straight ahead. Tongue out, panting hard, game to keep going even as his littermates looked for places to lie down and rest.

One-Eleven turned and rubbed her ribs along the side of the little pup's head and jaws—a rough jostle, not unkind, which carried his scent back through the pack as she nipped and roused the rest of them, towing them back onto the trail.

Wolves lived by their feet, not fangs.

CHAPTER 7

Trace sat at the base of a ponderosa pine, his hands bound behind his back with heavy plastic ties. Before him squatted the man from the bar, the black-bearded miner with the hatchet face and outsize knuckles. He no longer looked like he worked at the Chino mine—or anywhere, for that matter.

He wore tattered camouflage, cutoff cargo shorts, and a sand-colored chest rig outfitted with equipment pouches, first aid kit, compass, flashlight, and other essentials. His bare arms were small but powerful, strung with riverine veins and long lines of tattooed script. The soles of his desert boots gripped the rocks beneath wide calves and thick wool hiking socks. On his back, a small daypack with a compound bow strapped to the side. He looked like he all but lived out here, and maybe he did.

When Trace had first felt the prick of the knife, he'd gone crazy, roaring and twisting, trying to wrench himself free, but the man had anticipated his reaction exactly. He rolled Trace onto his back, hooked one leg across his stomach, locked that foot with his opposite leg, and cinched Trace in a knot of limbs. At the same time he applied a chokehold of some kind, palming the back of Trace's head. Trace's vision narrowed, tunneling toward darkness. The blood slacking in his brain. The man whispered gently in his ear: "Shh, cowboy. Eight-point-nine seconds and you're asleep."

By the time he came to, Trace found himself curled up on the ground, bound and stripped of his outerwear. The man led him to a small copse of pines, where he sat him against one tree, his pack and weapon against another.

Now he squatted before Trace, staring at him. His nostrils widened, as if scenting him. In his right hand he held a karambit—a wicked hook of blade, black as a bear's claw, which curved down from the heel of his hand. The skullcap was gone and the man's dark hair was tied high aback his head, bushy as a wolf's tail. His eyes bright and clear and slightly out of true, as if they took in more light than they should.

"Been tracking you ever since them first lobos you took."

"I got no idea what you're talking about."

The other man said nothing. His clothes were almost rags, as if he'd gone feral out here, though his black beard was combed long and sharp, shot with a single bolt of iron hair. No ranger or wildlife agent, that was clear. Not a local, either. More South than West in his voice, more mud than wind. He seemed both a stranger and some part of the place, at home in the backcountry.

Trace flexed against his restraints. "You some kind of law, that it?"

The man scratched his ear with his thumb. "Some kind, maybe."

"If you ain't, you got no right to hold me here."

"Right?" The man set his elbows between his knees and clasped his hands. The karambit hung down, the curved tip pointing at Trace like a stinger. "Well, cowboy, I don't recall nobody having the right to take this land from fifty million Indians lived here for ten thousand years before Christ was born in that manger in Bethlehem. Nor anybody having the right to wipe it clean of thirty million bison and lion and wolf. And I sure don't recall you having the right to kill a single one of the couple hundred legally protected lobos left in the whole world. In light of all that, you want to sit there and bitch at me 'bout a pair of plastic bracelets won't let you hit me in the face while I talk to you?"

Trace pushed out his chin. "I ain't playing this game. You can go ahead and turn me in to the law."

"Law? You keep using that word." The man duckwalked a couple of feet closer and crouched there, staring at Trace. Something rogue and outlandish about him, yet focused, too. Animal-like. "That kind of law, it don't interest me much. It comes and goes with the years, changes with whoever's in office at the time. No, I always been more interested in older laws, deeper ones, which this world has all but forgot."

He crept closer, tapping the point of the knife against his own knee. "Ought to bleed you out right here, that's what I ought. Leave you for the coyotes and ravens. Let the meat of you pay back a little of what you took. Pound for pound. That's a law would make sense out here."

He pressed the curved claw of the knife harder into his own knee, as if driving home his point. Trace knew he ought to tread lightly but couldn't seem to help himself.

He puffed out his chest. "Case you forgot where you are, this here is America. Pound for pound, eye for an eye—that ain't how it works in this country."

The man cocked his head. "You're so worried about how the world *should* work, friend, you ain't seeing how it's working right here in front of you."

Trace eyed the karambit. A blade built for flesh. "Oh, I'm seeing it all right."

His eyes crawled the words inked along the man's arms. Many were in olden scripts, as from the ages when they were first written:

Arch type of ravin.
Beast of waste and desolation.
They cut their teeth on history and grew fat on war.

Trace had seen some of the same lines on antiwolf bumper stickers and signs. Words that spoke of man's fear and hate of the wolf down through the ages. This man seemed to wear them like some kind of testament.

Trace cleared his throat. "You some kind of wolfman, that it?"

The man stared at him with unblinking eyes. "Had my own sanctuary once, my own pack. Animals saved from the black market, from drug dealers and no-count trash." He turned and looked east, his eyes thinned to slits. "Till it got took from me. Every one of us scattered to the four winds, lost or captured or killed."

The man's chest had begun to rise and fall faster. He paused, closed his eyes. A slow, deep breath, loud through his nose. It must have taken him ten seconds to let it out. Trace looked longingly at his pack and rifle leaning against the tree across from him—just feet away.

The man opened his eyes, calmer now. "I'd love to gut you out right here, leave you for the wolves and coyotes. But I had a close call a little ways back, real close, and I reckon I ought to pass on the good fortune." He pulled back the hem of his shorts slightly, showing the edge of several ghastly scars that tracked up his thigh—wounds that looked made with the claws of some wild beast.

"Jesus Christ," said Trace.

"Not Christ, a lion. He took me down to bone and saved me just the same."

Trace shook his head. "Man, you are something else."

The wolfman crept closer. "In return for your life, all I want to know is one thing."

"Yeah, what's that?"

"Who hired you out for this job?"

"Hired me?" Trace huffed. "I don't work for nobody but myself."

He wasn't dumb enough to snitch on the men in the pale hats, not to the first wolf-nut to menace him with a drawknife. But his anger got the better of him. The hot truth came bolting out. "Hell, I wouldn't need nobody to hire me. Feds revoked our grazing permits two years ago because we shot a collared lobo took down a calf on our land, and the investigators claimed the wolf we killed was miles away at the time of the predation."

"Maybe a lion done it."

"It was a wolf. No matter what the tracking data said."

"Then you killed the wrong one."

"There ain't a wrong one."

"The mate of the most famous she-wolf in the country might be the wrong one."

"Yeah. Just our luck. The footage that made her famous came out just a week later. Soon everybody and their mother knew she'd had to take down that bull all by herself because we'd shot her mate. So the feds made an example out of us. Slapped us with the maximum fine and the Forest Service revoked our grazing leases on top of that. It'd been a tough few years and we'd already had a lien put on the ranch. Had to start selling off the herd. Then the baler, feeders, calving pens, buggies. Anything that wasn't nailed down and some that was. In the end it wasn't enough. Bank seized the ranch. My old man checked out and my mama's back on her pills. Our family had been on that land a hundred years."

"Wolves been on it half a million, at least."

"They had their time. Now it's ours."

"Our time?" The man's voice sharpened. "Our time is the Sixth Great Extinction, my friend, or haven't you noticed? This here planet supported multicellular life for at least six hundred million years before we come along on two legs and completely fucked it. In the ten thousand years since we brought *civilization* to the world, other species been dying out at a thousand times the normal rate. Four of five wild mammals? Gone." He snapped his fingers. "Whether you believe it was God put them there or half a billion years of evolution, it'll be the crime of the cosmos to push them into extinction under our watch. Wolf, bison, elephant, rhino, tiger, all stand at the brink. And then there's us, thinking we're so fucking high and mighty, sitting on top of a world shattering beneath our own weight."

The man's eyes were wide, their yellowish whites splintered with red veins. Trace saw he'd pressed the knife hard enough into his own knee to draw blood. He pointed the bloody tip at Trace's nose. "All them wild-eyed end-times preachers were right, friend. Our time is nigh. And it's our own sins in which we'll burn."

Trace dug his heels in the dirt. "If the whole world's going to hell, what's it matter?"

The man put the knife back to his knee, picking at the bloody little welt he'd made. "Matters we don't take down the rest of the kingdom with us. And the wolf, it's special to me. No animal's been as hated, see, all the way back to the Holy Bible, to fairytales and nursery rhymes. Bunch of nefarious myths, cruel and untrue. They say the wolf is evil, that it kills for fun, kills more than it needs to eat. That it's a ravening monster, hungry as wildfire. It's a scapegoat, is what it is. It's all the evils of our own nature, projected on something else. When you hate the wolf, you don't but hate yourself."

Trace pushed his head back against the tree and drove out his chest. All his pent-up fury was busting loose, boiling under his skin. "Seems to me you're the high and mighty one, the one full of hate. For your own kind. Bet you'd rather be a wolf than a man. *I identify as a lobo.* You ought to get that tattooed on yourself, across your fucking forehead. You're lucky them wolves of yours never ate you for supper."

A sliver of blood had run down the man's shin, pooling in his sock. He didn't seem to notice. "A wild wolf ain't killed a single person in the Lower 48 in recorded history. You know that as well as I do. Lightning takes down more head of cattle each year than wolves. Ones they do take is mostly because the herd instinct's been bred out of modern beef cows. First sight of a predator, the dams are like to cut and run instead of circling up and facing down the intruder like wild cattle would. Like the old longhorns and aurochs done. Like bison still do."

"So you're an expert at ranching now? People like you, you don't know what it's like to live that life. Taking care of several hundred head of cattle whose lives are on you. Your responsibility. You're the one battling to keep them alive and healthy despite disease and drought and more federal regs than you can shake a stick at. More every year. Unending. All of it. Then they go and put predators back on the land. We're the ones paying the cost. Us. The people who actually live here."

"You graze your cattle on public land."

"Damn right. And we pay a pretty penny for those leases, too. On top of taxes. When's the last time you paid Uncle Sam his due, Mr. Wolfman?"

The bearded man shook his head. "You got a hard row to hoe, Temple. I ain't arguing that. And lobos don't make it no easier. But less than one percent of cattle losses come from wolves. And it ain't just about us, right now. It's about history. Extinction. What makes you hate a thing enough not just to kill it, but to eradicate its whole species from the face of the earth?"

"The rest of the earth ain't my problem. Like I told you, a lobo killed one of our calves. Ripped her apart. And shooting that animal near as not brought our whole family to ruin."

"That wolf didn't take your ranch, nor your father neither. It took one calf. It was men did the rest."

"Yeah," said Trace. "The same men put those wolves on our land in the first place, no matter how hard we were struggling already to make ends meet. Feds and a bunch of big-city voters don't know a wolf from a goddamn teddy bear. Don't know how they kill. Never seen a calf torn apart, her insides strung all through the grass. We drove out the wolves once. We'll do it again."

The wolfman nodded, curling his lips against his teeth. "I'm sorry you feel that way, friend." He set his hand on Trace's shoulder. Trace expected him to clamp down hard, driving his words in with his grip, his horned knuckles, but his touch was light. "I hope you find your way." A slight squeeze, as if they really were friends.

Then he rose, stowed the knife, and took up Trace's rifle. He dropped the magazine, cleared the chamber, and removed the rear take-down pin, hinging apart the upper and lower receivers. He hurled the bolt carrier in one direction and the charging handle in another, rendering the weapon inoperable. Then set it gently back against a tree and headed off into the woods. Head low, shoulders rolling like a boxer's, a slight limp out of that scarred leg. A shadow between the ponderosas, then gone.

Trace's mouth hung open. "Hey! Hey, man! You just lettin' me go?"

No answer. Just the wind through the branches, the buzz of flies.

Trace set his head on his knees and blew the pressure from his lungs. Elation rose in his blood. A weightless glow. Thank God he hadn't given up the men in the pale hats. He might've signed his death warrant for nothing, for some longhaired freak with crazy eyes and a scary knife.

Trace shook his head. He'd heard of people moving out to public lands, living inside national forests and federal wildernesses—lone hermits and small clans gone back to living like ancient peoples, preparing for civil war or civilization's collapse. People called them *outlanders*. He reckoned this wolfman was one of them.

He shook his head. "Whack job. More hair than brains."

The man had left Trace's pack against a tree a few steps away. Trace had his pocketboy in one of the outer pouches—a folding saw that would make short work of the cuffs. He got his boots beneath him, pushed his back against the tree, and rose to his feet. He stood there a few seconds, just enjoying it. This moment. The heady rush of near death. The glow in his veins. The pride. Then he headed for his pack, stepping between two large roots to retrieve it.

A metallic snap beneath his foot.

Later, Trace would recall this moment over and over, replaying the loop again and again, a circular film in his mind, as he looked for some sign he'd missed. A disruption in the duff and pine straw between the roots, an unnatural place in the forest floor, anything to tell him what was buried there.

What jaws.

CHAPTER 8

Trace lay shrieking, spitting through clenched teeth. The trap had leapt like a fiend from the ground to snatch his leg in its teeth. Urine burned down the insides of his thighs as he squealed and lurched, trying to yank himself free. He felt wrenched out of himself, like his mind or spirit might break out of his skin. Then he was on the ground, writhing, rasping for air.

He didn't want to look. As if not seeing might hold off reality. He wanted someone else to look for him, to tell him how bad it was, tell him it would be all right. But there wasn't anyone.

He looked.

Steel jaws smiled back at him, clenched in the mess of his leg. Blood everywhere, bulbing and oozing through his pants. An old steel mantrap not unlike the ones his grandfather had kept hanging on the wall of the barn, lined up like rusty shark's jaws. Some big enough for bear, lion, men. This one designed to catch poachers. The teeth just cleared the top of his boot.

He wailed through clenched jaws. Twisted to look up into the trees.

Wild scrawls of light, too bright. Down to the trap. It hissed in his ears. It told him how small he was. How soft. How hard the world when you slipped between its teeth. His vision dizzied. He retched onto his thin wool undershirt, hot on his chest, heaving until his stomach was empty.

He threw back his head, bile burning on his chin. "Fuck you, you longhaired feral fuck!"

His voice went nowhere. Died against the rocks and trees, cliffs and sky and steel trap. He was alone. His heart running away from him, his breath. Panic roared in his blood, crimping his fingers, ripping his mouth slack. There wasn't enough air here, he couldn't breathe.

He closed his eyes and imagined himself behind the scope of his rifle. His heart small, cold, hard. A stone, a pebble. He breathed in, breathed out. A pebble, a grain. He imagined leading the family horses to the upper pasture after supper—the place he always tried to go in his mind when he needed calm. Something a school counselor had taught him after a junior-high panic attack left him crippled in a bathroom stall. He tried to stay there in his head, floating between the warm barrels of the horses, their rubbery nostrils smoking in the dusk. He breathed in, breathed out.

Panic killed people in the wild. He had to focus.

Chop wood, carry water. Something Old Temple used to say. What to do when you were in hell. Keep going. *Chop wood, carry water.*

Trace wriggled over to his pack, rolled onto his side, and worked the pocketboy from its mesh pouch, fumbling open the serrated blade behind his back. He set the teeth against the plastic cuffs and strained. The binds popped. He sat up and tried the earlike levers, then wedged his fingers between the teeth of the trap, trying to pry it open. No chance. A coil-spring trap strong enough for a small bear, designed to be opened with special trap setters.

He tried to wedge the barrel of the rifle between the jaws, but the suppressor was too big to fit. He removed it but the barrel was too narrow for a pry. Next he pulled up the length of chain attached to the trap. The hidden links crackled up out of the underbrush. At the far end, hidden in a thorn bush, a three-pronged iron drag shaped like a grappling hook. A wolf or bear or mountain lion would catch one of the prongs on a root or rock or tree and become trapped at the end of the chain, or else tow the drag scraping and tumbling for hours, even days—a trail of agony easy for a trapper to track. A fate staring Trace dead in the face.

He set the drag in his lap. He had to outsmart this predicament somehow. He inspected the bronze shackle linking the drag chain to the trap. The screw pin had been soldered over, locking it closed. Same on both ends of the chain. The wolfman had thought of everything, it seemed. He'd left Trace thinking he was free, full of pride, only to lure him straight into the same jaws as untold thousands before him. Bears and lions and wolves and coyotes. Foxes and bobcats and beavers and badgers. Unfortunates, all.

Trace set his forehead against the drag and roared. A dam was busting inside him. The one that held back the fury over his father's death, his mother's relapse, the family ranch lost to the bank. Nobody was going to take his life from him, too—not without a fight.

He looked to the sun. It was the better part of five miles back to his truck. Two canyons, two river crossings. His pack and rifle would be dead weight. He'd have to return for them later.

He unzipped various compartments of his pack and made up a smaller kit bag to tie over his shoulder, full of what the old cowboys called their possibles: water, food, light, tools, first aid, map, fire makings. No sidearm—the man must have taken or tossed it. He set his pack and rifle back against the tree. Doubtful they'd be found anytime soon—not out here.

Trace took up the slack of the trap chain and coiled it around his arm, holding the cast-iron grapnel upended in his fist like some kind of medieval weapon.

Five miles.

He slung the iron hook into the earth and began to drag himself, slowly, along the ground. *Chop wood, carry water.*

CHAPTER 9

One-Eleven locked her legs, skidding to a stop on the narrow trail. The rest of the pack piled up in a whelm of dust behind her, the pups tumbling over one another on splayed forelegs and overlarge paws. Once they'd regained their feet, they ducked their heads under Dozer's bushy bulk, trying to see what had stopped their mother dead in her tracks. Their older brother, big as a small boulder, ever their refuge in the field.

One-Eleven stared down at the canyon on this edge of their territory. They'd come here for sanctuary, for deep shadows and jagged terrain, but a circle of trucks and trailers was parked in a turnout on the far side of the canyon. Beyond them ran the highway she never crossed, not since her first mate had been killed on the other side of it. Towns and ranchlands out there. Guns and men.

Graynose flared his nostrils, scenting the air rolling up out of the canyon. His eyes had begun to cloud since last winter, but his nose was still sharp, better than hers. He caught a scent and his hackles slowly stiffened. A line of horses and riders was moving down into the canyon, the dust of their hooves curling up from the trail. Sunlight rippled across the dark steel of their rifles. A hunting party.

She and Graynose looked at each other.

The old wolf turned his shoulders slightly, urging them toward the East Fork. Another refuge. Hikers sometimes there, drawn to steaming springs and lingering wildflowers, but few hunters. The vegetation still thick there this time of year. The pack could remain in the shadows, avoiding marked trails. The land would hide them.

One-Eleven resisted. Something pulled her back the way they'd come. They'd heard what sounded like men on the riverbank but no shots. A fracas in the brush. She wanted to know what was on their trail. Who. She wanted to investigate.

She looked back at the pack. The pups were still staring at her from around Dozer's shaggy bulk. The big yearling was built like a battler but liked best to sleep. Anywhere, any hour, even on his feet. Nothing deterred him. Rain, cold, hunger, even pups pulling on his tail. He could always doze. Find a patch of sunlight and stick his paws in the air. Once he fell asleep during an hours-long standoff with a large black bear over a muley carcass. The big wolf's sheer unconcern spooked the bear, who huffed a great plume of breath and ambled off, giving up the kill. Even now, despite the thick slaver dripping from his tongue, Dozer's eyes were growing squinty.

Graynose turned east again, trying to pull One-Eleven in that direction. He bobbed on his forelegs. *Not safe here.* The old wolf was bold, even reckless at times, but he'd traveled vast distances through the lands of men. Graynose had threaded high mountain passes and dangerous ranchlands, following logging roads and irrigation canals, sleeping in culverts and crossing highways in dead of night, roaming the outlands for years before he found her. He knew they needed to keep moving.

One-Eleven hesitated, caught between the urgings of Graynose and the pull inside her. The question, hooked like a hunger inside her. Who was hunting them? Their scent and shape. Their habits.

One-Eleven curled away from the canyon rim, leading the Dark Canyons back toward the heart of their territory.

CHAPTER 10

Noon. The sun burned high over the forest. Beams shafted down through the canopy, fracturing the shade. The early spike of adrenaline had worn off, and the pain, the pain, the pain. Deafening now. A claw hammer pounding on Trace's shin, every heartbeat driving a nail. His toes had gone numb, the blood flow crimped. Too long and he'd lose his foot.

The thought made his heart feel too big, tumbling out of control like one of those pinnacle rocks that came crashing down the canyon walls without warning, violent as a wrecking ball. He closed his eyes, trying to slow his breath. He thought of the dusk horses in the pasture again, the sweet steaming of their nostrils. But One-Eleven kept jumping into his mind instead. Her silhouette poised broadside in his scope, the dawn river riffling around her. Then the sight picture would jerk apart on him, scattering again and again. The same loop like when you had a fever.

Trace kept jamming sticks and rocks into the trap, trying to pry the teeth back even a fraction. He tried a narrow length of alligator juniper, one of the harder softwoods in the Gila, and managed to wedge it between the jaws. He hauled back on the checkerbark branch like a crowbar, feeling the wood strain and bow. The slightest lessening of pressure. He wedged a flat stone between the jaws, trying to preserve this tiny fraction of reprieve. He pulled out the juniper branch and felt around with his left hand, slippery with blood and grime, trying to see what he'd gained, what sliver of ground. The stone snapped out of the trap and the jaws shut on his fingers.

Trace shrieked and ripped his hand free, holding it in his opposite fist as he rolled and bawled. One of the teeth had taken a nasty chunk of meat from the tip of his middle finger, more than might ever grow back. He tore off a piece of shirttail with his teeth and knotted it over the wound, a bloody finger puppet.

Pain thundered between his hand and leg, back and forth like artillery inside him. When the trap had spat out the stone he'd felt the sickening *click* as the teeth touched his shinbone. He vomited again, just heaves now. A thick, yellowy slime on his mouth and chin. He needed water. He took up his canteen—only a tinny wash in the bottom. He'd drunk too much in the first hours when he was flush with adrenaline, thinking he'd be back to his truck by midnight, headed for the nearest ER.

He trickled a little water down his tongue. He'd be spending the night out here. No shelter, no weapon. The teeth driving ever deeper. He'd done his best to clean up the wound, but every hour increased the risk of infection. Panic came creeping back on him, circling, crackling around the edges of his mind like flames. Threatening to make a run right for the center of him.

He slipped the kit bag from his shoulder and took out the satellite phone he carried in case of emergencies. The rubbery antenna could overcome the lack of a cellular signal, shooting his voice into orbit and bouncing it down into the ear of someone willing to help him out of this canyon. He dug his thumbnail between the hard little buttons.

Who?

If he called 911, the first responders would be forest rangers who'd quickly back-follow his track and discover the pack and rifle. He'd become the prime suspect for the killings of the other wolves, given his personal history, current location, and the recent coordinates of the wolfpack. He couldn't call his father and grandfather, not even a sat line reached that far. No siblings, no close friends left from school. He was from a town twenty miles outside of the Gila National Forest, population 186. Fifteen people in his graduating class, drawn from four thousand square miles of district.

No girlfriend to call, no one in recent memory save for a few chance trysts with women from New York or Kansas City, Oslo or Berlin. Serious hikers who wanted to see the Mogollon cliff dwellings, backpack the nation's first federal wilderness, and listen for the howl of a rare Mexican wolf. Always the sense they wanted him only because he, too, was part of this place. A native. A real cowboy. Always a cold ache in the morning when they drove away in their camper vans or converted school buses.

Leaving the phone had to be deliberate. The wolfman must have known Trace had no one to call. Maybe he'd wanted Trace to know it, too.

Trace tapped his thumb on one of the keys, not hard enough to dial. The men in the pale hats had given him a contact number, but he knew what would happen if he called it. A squad of men in silverbelly hats, square-jawed with rifles and tac vests, wiping any trace of him from this canyon. He knew enough to know their ethic. Success or else. The group over the individual. Any security breach, cauterized. More than that, the wolfman would be watching, waiting to see who showed up. Little different than if he'd snitched—and once they found out, that would be that.

In fact, the wolfman probably hoped he'd call them. The very reason he'd left the phone.

Trace stared at the keypad. So many possibilities, yet none. He leaned his head back against the pine and chanced a glance down his leg, past the knee. The trap was still there, smiling red-toothed through the bloody muck of his pants. One-Eleven jumped again into his mind, poised in the dawn river, laced beneath his crosshairs . . .

Trace set his hand on his forehead. A bright heat on his palm. Tiny blisters of sweat along his eyebrows, as if his thoughts and dreams were bubbling to the surface, running down his face.

He looked back at the phone. One number he could still call.

"Mama?"

The voice on the other end of the sat line sounded scratchy, coarse. Not just the connection. "Who's this?"

"It's me, Mama. It's Trace."

"This ain't your regular number."

"It ain't my regular phone I'm calling from."

"You in jail?"

"No, ma'am. I just, wanted to talk to you." Trace could hear the roar of semis in the background, the belch of a jake brake. "Where are you?"

"Up near Albuquerque. Trying to get my medicine."

"Oh." Trace looked down his leg. "I was hoping you might be closer to home."

"I'll be back soon's I get my medicine. There's a doctor up here I'm trying to see. Supposed to be good, willing to help a woman in pain." She paused. "Say, you ain't got any extra cash you could loan me, do you? I'll get you back soon's I get my check next week."

Trace leaned his head back against the tree. A burn behind his eyes. "No, Mama. Not right now I don't."

She'd been a semipro motorcycle racer for most of her life, sliding a big Harley-Davidson flat tracker around the dirt speedways of the West. A wheeled bull rider gripping the wide, chrome horns of the handlebars as the machine bucked and squirmed beneath her, roaring for traction. Her outside elbow cocked high, her hammered-steel hot shoe kicked to the inside, skimming through the turns.

Her father and mother and siblings had all raced—it was in their blood. Trace had seen old photographs in the family albums, her face set hard behind the clear bubble shield of her helmet, her blond hair splayed wide in the wind. She was in her early forties when she wrecked hard at a track in West Texas and broke her femur in two places. After the surgeries, the doctors sent her home with a new painkiller, widely heralded as a miracle drug at the time.

OxyContin.

Trace was just a boy, but he remembered how sick she got trying to kick them. Greasy and fevered, writhing in the sour bedsheets like a possessed woman. She quivered and cursed and retched, fighting to survive the withdrawals, to exorcise the poison from her body. Often, Trace was afraid even to enter her room. He'd just sit in the hallway outside her door.

"Is she dying?" he asked his father.

The man leaned his back against the wall and slid down next to his boy, crossing his arms over his knees. "Some part of her is. And it's trying to bring her with it. But your mama is hard as nails, boy, you know that? Double tough. Tougher'n I ever was, ain't afraid to say it."

"Am I that tough?"

"I hope you don't never have to find out."

She'd been clean for nearly twenty years when she found Trace's father dead on a creek bank. He'd shot the wolf in the spring, during calving time, and turned the same gun on himself a year later, just after they'd lost the ranch.

The man had spent his whole life driving cattle from pasture to pasture, hauling hay and checking fence lines, catching calves caught in barbwire—sometimes too late. Battling each year to keep the herd strong and healthy, heavy enough in gross hundredweight to keep the operation afloat. His entire life rooted in the land, the hard sun baking the canyons and the torrents running dark and violent when the rains came. Eating lunches on the tailgate of his truck, parked beneath a big ponderosa pine, watching the cattle graze. Guiding the odd party of bowhunters deep into the Gila or Apache, where he could track elk and mule deer better than any of the hotshot outfitters.

A quiet man, he'd taken the federal reintroduction of wolves with only a few pained winces and extra bottles of antacids, the tablets ever rattling in the glove box of his old flatbed farm truck. Meanwhile, his own father—the infamous Old Temple—had gone truly ballistic, spewing ire until his heart gave out. But when they lost their grazing permits, it was like someone sucked out the man's soul. He was sixty years old and everything he'd worked for had been taken in a night. Still, he didn't rant or moan like Old Temple had done years before. He got to work filing appeals, selling off cattle and equipment, trying to keep the bankmen at bay. But he seemed brittle, shrunken, going through motions that barely nicked the sealed door of the family's fate.

Trace once sneaked home drunk from the bar and found the man bent over the dinner table, surrounded by crumpled bills and receipts and an ancient calculator, his drugstore reading glasses sliding down his nose. Trace had the urge to wrap his arms around the man, to squeeze him tight. But it seemed too dangerous, like he might collapse the crinkly newsprint of his father's skin, crushing him. Trace turned and tiptoed to his room.

When all the efforts to save the ranch failed, Trace's father went to the big creek behind the house when no one else was home. He meant for the current to carry him away, so neither his wife nor boy would suffer the fate of finding him, but his body washed up on a sandbank just downstream. Trace's mother found him there, his head emptied out by his short-barreled Marlin .30–30 carbine—the same rifle he'd used to take the wolf. Since then, it seemed like she was racing after him, taking whatever would get her there fastest.

Trace wiped his eyes with the back of his hand. "You talked to your sponsor lately, Mama?"

His mother's voice tightened. "You know I ain't."

Trace sat up slightly against the tree. "Mama, you told me last week you'd call your sponsor."

"I will, baby, soon's I get my medicine. Then I'll be in the right head to talk."

Trace tensed as another wave of pain rolled through him. It hammered and pulsed outward from the wound, like the metal jaws were gnawing on him, trying to crack his bones. Get to his marrow. His heart chased itself, tumbling around his chest. He breathed through his teeth, an audible rasp. For the first time in his life, he wanted one of those little white pills that did his mother so much harm. Now he understood them. How you'd give anything for space to breathe. Anything to dull the great animal of hurt inside you.

His mother must have heard his seething breath. "I know you're upset with me, son, but that ain't no way to act. I'm doing the best I can."

Trace's mouth spasmed and he clenched his jaws harder, holding the receiver from his face. He wanted to wail, to loose his hurt into the wild. It was too big to bear alone. A pain shared was a pain divided, people said. But his throat was locked against the sound.

He set the phone back to his cheek. "I know you are, Mama, doing your best. That ain't why I called. It's something else I wanted to ask."

"What?"

"You think Dad wasn't tough enough, doing what he done?"

She was quiet a moment, only the sound of the semis in the background, booming through the desert. "Your father was tough as they come. He wasn't weak, son, he was lost, and that's something completely different. Even the toughest get lost. Sometimes more than the weak do. They swim out farther from shore."

"You think you and me are lost?"

She sniffed again. "If we are, we got a right to be. But that don't mean we can't find our way. What did Old Temple used to say? When you're going through hell, keep going. We just got to keep putting one foot in front of the other. That's all we can do."

Trace looked down at his leg, the chain in his lap. “Chop wood, carry water.”

“That’s right, honey. Chop wood, carry water.”

“Yes, ma’am.”

CHAPTER 11

One-Eleven and the Dark Canyons hunched in the reeds upstream of the elk they'd killed earlier. Snouts low, watching the river. The shallow current bubbled around the fallen bull, carrying threads of the kill downstream. Only the vultures had found the carcass. They shuffled stiffly atop the mount of flesh and ganged along the riverbanks. Aware of no disturbance, it seemed. No men.

One-Eleven led the pack back into the trees, wending toward the source of her curiosity, a mind-hunger that drew her sure as fresh blood in the nose. Soon they were circling the high thrust of sandstone, nervous, sniffing and snorting over the messed earth. The remnant scent of rioting men. The wolves hunched their shoulders low to the ground, paws wide, as if moving beneath the low ceiling of a cave, ready any moment to bolt. They followed the scent-trail into the trees, finding the pack and propped rifle, the bloody crater where a trap had burst from the ground. One-Eleven could almost taste it, the tang of blood on steel. A chemical reaction.

She ran her nose along the furrow where the steel chain had been torn up from the ground like a root or vine and sniffed the sweat-blanched shoulder straps of the pack and rifle sling. She found two tracks leading off from the place. One light and scarce and fast, heading toward the rocky pinnacles and caves higher in the canyon. The other bloody and gouged and slow, with long scrapes and drags—the trail of something wounded, dying.

The pups snuffled and snorted about, high on man scents. Little Paw nosed the rifle. The muzzle scraped against the tree and the gun clattered to the ground, which sent the whole pack bounding and fleeing in every direction, jumping behind rocks and trees and brush.

Little Paw just kept going, leaping down the riverbank and charging the vultures there. They hissed and hopped away from him, floating up onto branches or boulders. One-Eleven and the rest of the pack followed, splashing down into the river to rush the vultures still standing atop the elk. The birds thumped away, bald heads rising over the river on heavy black wings.

This was a Dark Canyon kill.

The pack would feed before moving on, following the fresh bloodtrack through the canyon.

CHAPTER 12

The sun rifled red through the pines. Trace crawled along the stony trail, hauling himself on bruised elbows. Foot after foot, hips twisted to keep the trap from dragging, a caked anchor of blood and dirt. Yard after yard. Inching wormlike along the ground, through tangles of brush and blowdown, silty washouts, muddy creeks. Pain tolling through him like a church bell. His vision flickered, dizzied with bright orbs and lightning flashes. Worse, he sensed something monstrous behind the pain, haunting him. Not just death but the fear of it. To die this way. Weak, whimpering, afraid.

He closed his eyes. White jags blazed and forked against the darkness. Cruel energies pulsed through him, cutting into his softest places. Forces too big to contain, like they could break you from the inside out. He opened his eyes after he didn't know how long. The light was retreating from the canyon, sharpening the shadows. He took the drag hook in both hands and slammed it into the ground, then hauled himself after it.

He had a USGS quad map in his chest pocket but barely looked at it. He knew where he was. Knew he had no choice but to follow this crooked trail through the canyon. A direct bearing might be shorter on the flat surface of a map, but the terrain would be impassable. Jagged climbs and descents to crosscut canyons, barren crossings with no shelter from the cold night wind. The only water found in ancient stock tanks, which you couldn't drink without boiling. No, the only way out was this old backcountry trail, taking the right path whenever it forked. He just had to not quit and not die. As the hours wore on, those seemed more and more the same thing.

His mind had begun to range strangely, like it did sometimes before falling asleep. Old, forgotten tracings through lands of memory. He remembered a day in elementary school when they were playing Cowboys and Indians on the playground, a make-believe shoot-out between the swing set and seesaw. Trace was partnered up Garrison, his best friend, who had gold skin and a dirty blond rattail and one pupil out of round, almost rectangular—the work of a catclaw thorn. He'd worn a patch for a time, an aluminum one with little holes to let his wounded eye breathe. Trace remembered him swaggering square-shouldered down the hall, arms swinging loose, chin high, that eye patch the envy of every other boy in school.

Soon the battle moved to the little arroyo behind the schoolhouse, the dry creek they scrutinized after hard rains for treasures that floated down from the old homestead that once sat atop the hill. Apaches had razed the house back in the 1800s—or so people said. Nothing now but a square cut in the mesquite.

Belt buckles had been found in the sandy belly of the arroyo, door hinges and gate hasps and even the frame of a cap-and-ball Colt six-gun. Fire-blacked artifacts that washed down over the centuries, migrating inch by inch through the sandy soil, evading the metal detectors of potbellied men. It gave the arroyo a Wild West mystique. All the recess gunfights eventually made their way here, the cowboys and leathernecks and Green Berets fighting the

Apaches and Germans and Charlies for the history buried in the dry bed of the creek.

Trace and Garrison's adversaries were the Cruz sisters, Imogen and Ria, whose long black hair meant they always had to play the bad guys in such battles. It had toughened them. They were hard adversaries who aimed right between the cowboys' eyes, their gunfire shouted hard and loud from across the creek. *Pow, pow, pow!*

Trace and Garrison had taken cover behind a clump of cheatgrass, pinned down like Butch Cassidy and the Sundance Kid, the fire coming too hot to raise their heads. Trace looked at the other boy. There was something about Garrison, something he was born with that none of the rest of them had. A boldness. A swagger. A wild light. He would be the first of them to smoke a joint, fall in love, drive 100 miles per hour. The first of them to die. A heroin overdose.

Crouched in the cheatgrass, even Garrison was scared, round-eyed at the unexpected ferocity of the two girls. His square pupil looked the size of a bedroom window as he took in the direness of their situation. The two sisters were about to charge across the creek, put their finger-barrels to the boys' temples, and drop the hammers of their thumbs.

Bang you're dead.

Trace realized what he had to do. He took a big breath and clapped a hand on his friend's forearm. "Tell my mama I love her."

Then he leapt up and charged right into the oncoming fire, his front arm curled at his waist, as if cradling something heavy, his opposite hand rotating beside it.

"Ch-ch-ch-ch-ch-ch-ch!" he shouted. "Gatling gun!"

The girls, already halfway down the far side of the arroyo, locked their knees and skidded to a stop, daunted by the unexpected charge. They were tough adversaries but fair. They knew they'd been outmatched. They clutched their hearts, mashed their eyes, and fell back into the soft sand of the bank as if killed, their ponytails trailing them like long black feathers. Trace felt the sweet glow of victory in his blood. Nothing had ever felt so good.

Then he tripped over a rock and fell toward the bottom of the creekbed, throwing out his arms to break his fall. His right hand shot down through the silt and met something sharp buried there. He screamed and yanked his hand back to his chest, stunned to see the rusty spike of an old squarehead nail sticking out of his palm.

The demeanor of his former enemies changed in an instant. The two girls came scrambling down the slope and knelt around him. The eldest, Imogen, lightly touched his shoulder, true worry in her eyes. Meanwhile Garrison dropped down behind him, wrapped his arms around Trace's chest, and yelled in his ear.

"Pretend it feels good! Pretend it feels good!"

Trace had closed his eyes, feeling bright bolts of power rip through him, like lightning tearing through a black sky. A tree standing pale-crazed, glowing over a dark land. Hands touching him on every side, like sweet roots of blood.

CHAPTER 13

The bearded man squatted in a small cave high in a canyon wall, rubbing his hands over the flames of a small cookfire. Foodstuffs and supplies sat packed against the walls. A rope ladder ensured no one could surprise him here—one of several dens he kept around the Wilderness. The roof of the cave was blacked with the smoke of fires centuries old, and the place had remained untouched for years before his arrival. Firelight licked the walls. Ancient red pictographs flared and moved on the tanned musculature of stone, as if scratched in flesh.

Slender figures with outsize hands and feet danced before him, some with an antenna or horn protruding from the top of their head. The wings of a large dragonfly with a curlicue tail flickered like rotor blades. Small dots pulsed starlike against the stone, and at the back of the cave, barely lit, a series of sharp triangles that could be red mountains or wolf's teeth.

He didn't know what the ancient cliff dwellers here had believed, what cosmology once shaped their world. Beliefs in animal gods or otherworldly spirits, in the primacy of flesh or mind, man or nature.

Whether they were even the same people who built the dwellings farther downriver. But he felt more comfortable here in their ancient warren than in any house or room. Some people were born a hundred years too late. For him, it was ten thousand.

He made a meal of beans and salted venison, nodding to the muley antlers that hung on the wall across from him before he ate. He'd taken the large-eared buck with his bow, field-dressed the animal with his knives and homemade gambrel, and packed the meat here for dry salting. He hadn't eaten a piece of store-bought meat in years, not since his last stint in a state correctional facility. He killed or scavenged or peeled it up off the road.

He ran a perimeter in his mind as he ate. His van, hidden beneath camouflage netting several miles from here, gassed and ready for action. His other caches and caves. The supplies packed around him in the den, bulk foodstuffs and assorted materiel, clothing and tools and several crates of things built to go bang. He looked into the fire, thinking of the world that lay just beneath the skim of civilization. A hard land, cold and jagged, in which only the strongest and smartest and luckiest survived, and every day was a fight. For any battle, today or ten thousand years ago, among wolves or men, you needed allies. A pack or clan or nation, comrades or cavalry or overwatch.

Your allies didn't have to be your friends. But they had to respect you, and you them.

He finished the meal, licked the bowl clean, and set it back on its crate. Then he crept to the edge of the cave and looked out over the dusk-dark canyon. Somewhere out there, a man may or may not prove himself capable of survival. Elsewhere, a pack of wolves moved newly safe through their territory—but for how long?

He raised his head to the sky and swelled his chest with the coming night.

CHAPTER 14

Trace jerked awake. He'd heard something—*a howl?*

It was dusk, the sun gone, a world the color of smoke. He brushed the dirt from his face. He must have fallen asleep or passed out. He felt different somehow, like he'd awoken into a new realm, stranger than before, almost eerie. Or maybe something inside him had changed, so the world looked different to his eyes. Maybe the sudden loss of light—a mysterious gap in time, lost to dream.

He raised his torso on his hands and began to haul himself down the trail again, scraping across the ground, the chain rattling on his back. He tried to think of things to hearten him. His mother. No matter how the world had wasted her face, turned her hands knobby and teeth square, her eyes would still light up at the sight of him. That much he knew.

The canyon was widening, opening. He could hear the wind scraping over the high rocks. The temperature was dropping like a bomb, like always this time of year. The edges of things blurring, running fluid.

The hour between the dog and the wolf. As Old Temple used to say: "Time you cain't tell if that beast at the edge of the pasture is a friend of yours or an enemy."

Trace slammed the drag hook against rocks and roots, hauling himself on his arms. In the failing light, he saw the white button of scar shining on the back of one hand. The squarehead nail. He hadn't noticed that scar in years.

The trail bent toward the river, weaving down through cottonwoods and willows. The lock-jawed trap rasped along behind him, hanging on like a stubborn dog. He looked down at it and snorted. His jaw loosened. Before he knew it he was talking to the thing, using the same voice he'd use with a stubborn horse or mule.

"You're just a damn old bulldog, ain't you? Got a bone locked in your jaws and come hell or high water or the Second Coming of Christ hisself you ain't apt to budge a single inch. I see you, boy. I see you. Just a dogged old son-bitch, steel-toothed, hardmouthed as a sourmug, and I'm the poor SOB happens to own the bone in your teeth. Well, thank you. Wasn't for you, I might be tempted to rest or sleep or quit. Sorely tempted. Just lay down my head and sleep sweetly beneath the stars. But them teeth of yours are sure to keep me awake and moving. Yes, sir. Sourmug, that's what I'm-a call you from now on. Sourmug the Stubbornest."

Nuts to speak to a steel trap, but Trace didn't care. It brought him a strange glee, a mad delight. At the sharp edge of the world, you could talk to whoever you wanted, however you wanted. You could talk to the trees and stones, the stars and birds, the flesh that sheathed your bones and the steel that clenched them. Friends could become enemies, and enemies friends.

Soon the black river was running through the canyon before him, thrumming over its stony bed. His mouth gone gummy, his tongue hard and cracked. He wanted to slake himself on the whole river, drink it dry and feel the drunken swell in his belly. He crawled out onto the gravel bar. Scraping, rattling. He leaned over the edge and dunked his canteen, watching the spout bubble.

The water was still soot-dark from summer wildfires. No matter. He drank and drank. Cold enough to crack his teeth. He imagined the water branching through his veins. Moonshine made of snowmelt and dead fire.

"Get you some," he told Sourmug, pouring water on the trap, washing away some of the blood-thickened dirt.

Finished, he raised himself on his hands and looked at his dim silhouette in the water, wavering like a spirit. Something came roaring from his chest. He threw back his head and his throat convulsed, launching some deep part of himself into the sky. High and wild and lonesome. It sounded like the call of some animal. Alone, hungry, hurt.

Alive.

Trace hung his head between his shoulders, heaving, sucking back his wind.

A howl rose high over the canyon, echoing his own.

CHAPTER 15

An auction barn outside Silver City. Big as an ark in the night, surrounded by vehicles of every description. Family sedans and pony cars, shiny new pickups, and battered ranch trucks with cattle guards and gooseneck hitches—many covered in silver-gray dust. The men in pale hats had commanded him to this place, on this night. *Here your questions will be answered*, they said. *Such as they ever will.*

Trace slipped in just before they barred the doors. Inside, the lights were dim enough people couldn't clearly see one another. The speaker had already started. A tall cowboy in a silverbelly hat that shadowed his face—only the glowing squares of his eyeglasses visible, and a broad gray gunfighter's mustache that drooped to his chin. He wore an ivory-handled 1911 automatic in a woven holster on his hip and stood just where the auctioneer would stand, holding a microphone in one fist.

"You know what the promise of America was? No kings. Every man his own ruler. Master and commander of his own domain. Equal in rights if not in wealth. Free from oppressive regimes. That sound about right?"

Damn right it does, said the crowd.

"That's what our ancestors fought and died for, freedom. Freedom from tyranny and oppression, from enemies foreign and domestic. It ain't the wind that stirs Old Glory on her flagpole, it's the breath of dead patriots. Men who died to keep that flag flying. Men who died killing Redcoats and Indians, Germans and Japanese and Viet Cong."

Hell yeah, said the crowd. *Patriots.*

"But now we got a federal government acting like the old Crown, reaching from damn near two thousand miles away, from offices and boardrooms in Washington, DC, pointing out every last thing we can and can't do on our own land. They want to regulate us to death, to legislate us straight out of existence. Drain us dry and suck out the marrow. Every year it's ten more teeth in our backsides. Restrictions on water use, pesticides, fungicides, rodenticides, air emissions from animal waste. You know you got a problem when a government cares more about monarch butterfly migration than human mouths to feed."

That's the truth.

"Hell, we got a government went as far as to reintroduce wolves into our own backyards. *Wolves.* Those big-city libs and enviro-nuts think they're cute. They ain't the ones whose livestock and pets and children are put at risk. They ain't the ones whose ancestors worked for decades to clear every last one of the thieving savages out of this country. They might as well parachute a war party of Apaches on top of us while they're at it."

That's right. Or terrorists.

The speaker held the microphone cord in two fingers, whipping it around him like a roper might. "Hell, just two years ago, we had one of the most respected ranches in this state lose their federal grazing leases after they shot a wolf on the land. One single lobo. Feds said it was the wrong one. Can you imagine? Our grandfathers must be turning over in their graves, dying all over again. This ain't the country they fought and died to defend."

Hell no it ain't, said the shadowed faces. *It ain't right.*

Trace felt the wind of their voices in his chest. He'd been lonesome so long, eating dinner from tin cans and sleeping cold in the bed of his truck. Here was an entire barn full of folks as angry as he was. At his own story, in fact.

The speaker whipped the microphone cord around his boots. "Friends, that there's just the start of it. Just the tip of the teeth of federal overreach. Now we got the government running our southern border like it's two thousand miles of welcome mat. Hell, it's harder to get into Disneyland than the US of A. These federal officials and bleeding-heart politicians like our governor? They ain't the ones got to live with the *invasion* of illegal *aliens* coming over. It's a war and we're losing."

Damn right, said the crowd. *A war.*

"We ask for more boots on the ground to patrol the border and what do they give us? *Excuses.* An excuse must weigh a lot more in Washington than it does here. Here it don't weigh two ounces of jack shit."

I know that's right.

"Now they're talking 'bout outlawing private militias. They want to make patrolling and drilling 'illegal paramilitary activities.' We've got an international border porous as a got-damn sieve and they want to neuter our ability to defend ourselves. It's a travesty of the American way."

Hell yeah it is.

The speaker took a small black leatherette book from his shirt pocket. The size of a pocket Bible but slimmer. "Ladies and gentlemen, I keep this sacred document here, against my heart, so I won't forget what it means to live in a free state." He licked his thumb and opened the book and read from the onionskin page. "I read to you the Second Amendment of the United States Constitution. 'A well regulated Militia, being necessary to the security of a free State, the right of the people to keep and bear Arms, shall *not* be infringed.'"

The crowd roared as he turned the book around and moved it back and forth like a picture book. "Friends, our founding fathers knew our militias were the last and most vital safeguard of a free state. And they want to take them away from us. They want to strip the American Everyman naked, unable to defend what's his. I ask you now, are we going to let them?"

Hell no we ain't.

The speaker patted his hip. "There are people who say Texas never should've joined the Union. Should've stayed an independent republic, same as it was back in the days of Sam Houston. Back then, Texas claimed the territory all the way west to the Rio Grande here in New Mexico, not fifty miles from where we stand. The Republic of Texas, it was. Its own country. There are people who say it should be that way again."

A high yawp from someone in the crowd, a battle cry. The speaker held up a hand. "Maybe, in the not-so-distant future, a free state like that might be possible again. An independent republic. For now, we got to start taking back our rights, inch by inch, day by day. Widening the gap between us and the rest of this country. Living to our own values."

Amen. 'Bout time.

"Look around you, friends. What we have here is an invisible brotherhood, a vast empire spread across this state and well to the east, across Texas and beyond. Even to Wall Street and Pennsylvania Avenue. Men who watch out for one another. Who know when to lend a hand, and when to look the other way. They can't root us out because we're each our own man, largely unknown to the others, bound by a common set of values."

That's right.

"We're men who value family. Men who love this land. Men raised to protect and defend what's ours, and our neighbors and their neighbors on down the line. We're men who oppose tyranny. Tyranny in wolf's clothing or a thousand-dollar suit."

Damn right.

The man turned on the heel of his boot, whisking the microphone cord around his knees. "What do we do? A lot of it I can't say into a microphone, that's for sure. We are the ghosts in the machine. But I will tell you we operate a network of units prepared for rapid deployment to community crises across the region, from natural disasters to active shooters, private border patrol to riot protection to voting poll security. Some of you here in the crowd tonight are already members of those units. Ready to combat problems the government can't or won't—and to oppose the government itself, if need be. Others of you could be selected for those units in the future, should we deem you have the right skills, mindset, and willingness to serve."

Men sat straighter and tamped down their hats, as if to show their readiness.

"We're working on long-term strategies as well, measures to ensure the lasting freedom and security of our members, their families, and other like-minded people of the region. We're working to create an independent stronghold against the forces of government tyranny."

Thank God someone is.

The speaker nodded. "You might read things in the paper and wonder if we're behind it. Probably we are. Or you might have us come to you someday, asking if you're willing to look into something for us or make a wide turn around it."

The man held up a silver medallion the size of a half-dollar. It looked like a challenge coin—the kind some military units and secret societies issued to members and friends, used to prove one's bona fides. On the coin, the severed head of a wolf, the furred neck dripping blood. Like the bust of a beheaded king or queen or president.

"There are men and women in high offices who carry one of these coins. Others who work the humble beat of city streets. People who work cows for a living and people who manage multimillion-dollar hedge funds. People united in common cause. Freedom. By your willingness, now, tonight, to give of yourselves, to support the cause and take home a medallion, you will be part of the Free West, and its victories will be your own."

A dark rumble of applause filled the auction barn. A sound that grew and grew, rattling the boards, thundering under the roof. When it seemed it could get no louder a high yawp rose from the outer night, like the cry of a man but higher, louder, piercing the plank walls of the place. The crowd fell silent, no longer clapping, their hats rising ever so slightly over their prickled scalps—

Trace started awake. Above him, a howling of wolves. An eerie chorus, almost supernatural, like the singing of ghosts. He'd nodded off again, gone tumbling across old memories and dreamlands. The wolves had awoken him, penetrating his sleep, as if trying to sound him out of the canyons. He wiped the slime from his face and crawled on.

The night passed before him in a dark violet glow. The high desert of Apacheria burning pale beneath the moon and Sourmug hounding him every inch. The pain a living thing inside him. Kicking his shins and gnawing his bones, driving him outside himself. At times his mind would float out of his head and he could see his body crawling along the stony path by the river, as if looking down from a pinnacle or canyon ledge. Strangely, even as his nerves shimmered with fear, the howling wolves made him feel less alone. They knew what he was living now. They knew cold and hunger, death and agony. They lived their whole lives out here, shelterless but for spring dens and thick coats of fur.

The black river rumbled beside him; the ponderosas creaked and shivered. The stones and roots were hard and cold beneath his hands. The wind scraped and tore over the canyon walls. His eyes were wide open, dilated to capture the scantest light. He thought of how well wolves must see the world at night, not darkness but a kind of long twilight. The stone glowing for them, the river bright.

He forded the Middle Fork on his hands and knees, the cold black sluice breaking white around him, so cold he couldn't breathe. On the far side he collapsed into a ball and began to shiver. He clenched his teeth but his jaws still spasmed. He had to keep moving, he knew. He set his forehead to the ground, letting the cold fill his skull until it ached, drowning out thought. Then he lifted his head and looked down at the bloody trap.

"All right, Sourmug. Enough lazing."

Before him, the trail veered to ascend a steep slot in the canyon wall. From there it would cross high ground to meet the West Fork of the river upstream of where he'd parked the truck. He took up the drag and began to climb. Inch by inch, his breath coiling from his mouth. The path dusty and rocky-ridden, steep enough at times he had to hug the earth, arms shaking, trying not to slide back down the trail. His heart beating too fast, too hard. He laid his cheek on the ground and tried to slow his breath, deepen it, waiting for the stars and orbs to clear from his eyes.

The moon was high when he emerged onto a wide tableland. The trail slithered off through a meadow of sparse timber, fire-blacked from an old burn. The trees weaved slightly before him, aching. Branches thin and dark against the sky, needles shivering. More than a mile to the West Fork of the river, and no place to hide.

Trace was halfway across the meadow when he caught movement in the corner of his vision, a shadow in the grass. When he turned his head directly, he sensed nothing, no sound or movement. A scratch of nails on stone, if that.

The wolves hadn't howled in a long time, he realized. An hour or more. The black-scarred trees bent over him and he began to sense other creatures in the night. Dark hackles through pale grass. A puff of breath. He couldn't be sure what he saw, heard, sensed. Whether he was hallucinating. The world was rippling around him, thumping with its own blood, seen as through dark-running water. Fear dashed his veins.

Trace laid his forehead to his arm, breathing hard. The thin muscles of his back squirmed around his spine, twitching with adrenaline, as if they could shield him. As if they weren't meat themselves. Wolves didn't attack humans, but these were not normal conditions. A man in their territory, bleeding. A man who'd tried to kill them—why shouldn't they devour him?

There were mountain lions here, too, and bears, and monstrous creations of his own imagination—creatures distorted with dread, darkness, pain. Fearsome werewolves and black cougars and varied ghosts of beasts and men. The very trees seemed to warp and bend around him, sinister, capable of dropping a limb on him, crushing his spine. He had no weapons to defend himself, no long teeth or sharp claws. Only the grapnel, held like a wilted iron bouquet.

He breathed out slowly, letting the tension smoke from his mouth. Emptying himself. Quieting. His breathing slowed. Whatever was out there, in the darkness, knew fear as weakness. Could scent it, hear it, see it. Fear was their cue. By turn, that which was fearless was strong. A creature best left alone.

He'd seen it once on an elk-hunting trip in Montana. From a ridge, he'd watched a string of wolves flee a giant blond-brown grizzly whose kill they'd tried to poach. The bear was fast over short distances. He was gaining fast on the stragglers when one of the juvenile wolves whirled in place and squared off against the woolly boulder. The six-hundred-pound bear skidded to a halt on its haunches and stared at the little wolf. The sharp hump of muscle between the grizzly's shoulders heaved up and down. The bear didn't look afraid so much as confounded.

What kind of pup was this?

Trace exhaled again. Letting the fear run free of his rib cage, out into the night. Letting his heart go down to a cinder, the same as he did behind his rifle scope. His body running cold, heartless, slow—an eternity from breath to breath. Long enough between heartbeats to draw that three-pound trigger like a tiny bow.

Bang.

Trace lifted his head and began to crawl again. He exhaled into the space around him. Tried to create a breadth of calm, inflating it around himself like a balloon. A tent or shelter. With practice, a house or temple. He used the drag like an ice ax, cracking it down and pulling himself after it, letting it sound through the night. He crawled through the long arcade of blackened trees and descended into a side canyon, a diagonal offshoot of the West Fork of the Gila River. The hoodoos stood like weird towers above him. The canyon stream was bone-dry, a bed of stone.

The trail fell into a darker plane of night, colder, the moon lost behind the canyon rim. The trees grew stranger, more stunted and twisted, sun-starved. They loomed at odd angles, reaching for scant rays of daily sunlight. The iron prongs rang between the walls in violent echoes, clashing and fighting in the canyon. An eerie thunder, like old battles heard on dark nights. History at hand, happening right here around him, ringing. He was part of it, built of the same stuff as the wolf and lion and bear. Their stories half a million years deep in this place.

Deeper.

Then he was out of the side canyon. He lay on a high spur overlooking the West Fork. A black blade of river roving through thin bristles of pine. Jagged cliffs of moonstone tuff rose nearly vertical on both sides, sharp and pinnacled, formed from volcanic ash so hot it welded into rock. The cliffs went hundreds of feet under the ground, he knew, whole other planets buried beneath the surface. In the spring, freshets of snowmelt came roaring through the canyon with enough force to uproot trees and tear apart bridges and carry off unwary hikers, bashing them against cliff walls.

"Two more miles, Sourmug. Got that in you?"

He gave the trap a moment to reply.

"I thought so."

Trace began the descent. The trail was steep and loose, better suited for pronghorn antelope or desert bighorn or rangers in good boots. Rocks and gravel and clods of dirt cascaded beneath him, clacking and bouncing off into lower darknesses. He deepened his breath. His heart a stone, his blood slow, circulating no faster than the dark gleam of the West Fork far below. He paused at a nasty switchback, nearly vertical, gathering himself.

"All right, Sourmug. Tough going ahead. Let's focus, keep it tight. We got this."

He started again. Crawling, picking his way down the steep decline. Then the trail broke loose beneath him, a cascading wash of pale dust and stone, and he fell.

CHAPTER 16

One-Eleven froze. A violent clatter in the night, a tumble of earth and rock. A shriek from the canyons. A man. The rest of the pack drew up tight around her, a halo of swirling fur, ears cocked sharp.

She led them toward the sound, slowly now, trotting light-pawed, leaving but faint tracks. She was following the trail of the wounded man who moved on four limbs instead of two, dragging himself along the ground like a snake. She and the rest of the Dark Canyons zigzagged along the trail, back and forth, crossing and recrossing, swinging wide to scent the surrounding corridor, scrutinizing every living thing to come this way. One-Eleven paused often, listening. Where there was one man, there were often more.

The pups mimicked her, scenting the same stones and scrapes and trees she did, pausing to listen to the same sounds. Stiff-eared, chests puffed. Sometimes they made a show of following scent trails of their own, their square noses smashed to the ground, snuffling hard, blowing their out-breaths through their mouths. Little Paw would vanish into the darkness, off on studies his own, only to reappear just before

One-Eleven chased after him. He pushed her right to the edge of her limits, testing them. He'd return wide-mouthed with brambles tangled in his coat, dirt pasted on his nose, or the burped remnant of something dead on his breath, which spurred the other pups wild with envy.

Now the little wolf came trotting high-pawed from the darkness, head tilted, holding something in his teeth. A large stick, so big one end dragged in the dirt. One-Eleven leapt toward him, ready to trounce him for hauling out a plaything while the pack was on the move, but the scent of the stick stopped her dead.

She rammed her nose along the dark-damp wood. Urine, but not from the man they were tracking. This one hydrated, healthy, unstressed. A fresh scent, no more than an hour old. Cautious, she followed Little Paw back the way he'd come, arriving at the spot where he'd found the stick. She and Graynose circled the area, noses to the ground, sniffing brush and boot prints, learning what they could of this second man moving through the territory—the other one from the riverbank.

Scarce scent of the outer world on him. Most hunters smelled of things alien to the Gila: soap and smoke, whiskey and gun oil—scents that made them easy to track and avoid. They traveled well-beaten paths and left ragged trails in their wake, broken branches and kicked-over stones, plastic wrappers and burned matchsticks.

This man had the musk of something wilder. A creature One-Eleven had never encountered. She and Graynose traced his coming and going, up and back in both directions. His trail light and clean. No waste, scarce sign, harder to follow than most.

A thing better left alone.

One-Eleven steered her pack back toward the canyon. Soon they'd know if a man lay dead on the rocks.

CHAPTER 17

Trace hung upside down against a bald thrust of canyon wall. The trap chain was stretched taut above him, the grapnel hooked to some rock or root he couldn't see. Past the bloodied toe of his boot, the night sky was just paling, the stars disappearing from right beneath his feet. Rivulets of blood crawled up his leg like columns of ants. He tilted his head back and the black snake of the West Fork River seemed to spill from his own mouth, slithering through the rocks hundreds of feet below him.

He screamed.

He pawed for his kit bag but it was gone, lost in the fall. He turned his head and ejected a watery vomit down the rockface beside him. Again and again, retching, his vision starry and red. His eyes rolled back in his head. He saw a pair of dark birds circling high above him, black-winged in the upper sky. Ravens. They took him back to his father lying on the sandbank behind their house, staring dead-eyed at the carrion birds wheeling over him, a grinding whirlwind. Then even farther back, to the day they took the wolf.

The animal had been haunting the edges of the property for days, a lone silhouette skating along ridges and tree lines. At night, he howled over the place, as if singing the blues. In the morning, paw prints in the roads and creek banks. They kept the dogs inside.

Trace found the kill in the upper pasture, beneath a gyre of ravens. A calf. He dropped out of the saddle and stared. Death was everywhere on the ranch, all the time, but not like this. Like the yearling had stepped on a land mine. Trace's cheeks burned. This was their herd, their stock to protect. Their brand seared on each animal's rump.

He radioed his father on the two-way.

The older man was just pulling up in his battered longbed when a wolf appeared on the edge of the pasture, gnawing a bone like a dog. A remnant of the calf, most likely. Trace's father stepped out of the cab with his .30–30 already in hand. He levered a round into the chamber and threw down across the hood, resting the barrel in the crease of his hat. Two hundred yards away, the wolf raised his head and looked at them, holding the bone between his paws.

Trace looked at his father. The older man was white-knuckling the rifle. His anger radiant, coming off him like gasoline fumes.

Trace licked his lips. "He's got to be caught in the act."

"The hell you call this?"

"We ain't seen him do it. And he's got a collar on him."

The sweatband of the man's battered Resistol had made a thin, damp-dark crown around his head. His bald spot shone through a whorl of gray. Trace hadn't noticed how big it had grown. His scalp pinkish, spotted. He'd already had several lesions burned off his face. He pursed his lips and slowed his breathing; the barrel seemed to stretch across the pasture.

Trace lowered his voice. "We don't know it was him."

"It don't matter. They're all the same."

"There'll be an investigation, old man. Stories in the papers, threats from the greenies. Feds don't rule it justified, we could lose our grazing permits. The whole ranch."

The older man didn't raise his head. "It's what we done for a century."

That was true. The very reason Trace had never seen a livestock kill like this one—the wolves had been removed from here, from the whole American West.

"Just because we done it that way—"

The shot clapped across the pasture.

The wolf rolled, legs flailing at crazy angles. A plume of dust. Then still. Just the sound of the cattle lowing at the bottom end of the pasture.

They stood over the animal. A clean shot in the shoulder, right through the heart. A red patch of entry in the cinnamon fur, the tongue pink-crinkled between the animal's teeth. Trace looked at the heavy leather radio collar. They were built to be tamperproof, but he'd heard stories of magnets taped to them to block the radio signal, or collars cut and cast into caves or rivers or wells. Others dropped in the beds of pickups at interstate truck stops, only to be found hundreds of miles away, wiped clean of fingerprints—always a good chuckle from the tellers of such stories, swirling their beer at the bar.

Trace looked at his father. "What you want to do?"

The "3-S Treatment" hung unsaid in the air: Shoot, shovel, and shut up. One of the oldest codes of the West. His father knelt at the side of the wolf, silent, looking over the animal. He shook his head. "What the law dictates. Call Game & Fish."

They called from the satellite phone the old man kept in the truck for emergencies. No cellular signal for miles. Game & Fish said state and federal agents would be dispatched immediately, though it could take up to forty-eight hours for them to arrive on site. They said to leave the carcass be. Not even to touch it.

That night Trace and his parents sat around the dinner table. No moon. The windows dark as blackout curtains. A dread had descended on the place. They were scraping their way through supper when the same howl rose over the land, as if singing for the dead.

They froze, as if they'd heard their own names called.

Trace's eyes snapped open. He was howling, hanging upside down on the side of the cliff. The chain still stretched over the rocks above him, caught between ancient crags jutting toothlike against the sky. He howled louder, harder, his vision shattering into red orbs and blazing stars. He was a creature thrust out of itself, apart from its cobbled cage of bone and tissue. A spirit bursting into some other space, like flint to spark.

When Trace came back, it seemed he'd been gone a long time, but the light was unchanged. Something caught his eye, movement on the trails above him. He watched a string of shadows descending the switchbacks, pouring down like liquid, a sluice of fur and hackles and shoulder blades. Wolves or not wolves, airy things, creatures of ash and smoke. Only their bright eyes apparent, wisps of light in the gray. They passed on the trail above him and vanished into the predawn darkness. No sound, no scrape or clatter of stone. Silent as wraiths. There and gone. Trace felt their going like a sledge in his chest, a ringing hollow. Big as an empty house, a dark home. Everything gone.

For a few moments, he hadn't been alone.

Then something shifted on the ledge above him. A figure rose silhouetted against the first dull streaks of dawn. A thing cloaked in shadow, wearing it like a shroud. The set of the shoulders looked familiar, like he was looking into the dark mirror of a river or well.

"Old man?"

A loud crack from the rim, as if a rivet had popped loose in the world. Then he was falling again, the slope twisting and rolling around him, a skittering tumult of stone and dust and scrub, trap and chain and hook ringing in the maelstrom and his hands flung wide, clawing for traction, anything to slow his descent, fistfuls of grass and dirt. He slammed onto the flat ground at the bottom of the slope, covering his head as the drag hook came crashing down after him.

He lay heaving, waiting for the damage to make itself known. The bones knifing through his skin, the fractured skull or punctured lung.

Nothing.

He opened his eyes. A galaxy of small golden eyes floated around him, swaying slightly. He could hear their dry whispers in the wind.

As if he'd been found. Saved. No longer alone. He blinked his vision clear. Not eyes but wildflowers. Hundreds of them. A patch of yellow brush blooms balanced on thin spines, shivering, whispering. Alive. If he died here, he thought, tiny threads of himself would be sucked upward through their stems, blooming gold in darkness.

"Not so fast," he told Sourmug.

He rolled over slowly and began to crawl from the bed of wildflowers. The West Fork riffled through the darkness. He dragged himself across stones and gravel and the cold hard mud of the banks. Dawn was breaking, steely jags ripping through an ashen sky. He leaned over the river and cupped handful after handful to his mouth, slurping and sucking the cold clear water.

Then he was crawling again, turning downriver toward his truck, east into the rising sun. Dawn came roaring into the canyon, a lightning flood that broke against the stone spires of the canyon rim and crashed down through the trees, casting long spears of shadow from their trunks. The river hummed beside him, still in darkness, and he looked down to see prints wending their away here and there along the riverbank, still fresh.

Wolves.

So they had been real. They were traveling the same direction he was, had overtaken him during the night. He placed a hand into one of the tracks. Four inches wide, bigger than his palm.

Then he was moving again, crawling, dragging Sourmug, the chain scraping and rattling on his back. Easier here, the stones worn smooth from generations of spring thaws, eons of freshets and floods. Some, small as his thumb, might have been stone pinnacles perched high over the canyon. Once the towering roosts of ancient ravens or raptors, held now in the palm of his hand.

He rounded a bend in the canyon, entering a narrow gorge. The walls darker here, red-brown, formed from sandstone and silt and volcanic ash. The sun ripped across their rough faces, irregular strata of light and shadow. Trace felt exposed, watched. High in the canyon walls hovered the dark caves of ancient cliff dwellers, recesses gouged like eye sockets in the rock. They were full of stone ruins. Vestiges of the Mogollon people, abandoned even in the time of the Apache, who left them untouched. Geronimo, born at the headwaters of the Gila, must have heard tales of their origin as a boy, stories of the ancient cliff people with their thin ladders and fortresses carved from stone. A people vanished.

The caves caught the light, staring back blindly at the sun.

An hour later, Trace glimpsed his rig in the distance. An explosion of relief at the sight, as if death had spread its heavy dark wings and lifted from his shoulders, releasing him from its talons. He'd never been so happy for the cramped camper strapped onto the back of his truck, the thin mattress and stuffy air.

"We made it, Sourmug."

The words sounded brittle as he said them, so he shut his mouth. A coldness came creeping over him as he slithered along, unexpected so near to safety. He looked over his shoulder for something circling overhead or stalking his flanks. Watching him. He could see himself like he might be seen. A young man whelmed with hurt and fury, bitterness and ire. Animated by such forces. He saw the sadness of it. The smallness. Somehow it seemed a previous life, as if he'd died back there in the canyon.

The last stretch was brutal. Everything he'd been holding back, trying to keep corralled, came busting loose. Tears and fear, waste and desolation. So much loss, whole histories buried in the earth beneath him, flowing in the black river, singing in the cliff ruins. A world howling. He could hear it.

Then he was at the truck, pulling himself along the side like a drowning man, grasping for tube bumpers and step rails. Panting, heaving. He made for the tailgate, where he kept a key hidden in a magnetic box. He rounded the rear bumper, the blood pounding in his face and ears. He half expected to find the wolfman waiting with his knife or a man in a pale hat, a round chambered just for him.

What he found instead: a hacksaw, a quart of antiseptic, an amber pill bottle of antibiotic, and a pint of Wild Turkey bourbon, lined up like offerings at a gravesite.

The wolfman, it had to be.

A shiver wracked him, as if someone had unexpectedly touched his shoulder. Trace turned and looked back at the dark canyon out of which he'd crawled, the drag marks in the dirt. The surrounding ramparts, dark and light, like a vast crumbled fortress. Nearer, stuck on the toe of his boot, the head of a single wildflower.

Trace lowered his head and bawled.

BOOK II

CHAPTER 18

Murdoch stepped down from the bush plane, removed his silverbelly hat, and lifted his nose. The sting of dry pines, distant pinyon smoke. The brown grass of the landing strip shivered beneath him. Late fall in New Mexico, no snow yet.

He'd flown VFR—visual flight rules—which meant no federal requirement to file a flight plan. Nor would there be any record of the aircraft hangared here, as this remote property was owned by a friend of The Ranch—the headquarters of the Free West. He turned and pulled his pack from the plane, standing it on the edge of the hatch door as he threaded his arms through the shoulder straps. His rifle was attached to one side, a custom semiautomatic chambered in .308 Winchester, the twenty-two-inch carbon fiber barrel tipped with a Class III suppressor—a weapon that had brought down all manner of beasts, all over the world. Some with four legs, some two.

Murdoch hefted the pack, clipped and tightened the chest strap, and headed for the old Quonset hut to which he'd been given the key.

Inside, a 4x4 camper van rented under a false name, in cash, packed with a list of provisions he'd provided.

Murdoch had warned the old men of The Ranch not to hire out a local hunter for this operation. But they hadn't listened, had they? A table of them squinting beneath their own pale Stetsons, crossing their arms, thumbing their chins. They had a poetic streak. The old men liked the idea of the only son of one of the oldest ranching families in the land handling the job, following in the steps of his forefathers. A job they'd tackle themselves if they weren't so damn old—or so they imagined. Given the boy's history, they expected a lot of people might sympathize with him if he got caught or killed.

Look where that had got them.

Murdoch, in contrast, was not born of this place. Far from. But few knew the land like he did. Few could read it like a book, interpreting the language of sign sure as cuneiform or hieroglyphics, tracking down wolves or lions or men across high desert or great plains. Perhaps some of the old Apache hunters were his equal, or the great hunters of the civilizations before them. The Mogollon or Mimbres, armed with spear-hurling atlatls, or the nameless peoples that once hunted woolly mammoths and prehistoric camels in this country, facing down cave lions and dire wolves and other such predators.

Murdoch set his pack on the passenger floor of the van and cranked open the hangar doors. He stood a moment in the vast rectangle of light, his hands on his hips, surveying the rugged landscape before him. High mesas and deep canyons, rolling hills and the ten-thousand-foot peaks of the Mogollon Mountains. Really, Murdoch couldn't fault the old men of The Ranch too much for their aesthetics. After all, they'd brought him here. Now he'd be hunting not just wolves, but the greatest prey of all.

Man.

CHAPTER 19

Trace steered his horse, Camo, through a shivering glade. The sky, a deep cobalt, stretched cloudless over the reddish buttes. A low noonday sun. It was late November, some eight weeks since he'd been caught in the trap. His legs rode beneath a pair of heavy leather chaps, the still-scarring wound encircling his calf like a shackle that never came off.

His lower tibia had been fractured at an oblique angle, but not displaced. The doctors set the bone and gave him a titanium plate to keep everything aligned. He was out of the cast and the latest X-rays showed the bone knitting well. He was supposed to be wearing a plastic brace, which lay buried in the back of his truck, and do as much weightbearing as the pain would allow, which varied from day to day, hour to hour.

Fortunately, he had Camo to take up the slack. She was a paint, her amber coat splashed white. A lightning blaze between her eyes. She blended well with the autumn terrain of the floodplain. Brown grass and skiffs of pale deadwood, firs and pines dark on the hillsides. She wasn't his horse, exactly, not on paper. She was from the Cruz Ranch—his new employer. The ranch's cattle herd was arrayed on the far side of the river, grazing, a spread of sepia hulks under the sun. Trace was hard on the trail of the Dark Canyon pack, only minutes behind them. Their prints wended neatly across the soft earth, nearly burning they were so fresh. He'd crossed their tracks several times in the last few days, but he'd yet to sight them.

One-Eleven was not known for hunting cattle, but Trace could clearly recognize her prints. Whereas the outside toes of dogs tended to point outward from the heel pad, wolves' toes pointed straight ahead. But the outside toe of One-Eleven's left forepaw was splayed out to the side, broken at some point in her life and healed at an odd angle—a signature.

Often the tracks of the pack were loosely woven, meandering freely as members explored various scents or signs. The alphas would stop at known scent posts to sniff and mark and scratch their scent into the ground, keeping their presence known. But the Dark Canyons were traveling fast now, moving in single file, each wolf nearly stepping in the tracks of the one ahead. Their strides long and unbroken—a cycling gait they could sustain long enough to chase down nearly anything that ran on blood, batteries, or gasoline.

Now the tracks veered across the floodplain, weaving through the sage and down into the brown splash of a shallow creek. No prints emerged on the far bank, so they must have turned to trot along the creekbed itself. Trace rode Camo up out of the water and followed along the banks, stony here but at least the horse could see where she stepped.

His heart was tripping along in his chest. After he crawled out of that cliff dwellers' canyon those weeks ago, he'd felt a wild, killing lonesomeness. As he spent his days healing in the back of his truck, eating antibiotics and swabbing his wounds with antiseptic, he just wanted to be back in the Gila, in the woods. The backcountry. It was like a fever inside him, blistering his skin with sweat. As if he'd been bitten by some rabid thing. He wanted to return to the story, the one happening right here.

The wolves.

He might not be as crazy about them as the wolfman, but he had an idea that hadn't been tried in the Gila as far as he knew. One that might give him a new role out here on the range, a new purpose.

One hundred yards down the creek, the wolves' tracks emerged, arrowing straight toward the herd grazing on the other side of the gold-leafed willows and cottonwoods. Trace hupped the horse out of the draw and through the trees, out onto the broad brown slope of grama grass where the herd had been grazing. He found them bunching, drawing down into tight little groups. The fall-born calves at their center, protected, as the wolves watched from the tree line.

These were Imogen's beeves. Imogen Cruz, with her black gambler hat and dark fingernails and tattoos of arrows and moons and animal skulls. She'd crossbred her stock with some of the feral cattle rounded up from the Gila National Forest and bought cheap at auction. The idea being that any runaway beeves surviving on their own in this country must know how to deal with wolves and other predators—something bred out of most domestic cattle over the years, as they hadn't had to deal with native predators for generations. Something wilder was said to be in the blood of these cows, their herd instincts well intact.

The Cruz steers lowed unhappily as they watched the lobos. Trace could almost sense the collective tremulations of the herd, the nervous energy flickering across their backs. But they were holding their ground, their collective breath fuming beneath the cold fall sun. Wolves were unlikely to attack a large animal that stood its ground, and they couldn't go after such a dense cluster of cows. They needed to cut an animal from the herd, get it alone, or else cause a stampede, spreading out the cattle and exposing their flanks.

Trace wore a large pistol at his hip, a five-shot revolver loaded with .410 buckshot, and he rode with an old pump-action Winchester shotgun in a saddle scabbard, loaded with something else. When he'd driven through the gates of the Cruz Ranch two weeks ago and up the long drive to the big adobe hacienda, he was operating on little more than a dream he'd had, a vision of returning to wolf country. He'd limped up to the front door carrying his hat in his hands, wearing his only good shirt, and been told *La Maestra* was out in the vehicle barn. He found her buried elbow-deep in the guts of an ancient Farmall tractor, her blue-black hair roped into a ragged ponytail that hung over one shoulder.

Trace removed his hat. She did something to him. Always had. Like her very presence changed his blood chemistry, made him jumpy and shallow of breath, hyperaware of detail. Ever since that day in the arroyo, when she'd touched his shoulder and Garrison had hugged him and he'd felt rooted, loved, even as the rusty nail screamed in the meat of his hand.

He looked at her. Strangely, his eyes always went to her hands. She had deep creases over her knuckles and broad, bluish veins on the backs of her hands. Her fingers were marked with crude tattoos of suns and stars and moons that reminded him of the petroglyphs carved into the stone walls of the Gila. The feeling was like when he came across a bear or wolf or lion in the wild—something that could kill him if it wanted.

Trace licked his lips; his mouth was full of cotton. Then Imogen looked up from the tractor and a smile broke across the wide wings of her cheekbones. "Well, if it ain't Trace Temple." She set her hands on her hips and blew a black tuft of hair from her eyes. Her face glowed. "Come to see little ole me."

Now Trace was going to learn if it would work, the idea he'd proposed to Imogen that day: range riding. Not a new idea, exactly. There'd been range riders since the first six cows arrived in the Americas on a Spanish galleon. Riders who stayed with the herds, lived alongside them, guarded them from rustlers and wolves—a continuous human presence on the range. But they'd begun disappearing along with the big predators, replaced with cowboys who tended to sick and injured stock, drove them from pasture to pasture, and herded cows to market, but bunked back on the ranches.

Now there was a movement to bring range riders back. They could locate and remove any elk or deer or livestock carcasses that might attract predators. They could report sick or wounded members of the herd, fix broken fencing, and maintain range health by driving stock toward better pasture. Prevent them from overgrazing or roaming into protected watersheds. They could track wolf movements in the area, learn their runways, and check their scat for livestock predation. Their very presence, in theory, would deter predators.

Imogen had been reluctant at first. "I like the idea. I've been following what they're doing up in Montana and Wyoming. Range Rider Programs. RRPs. But we don't have the state subsidies for it here. You know how thin-stretched we are these days. I don't have hardly anything to pay you."

They were sitting on the side porch of the vehicle barn, drinking home-brewed tea from a bottle in her cooler. Trace nodded. "I don't need much. I'll be living out there with the herd most of the time, and I've got my camper truck. Just help however you can. If I can prove it's working, we can figure out how to pay for it. If it works, you'll have money to spend and other ranches will follow."

Imogen looked out across her place, the outbuildings and corrals. Her dark eyes went down to slits, sighting far into the distance. "My great-great-granddaddy was a vaquero in the time of the great longhorn droves, did you know that? Days when there were vast herds of *criollo*, cattle of the country, descended from runaway Spanish cows that survived in the wild. Those were some double-tough cattle, disease- and drought-resistant, horns wider than Humvees on some of the steers."

She swept her hand across the horizon. "To hear it told, they used to round up herds big as inland seas, ten thousand head and more. So many their horns attracted lightning. When a big boomer came down on the prairie, blue-white fire would go racing across the points of their horns, balling and crackling around wagon wheels and the brims of men's hats, sparking from the ends of their whips. The very air wired to blow. No one would utter a curse, not with God's wrath so close. After a storm, the vaqueros' faces would be blistered, especially the side that faced the herd." She nodded. "Those droves ruined my great-great-grandfather's face, scarred and pocked his cheeks, but it's how he got the seed money for this ranch."

Imogen stuck out her jaw. Something renegade in her eyes, an edged gleam. "People act like I'm being so progressive with what we're doing out here, crossbreeding with ferals and such, but a lot of it's really trying to turn back the clock, creating a herd better suited to a harsher climate and natural predation. Strikes me what you're trying to do with the range riding isn't much different, operating more like the early vaqueros and cowboys who pretty much lived on horseback."

"That's one way to see it," said Trace.

"My old man would hate it."

"How come?"

She shook her head. "He had this idea of a moment in time when everything was better. The wolves and lions and natural predators all gone, hardly any regs on water use or animal treatment or agrichems. Only the barest oversight. Back when times were easier. As if they ever were. And things don't stay the same anyway. Everything changes from one moment to the next. That world wasn't sustainable. We know that now. He was just stuck, unwilling to turn toward anything but some gloried slice of time that might never even have existed except in his memory of it."

Trace nodded. "I think there's a lot of people stuck like that. It's a hard thing to push against."

"I loved that man. I really did. But that ain't gonna stop me from evolving this place toward something that can better withstand whatever comes down the line."

"What does that mean for me?"

She looked at him, eyes aflash. "For you, Trace Temple, it means I'm gonna give you a shot."

Trace slowly drew the shotgun from his saddle scabbard and laid it across his lap, his finger curled on the outside of the trigger guard.

"Here we go."

He rode out toward the wolves, cutting between them and the herd. The Dark Canyons bolted before the man on horseback. They darted into the cover of the willows and cottonwoods, their shapes flickering through the broken cover of trees and brush, shadow and sunlight.

Trace sat the horse on the gentle slope, watching them. They were perfectly camouflaged for this country. Traces of gray and brown, buff and ocher, like chipped pieces of the land itself. They moved back and forth in the trees, wary. Trace and Camo cast a single jagged shadow before them, stunted and strange, like someone's painting of a dark horse and rider. A thrill crawled through his veins. A tingle in the shackle of scar tissue. They'd done it, he thought. What he'd told Imogen they could. The wolves were at bay, any thought of attack thwarted.

Then One-Eleven stepped from the trees, plainly into sight. Her fur silver and rust, legs dark-brushed with mud. She looked right at him.

Trace's heart jerked in his chest.

The she-wolf lowered her head slightly. Her large gold eyes bored straight into him, like she was waiting for him to do something. To speak or yelp or howl. To fight or run. It occurred to Trace that she might remember him from the day of the trap, the wet rag of him brushed all through her territory. His scent. Could she know he'd been hunting them then?

"I'm sorry." His own voice a surprise to himself. "I ain't after you now, not like that. But these cows, you got to leave them alone."

The she-wolf's ears swiveled, as if searching out the meaning in his words. Her head lowered yet farther, between her long front legs and outsize paws. Not a submissive gesture but focused. Her senses drawn down on him, aiming.

He tried hazing her, waving one hand.

"Git! Y'all go on!"

The wolf didn't move. Trace felt the shotgun across his thighs. It was loaded with 21-ball rubber buckshot, an averse-conditioning round designed for predator control. Nonlethal, though it could blind or maim at close range. A riot gun for wolves and coyotes. A last resort. Not the relationship he wanted to have with these wolves—not what he'd imagined lying in the back of his camper, recalling his bloody crucible in the canyons. But.

"Git! Go!"

The she-wolf didn't budge, her four legs planted firmly beneath the noon sun. She was staring him down, the pair of them locked into some kind of standoff.

Trace thought of the men in the pale hats who'd shown up while he was bedridden in the back of his truck. One of them had rapped hard on the camper door. When he opened it, Trace found three of them standing there with their palms resting on their holstered .45s, casual-like. Faces shaded beneath their thousand-dollar hats. Eyes masked behind mirrored sunglasses.

"Missed your check-in," said one.

"How'd you find me?"

"Lucky guess, I reckon." The man smiled. Square coffee-stained teeth, healthy gums. *We can find you anywhere.* He nodded toward Trace's leg. Trace had the splint and dressing off for cleaning. The tooth marks of the trap gleamed with antibiotic ointment.

"Reckon you stepped in something you wished you ain't."

"It wasn't plan A."

"Nor plan B, I imagine."

"Nope," said Trace. Weeks ago, he would have said, *No, sir.* They both seemed to hear the difference. The man squinted, his crow's-feet tightening outside his sunglasses. "Surprised a seasoned woodsman like yourself would get himself caught in such a trap as that. What was it?"

Trace nodded to where Sourmug hung on the camper wall. The man leaned in to see, whistled. "Outlaw trap. You think it was set for you? One of these goddamn ecoterrorists?"

Trace thought of the wolfman who'd stalked him, trapped him, and made him drag himself miles and miles back to his truck—only to leave medical supplies for his recovery. Some of the very salves and medicines he was using now.

"No," he said. "It's an old mantrap, could've been left on that trail for decades, deep buried. Just blind bad luck is all."

The man grunted, turning to glance back at his two comrades. They didn't seem big believers in luck. "When can you get back out there?"

Trace swallowed. "I'm not going back out. I decided."

"You decided?" Again the cowboy swiveled slightly, looking at the others. Their hands resting on the butts of the double-stack automatics holstered high on their belts. The man smoothed his mustache with his left hand, showing those square brown teeth. "Hate to tell you, son, but this job, it ain't one you can just *dee*-cide to walk away from."

Trace was in his underwear, his bare leg spread out before them, oozing and discolored. Knowing they might come, he had the five-shot revolver concealed under the flat bottom of his bolster pillow. Inches from his hand.

"Your money's under the foot of the bed," he said. "I ain't spent a single dime. Take it all back. That's a good deal. You get what I already done for you for free." He made no move to get the bag himself, unwilling to draw his right hand too far from the bolster pillow.

The man sniffed. "What you done for *us*? No, son, you ain't done nothing for us. Not a single damn thing. You done what you done for your country. Us? You best forget all about us." The old cowboy lifted his right hand from his belt and aimed his index finger dead center at Trace's forehead. "You best wipe your mind clean of *us*."

Then he leaned into the camper, reached under the bed, and pulled out the black leatherette duffel bag. He felt its weight, then handed it back to one of his comrades.

"Better be all there."

"I said it was."

The man shook his head. "I didn't know Old Temple's blood had run so thin. First your old man, then your mama, and now you."

He leaned and spat, then turned on his heel and walked away, striding between the pair of armed men whose eyes remained fixed on Trace, hands on their guns, as they slowly backed away.

"Git!" cried Trace again. "Go on, wolf!"

He lifted off his hat and waved it, trying to haze her. One-Eleven hardly reacted. She just watched him, ears swiveling, tail stiff. He could sense the uneasiness of the herd behind him. Snorting, hoof-stamping. The very presence of predators was known to curb weight gain in calves and the reproductive output of their mothers—the stress of it. If they broke ranks or stampeded, the wolves would give chase, unable to resist their prey drive.

"Come on, girl," said Trace, talking through his teeth.

People always said God or the universe stepped up for those who took a leap of faith, but Trace knew it wasn't that easy. The world was hard as the teeth of a Duke #16. A bear trap. No one liked to think they could get stuck in the jaws of something they couldn't quit or leave or get free of. But how many millions—wolves and bears, elephants and people—got caught in something and never got out? Steel traps or wire snares, addiction or debt or love or war.

Trace stared back at One-Eleven. She was not some magic animal. She was a predator like he was, one well-made for this country. Dire wolves had hunted the continent for eons before his own species first came marching across the Bering Strait land bridge and bred their way across the new continent, hunting mammoths and mastodons alongside the wolves and cave lions and saber cats. She was trying to read him, it seemed. Whether he was a threat. She didn't seem to realize he could reach across the thirty yards between them in an instant, too quick to flee. That he did have that magic in his hands, that power.

Or maybe she did know.

The herd would break soon; he could sense them coming to some edge. They were only so tolerant of wolves this close. He had to get rid of the pack now. The she-wolf watched him, waiting, her senses fixed on him.

Trace decided what he had to do.

She was gone the moment he lifted the gun.

CHAPTER 20

Murdoch lay on the knob of a forested butte. He'd been here since before dawn, lying prone as he glassed the high valley. He'd watched the cold blue timber slumber beneath a sea of mist, quiet in the predawn. Then the sky lightened, paled. The sun broke over the horizon and jags of light burned down into the valley, triggering the birds to sing.

Murdoch was not his real name. His real surname did start with an M, but he doubted anyone within this entire 558,014 acres of federal wilderness could pronounce it right. None of them would ever know it anyway. Not even the old men of The Ranch.

As a boy, Murdoch had spent more time fishing than hunting. The best moments of his childhood came alongside his grandfather on a moldy sofa set beside their little river, waiting for the carp to bite their bread-baited hooks. A stone footbridge stood nearby, said to be a thousand years old. But when Murdoch was thirteen, NATO warplanes bombed that bridge and the rest of their village, shattering everything into blackened shingles and rubble, gaped concrete and twisted rebar and bloody body parts. His grandfather was killed.

Murdoch spent the next winter scrambling over broken chunks of the bridge to hunt what scarce game was left in the forest. His grandfather's bolt-action Mauser strapped across his back on a length of twine, his boots wrapped in plastic garbage bags to keep out the snow. He brought home animals rib-raked and lean for the family table, honing his fieldcraft with the intensity of a starving creature—skills that would serve him well in years to come. He would spend the rest of his life earning his living with a rifle, in one way or another.

Still, all that fishing had taught him something. Patience, perhaps. The state of waiting. Sometimes for hours, sweating or shivering, believing your prey will walk into view, appearing like something you love. Though he still preferred the stalk, a kind of active meditation. All the senses elevated like the finest hairs from your skin as you wended through winter woods or bombed streets. He knew this operation would require both, to stalk and to snipe.

The land was fuming below him. The mists sun-flashed, whipped like volcanic gases from the canyons. Murdoch folded the tripod of his spotting scope and broke down his camouflage hide, then heaved his pack to his shoulders. He'd sighted elk farther up the valley where it narrowed into a red-rock canyon. He began walking down the edge of the butte, keeping in the cover of the trees, pausing now and again to lift his binoculars. The shadows of the evergreens fell slanted in the valley, sharp as arrowheads beneath the rising sun.

He'd spent the last day and a half hiking in. Few hunters roamed this deep into the federal wilderness. The nearest road was too far, the terrain too rough. You had to pack in everything you needed for several days and camp along the way. Nothing mechanized was allowed here, not even a pedal bike. Only the most dedicated hunters were willing to put in the time and effort to make a kill this deep inside the wilderness, field-dress the animal, and haul out the meat on their backs.

That made the area perfect sanctuary for late-season bulls. They were in a survival state now, done chasing cows, looking for somewhere to hide until the end of rifle season. A fortress of deep woods and hard terrain. No more bugling or racking antlers with rivals. The old bulls became creatures of shadow this time of season, venturing out only at dawn and dusk, wary as ghosts. Their racks, which had burned atop their heads like crowns of fire just weeks ago, had become brittle things to hide amid the trees.

A spooky time, this late season. Winter loomed on the horizon, heavy and chill. The woods were strange, nervous. Sound seemed to travel for miles. Murdoch caught a big bull with his naked eye. The elk was standing beneath the shadow of a tall ponderosa pine perhaps five hundred yards away.

Murdoch set the timer on his watch.

Sixty seconds, his standard.

He sank to one knee, unclasped the waist and chest straps of his pack, and slipped one shoulder free, letting the pack rotate to his strong side as he placed both hands on the rifle. One held it steady while the other cleared it from the side of the pack. Two snaps. He set the rifle on its bipod, pulled the rangefinder from his chest rig, and lased the target.

Five hundred and six yards.

Murdoch pulled the ballistics solver from his chest pocket, inputted the range, and received a firing solution. Then he lay prone behind his rifle, dialed the windage and elevation into the scope, and flipped up the caps at either end, setting his eye to the lens.

The elk leapt into the narrow sphere of vision. A six-point bull, known as a royal. Seven points an imperial, eight a monarch. A royal would thrill most hunters, a proper trophy. But no fever touched Murdoch, no blaze of blood rushed to his face or fingertips. He exhaled, letting the rifle settle into the natural cradle of his arms. Then he laid the crosshairs over the bull's shoulder, where the heart was. Exhaled again, fine-tuning the scope's parallax. Exhaled a last time. Squeezed the trigger.

The suppressor muffled the initial shot—a muted chuff—followed by the supersonic crack of the high-velocity round punching past the sound barrier, which nothing could suppress. The elk went down and didn't move. A good shot. Murdoch rolled his wrist to check the timer.

Forty-seven seconds. Well within his standard, plenty of time for a follow-up shot if necessary.

None was.

Murdoch didn't hike down to the elk like a normal hunter, who'd field-dress the animal and pack out the meat for his deep freezer. Instead he safed his rifle, retrieved an energy bar from his pack, and settled in to wait. His prey would come to him, like carp to a bait hook.

CHAPTER 21

One-Eleven looked to the distant ravens swinging against the sky. The large black birds often soared in her wake, waiting for the leavings of her kills, or else flew on ahead of her, scouting wounded animals or carcasses. Now they circled several miles to the west, over the high and dense terrain where big bulls tended to roam this time of season.

One-Eleven led the pack in that direction. The loose echelon of them trotted through the trees and across the meadows, zigging down the steep sides of the canyons, through the cold, dark waters at their bottoms and out again. Their paws ever moving, churning up craggy paths and ledges no wider than their own trundling shoulders.

That morning, she'd come across a man whose scent she recognized. The same one who'd crawled all through the canyons in the early days of the season, when they were being hunted. He'd returned. She found him with a herd of cattle that didn't flee before her, nor did he. Strange. One-Eleven was curious, but first the pack needed to eat.

Days and days since their last meal. Their bellies sucked up tight to their backbones. When they came across old kill sites, slaver smarted beneath their tongues. They'd dug up old caches, cracking black bones for marrow. It wasn't enough. The elk and antelope were nervous this time of year, crackling through the fallen leaves and brittle brush. Harder to stalk.

Closer, she could see the ravens worked up over the trees, dropping down and bouncing up again. Flighting like they wanted something they couldn't have just yet. Something still alive or newly dead, too tough for their beaks. A wolf could tear such a thing open.

Graynose shadowed One-Eleven, his black form whisking along beside her. His frosty muzzle flickered through the late sun and purple shade of the canyons. A nudge in her chest when she looked at him. A surety. A part of her, sure as the younglings that followed. She led them upcountry, the land rising beneath the bows of their chests, growing sharper as they climbed. Rougher. The trees taller, denser, clustered along high meadows where cattle grazed during the summer and bull elk crept this time of year. Low-light creatures afraid of their own hooves, trying to hide their antlers among the trees.

The shadows were at their longest, shooting long and irregular from every tree and rock and ridge, when One-Eleven led them to the edge of the meadow beneath the ravens. A bull lay in the grass just beyond the tree line, dead. High overhead, the dark flecks turned and swiveled, their shadows flung miles distant. A few of the birds had come down to chance what they could, the eyes of the bull and the small round wound in the shoulder. One-Eleven scented the fine spray of heart's blood in the brush behind the bull. She thrust her face among the dried spatter, huffing. The others were swarming around her, telling her they wanted the bull.

One-Eleven faced the direction of the elk and went rigid. Her ears rose to full height, the veined flaps of flesh pivoting here and there, tuning to the woods and meadow and opposite ridgeline. Her eyes went round, unfocused, open for any movement out of place. Her nostrils flared, winging the dusky air into her nose.

Something wasn't right.

The young wolves pushed against her, licking her jaws, telling her they were hungry. She ignored them, snapped one of them back. Graynose looked at her and the bull and back at her, dipping his head. Coyotes would find the carcass soon. Perhaps a bear or the big lion that roamed this territory. Still One-Eleven didn't move, planted on stiff legs. Something wasn't right. The elk had been killed where it stood, heart-struck. The work of men. The pack often feasted on gutshot elk found dead in the forest, miles from where they were first wounded, but men never left clean kills where they lay. They quartered them with sharp knives and carried off the fresh meat. This bull lay untouched, intact but for the bullet wound.

A trap.

Lobos of her bloodline had avoided rifles and traps and poisoned baits for generations. They'd divined steel traps boiled in oak leaves and buried beneath layers of pan-sifted dirt, laid by men who knew the land as well as any man could. They'd outmaneuvered hounds and hunters and Thunderbirds. Her ancestors the sharpest of their kind, the fittest. They had to be.

The ravens ganged in the branches overhead, gurgling and croaking, impatient. The other wolves, even Graynose, kept crowding her, running their ribs along her legs and shoulders. Hunger big as canyons in their bellies.

She was pack mother. Leader, not law. She could snap and bark the pups into place, but they were nearing her own size now, if not maturity. Still pups in her mind, but they grew larger by the day, more their own wolves, and Graynose was her rough equal. He was stronger, she cleverer. He larger, she faster. Their hearts the same size, game and bold. But a streak of something reckless ran through Graynose, who'd left his birth pack as a young wolf and ventured down from the north country. He'd crossed vast miles of hostile country, ducking beneath headlights and gunshots, digging under barbwire fences or leaping over them, living alone for years until he found his way to the Gila. To her.

The sun lanced red through the trees, silhouetting a line of leafless trees along the opposite ridge. The meadow had welled with deep twilight, darkening fast. The ravens cawed in the branches. Graynose looked at her, then licked his teeth and stepped out into the meadow.

CHAPTER 22

"You got dinner plans?"

Imogen, her voice crackling over the two-way radio. Trace whoaed the horse at his little camp by the creek. The sun just down, a reddish glow on the horizon. Trace had been telling her of his encounter with the Dark Canyon pack. That was one of the range rider selling points: someone to report what was going on in the field, to keep tabs on the whereabouts of any lobos, lions, or bears in the area. The ranchers received GPS data on the wolves from the state, but it was often twenty-four to forty-eight hours old—a wolfpack could travel a hundred miles in that time.

"Dinner?" He held the walkie-talkie sideways so the rubber antenna wouldn't catch his hat brim. "Oh, got a real cowboy special tonight. Canned pork-n-beans."

"Fine dining," she said.

Trace swung down from the saddle and staked out Camo to graze. "It'll eat."

The radio crackled. "Why don't you send me your twenty? We made a little too much tonight. I'll run you out a plate."

Trace dipped his head and keyed the mic. "You sure? I'm a good few miles west of the ranch."

"Hell, I had paperwork all day. I need to get out the office."

Trace sent her the coordinates with his GPS communicator. Once they signed off, he looked around slightly panicked at his camp, as if he had a whole apartment to tidy up. But there wasn't much he could do. Not much of anything, period. A firepit, a folding chair, an old canvas wall tent—some dirty clothes in there, but he couldn't imagine she'd be seeing the interior of that flimsy establishment. So he sat on a rock by the creek and worked the boot off his left foot. It was swollen from the long day in the saddle, the skin itchy as the shiny scars came in. A few remnant scabs still shedding. He peeled off the sock and laid his bare foot in the creek, so cold his whole body quaked.

The flat stone beneath him still held some remnant warmth from the day's sun. Trace lay back on it. He wanted to double-check the camp one more time before Imogen arrived, but the warm stone felt so good, almost like another body, and his head was growing heavy. The day's encounter with the wolves had burned up more energy than he thought. Exhaustion fell over him like a heavy quilt. His foot was beginning to numb in the creek. The water running cold and black and swift. Trace closed his eyes. *Just for a second.*

His mind began to drift, his thoughts growing fluid, strange. Behind closed eyes, he could see dark, jagged fragments embedded in the wound, like shrapnel or teeth. He watched them begin melting into the current, whirling downstream. Dark shards of himself pouring down through the zigzagging creek, swirling against boulders, streaming between rusty stock tanks and abandoned mining equipment. The waters forking and branching as they went, spreading through the land. Soon he was afloat the current himself, bobbing along beneath a dark sky. A high red moon shone on the water, turning it thick and molten, warm as blood. He realized he wasn't in the creek now but inside himself, his own body, riding the arteries through the vast country of his interior, the branching vessels and capillaries. They seemed the same, somehow. Blood and a river.

He started to paddle for shore. He wanted to see more, the terrain of these dreamlands. Moon dust and dark trees in the distance. Vast lands unexplored. In the distance, against the trees, a pale wolf. But he was slipping past, carried away faster than he wanted. Too fast. His limbs churning underneath him, not strong enough in the current. He tried to raise his voice, to call out to the animal, to howl for help, but there was blood in his mouth; he'd sucked it down on accident. It filled his lungs like a scream.

Trace roared awake, coughing and grappling for the surface. He opened his eyes to find Imogen standing over him, rearing back before his outflung arms, one hand on her hat like a bull rider.

"Whoa!" She held out her free hand. "Whoa now."

"I'm sorry," he said. Cold air in his lungs, not fluid. He pulled his foot from the creek. Stone-blue, bloodless. "Damn, I was dreaming."

Imogen shook her head. "That's all right, I startled you."

"Damn." Trace heeled his hands into his eyes. "I fell deep, didn't I?"

"My old man always said you can't trust a man don't dream aloud." She sat back on his single camp chair. "Of course, he used to sleepwalk around the house in his pajamas, talking about beef grades and pissing in the potted plants."

Trace found his hat and set it back on his head. "Better than doing it awake, I reckon." He swiveled around to look at her where she sat in the chair. Her black hair lay all jagged around her shoulders like a buffalo collar and she had the curved wire handle of a Dutch oven hooked under one finger, the cast-iron pot set between the black toes of her boots.

"What you got there? A whole pot?"

She cocked her head. "You don't know what today is, do you?"

Trace squinted one eye and looked around at the creek and pasture like they might have the answer. "It's a weekday, ain't it? Like, Wednesday?"

"It's a Thursday," said Imogen. "It's Thanksgiving."

"Damn." Trace rubbed his chin with the back of his hand, looking out across the darkened land. "Reckon I lost track of the days out here."

"Lucky for you, we don't lose track at the ranch." She tapped her boot against the side of the Dutch oven. "Brought you what's left of the Cruz family *chili picante con pavo.* Thanksgiving tradition."

"Turkey chili? You didn't."

"I did, too. Same recipe for a hundred years, or so it's claimed. Got a little cold on the ride out, though."

Trace nodded, pulled his boot on, and stoked up the fire, feeding in larger and larger sticks from his woodpile. Soon it was crackling and spiking, sending up embers. They set the black-iron pot on the grate. Trace pulled up the stump he'd been using for a breakfast table and sat down beside her. He rubbed his hands together, looking around at his meager encampment. "I just wanted to thank you for giving me a chance out here. It really seemed to work today, like it was worth it."

Imogen pulled her legs up into the camp chair and crossed them, boots and all, rocking slightly on her sit bones. "Hell, I should be the one thanking you. I didn't realize how good it would feel to have somebody out here keeping tabs on things. I'm sleeping better already."

Warmth in Trace's chest. He reached into the inner pocket of his vest for the small tin flask he carried, his father's initials engraved on the side. "I wasn't expecting company. Can I offer you a drink at least?" Just as he said it, he caught himself. "Sorry, I forgot you don't—"

To his surprise, she took the flask, scented the spout, and set it to her lips. She swallowed with her mouth slightly open, teeth just visible, venting the fumes.

"Mezcal," she said. "My favorite."

"Really? Mine, too."

Imogen handed back the flask, their fingers touching. "I just don't drink in bars, not in years. Only at home. Or with people I trust." A hardness to those last words, her jaw jutting out. Old hurts maybe, rocky under the surface. "So what was it like out here today, encountering them in the wild?"

Trace took the flask and had a small swig of his own. They were just downstream of the pasture where he'd crossed paths with One-Eleven and the rest of the pack.

"It was strange. Definitely some kind of communication going on. They were probing, I think. Trying to figure me out. People think they're just vicious creatures, savages, but if you're around them at all, you can't help seeing how intelligent they are."

"They must be, they survived out here this long."

Trace nodded, looking out into the darkness. "I know that's right."

"You think they'll be back?"

Trace chewed his lip. "Well, your leases here are in the eastern edge of their territory, even your winter pastures, so it's likely. That said, One-Eleven's got no history of predation. I think it was more I'm new out here, and they came to check me out. We'll see."

Imogen lifted her hip, pulled a bandana from her back pocket, and leaned to raise the lid from the oven. A bloom of steam. "Should be getting close. I forgot a spoon, you got one?"

Trace grimaced, lifting his hip to pull an ancient four-in-one camp utensil from his pocket. "Only this." He unfolded the spoon for her. "I can use the fork side."

She flashed her eyes at him. "Please, you think I got cooties? This here is real chili, *sin frijoles*. Fork wouldn't do it justice."

They took turns eating straight from the pot. The turkey chili was high heat, perfect for a cold night. The moon hung low over a distant ridge and the creek ran dark before them. In the morning it would have crusts of ice along the edges. Trace took a bite of chili and handed her the spoon.

"You ever think about Garrison?"

Imogen nodded, scraping the side of the pot. "A lot, actually. Even more in recent years. You know, everybody thought my parents forced me to go off to boarding school." She shook her head, still working the spoon. "Fact is, I hardly fought them. I was scared. I could see the way he was heading, same as his old man, and I was scared of going that way with him. If I stayed, I knew I would. When I was close to him, I couldn't help myself."

She shook her head. "I carry a lot of weight around about that. That I left. It hangs on me, always will. When I heard he OD'd, I just went off the tracks. I was living in L.A., modeling, dancing, just out of control. Pills, parties, cocaine. Really just punishing myself. It was my dad getting sick that finally pulled me out of it. He was in so much pain, and I didn't want to hurt him any worse, going the way I was. I came home."

She looked out into the night. "Out here, the ranch, it saved me. Righted my world. It's a hell of a pain in the ass, it really is, it'll put lines in your face like nothing else, but it's something of your own, you know?"

A sting behind his eyes. "I used to. Since we lost the ranch, I been pretty rootless, just blowing around, boondocking, living out the truck. Nothing but wheels under my feet. That tent pitched right there, that's probably the longest I stayed in one place in a year."

"Well, I'm glad you're here now."

The words made Trace's belly warm. She'd been a grade older than he and Garrison back when one year seemed an age, a whole different plane of existence. A huge gap, just incredible to cross. Now they found themselves out here where such divisions meant nothing.

When they'd finished scraping the pot, Trace walked her back to the ranch buggy she'd driven out, a small all-terrain vehicle with a bench seat, racked rifle, and long radio aerial. The moon was higher now, free of scud. The floodplain glowed silver, an alien moonscape. Trace set the pot in the bed of the buggy and turned toward her, removing his hat. A sudden ache at her leaving. Her dark eyes shone and she seemed to bow slightly toward him. Trace leaned in, close enough he could feel the warmth of her, an aura that drew him sure as fire in the night.

He opened his mouth, as if to say something. Maybe to kiss her. But a howl came flying down from the black mountains to the west. A voice hurled long and wailsome across the plain, like the keening of some prehistoric ghost.

CHAPTER 23

Murdoch walked across the meadow, fall grass crackling, his rifle cradled in one arm. Above him the stars shone wild across the ragged band of the Milky Way. Distances too vast for his species to comprehend. Just numbers. As a boy he'd liked math, physics, geometry. The ability to define and calculate invisible truths and forces. Gravity, bearing, pressure.

The orthodox priests of his boyhood couldn't predict when their Christ would return or the true trajectory of a soul after death, but simple arithmetic could calculate the drop and twist of a bullet fired spiraling across a thousand meters of atmosphere to land in the heart of an elk or bear or man. Equations could produce the launch angle of a rocket shot across seven months of space to land a rover on Mars. Algorithms were already predicting the recidivism rates of potential parolees, forecasting their trajectories through the outer world—whether they would land again behind bars, and when—while predictive analytics could determine which drivers were most likely to be involved in accidents.

With enough data and computing power, something close to God emerged. Many scientists now held with the theory the universe itself was but a simulation, a reality created inside a quantum computer. The chances were higher that we lived in a virtual world rather than a physical one. To Murdoch, that did not seem very different from living beneath the eyes of an all-seeing god. No matter the cosmic model, he knew he was an outlier, a creature without the innate hindrances of guilt or conscience or resistance to violence. And more, he knew his place inside this matrix. He was an instrument, a precision weapon that could be directed at men and beasts, even species and nations.

A snap in the brush and Murdoch knelt in place, listening, watching. Nothing. A hare or shrew. He rose and continued across the meadow, his figure casting a shadow beneath the pale of the rising moon.

The wolves had first come out of the trees at the cusp of nightfall, sniffing at the dead bull. High on the ridge, Murdoch thought he'd have enough light for a shot, but it took them a long time to quit dancing around the animal, scenting the carcass, and investigating the surrounding area. By the time they settled down and tucked in for their meal, it was full dark.

Murdoch had prepared for such an eventuality. He mounted a thermal clip-on sight to his rifle's forward rail system and zeroed it with his day optic, mating the crosshairs. A new world became visible, a twilight realm where heat signatures glowed white. The warmer the object, the brighter. He could see the cold-dark carcass of the bull elk, drained of warmth, and the white-hot shapes of the wolves dancing like wraiths around the fallen hulk, their jaws covered in black masks of cooled blood. He counted them. One was missing. The one he wanted.

One-Eleven.

There. She was hovering in the woods behind them, glowing in his scope, a ghost in the trees. Strange she wasn't feeding alongside the rest of the pack, that she hadn't even stepped from cover. Murdoch zoomed in on her.

He'd done his homework. He'd read accounts of the old outlaw wolves said to have an uncanny sense of traps, poison, danger—Las Margaritas and Old Three Toes and Lobo himself, King of Currumpaw—animals that seemed to harbor a true sixth sense, evading the most veteran trappers and hunters for years. Roy T. McBride, one of the most revered trackers of the century, said he just couldn't comprehend how Las Margaritas could avoid traps set so well they *could have been born there and not any better concealed*. It took McBride eleven months of focused pursuit and several thousand miles on horseback to catch that single outlaw wolf in the state of Durango, Mexico.

Some said One-Eleven was of similar blood, but Murdoch doubted such tales. They were inevitably written by the victors, the men, who always held their own skills in high regard. He'd heard a proverb during his time in Africa: *Until the lion learns to write, every story will glorify the hunter.* Probably a mistranslation, but it rang with truth. The more mythical the animal, the more celebrated the hunter who slayed it.

Then One-Eleven perked her ears and looked across the meadow, staring right in his direction. Murdoch, hardened as he was, felt a weird twitch of unreality at the sight. It started at the base of his skull and crept down his neck. The sense of a slight wrinkle in his world, a shift—this wasn't the reality he'd thought. In that world, there was no way the wolf could know he was here. He was downwind, nearly half a kilometer away, hidden in darkness and camouflage. And still he didn't have a clean shot. The she-wolf was too deep in the trees, screened with limbs and brush, unwilling to step into the clear.

Murdoch waited behind his rifle, prone, one knee hugging the ground. Soon her hunger would overcome her, he thought, drawing her out of the woods. The others were feasting, gorging on bloody chunks of elk. Some of the meat they would cache, burying it for harder months to come. Old meals they could dig up during thin times.

The moon rose higher. The she-wolf still hadn't emerged from the trees, but Murdoch didn't mind waiting. Much of his life had been spent in such blinds, in the high windows of bombed-out apartment buildings or deep in the bush, waiting for his quarry to appear. Once he'd shot five enemy snipers in a single day, each one slithering into the same culvert where a dead comrade had been dragged away. Murdoch found it offensive. Each one crawling right into his crosshairs. They must have been ordered to do it. He didn't feel sorry for them, but how he would have enjoyed putting a bullet in the brain of their commander, eliminating his thread from the gene pool. A service to the species. Alas, such men rarely raised their own heads over the wall.

A pale slash of heat in the scope. One-Eleven bounded from the trees, grabbed a big piece of meat, and wheeled back into the woods—much too fast for an accurate shot. Then she dropped the meat. One of the young wolves, then another, turned and followed her into the cover.

Murdoch smiled. The bitch was savvy. He'd not come across such an animal since his time in the Russian taiga, hunting a man-eating Amur tigress that eluded local authorities. It had started when a local poacher shot the animal and stole part of her kill. The bloodied tigress tracked the man back to his remote cabin, devoured him, and then began hunting down a string of men connected to him. She'd annihilated most of a local poaching ring before Murdoch's arrival. The tiger's sheer intelligence prickled the fine hairs at the base of his skull. Once he found a mattress she'd dragged from a poacher's hut and lain on for hours, waiting for the man to return home. Some said she ought to be left alone to finish her work. But he put a bullet in her, the same as all the others.

Murdoch shifted his aim to the wolves still gathered around the elk. He might not be able to take One-Eleven tonight, but he could wound her just the same.

He moved his crosshairs to the old male wolf.

CHAPTER 24

One-Eleven howled. She stood on the bare tuff of a promontory and howled over the nightland. Over ragged blue canyons and flickering streams, moonstone bluffs and broad plains. Behind her, the pack raised their own voices, higher and sharper, a wild chorus of wails.

They howled Graynose. Meat-getter, blood-bringer. Father wolf.

One-Eleven had been in the woods with the piece of elk, her young gathered around her, working on the big hunk of meat, when there came the lightning-crack of a shot. She bolted at the sound, fast and deep into the woods, pulling her pack from the danger. They might have run for miles if she hadn't stopped on a small ridge and turned broadside to look. She had to see.

Graynose lay motionless beside the elk, his side bloodied. One-Eleven huffed the air for him, his scent, a last shred of him, but they were upwind. No trace of him on the air. Nothing. Her body quivered, quickening, her flesh telling her what to do. She turned and ran, leading the pack from the gun.

Now they stood high on the ash tuff and howled. They howled

father wolf, elk-killer, meat-maker. They howled Graynose, warmth-giver, mouth-licker. They howled for him again and again, in unison and apart, ribs heaving, ears slanted back, mouths made into little circles. A pale fire of breath burned just above their snouts, sending up their voices. The young wolves believed their howling would make him come, summoning him across miles of canyonland.

It always had.

The fire of their breath died out. The last of their howls traveled far into the distance, bounding off the rocks. They stood splay-legged on the tuff, weight forward, listening to the land beneath them. Their jackrabbit ears pivoted this way and that, trying to catch the sound of him, a lone echo of the pack.

Nothing.

One-Eleven stood rigid among them, ears cocked high. Dozer and the pups turned to look at her. They rubbed their heads against her shoulders, along her sides. Their snouts still bloody. She ignored them. She remained fixed in place for a long time, listening. Then she turned and led them off the tuff, back into the trees.

CHAPTER 25

Murdoch stood over the wolf. M997. The gray-nosed alpha male of the Dark Canyon pack. A clean shot through the heart, sent from 506 yards—the same distance as the elk. The rest of the pack had fled at the supersonic crack of the bullet. Murdoch had waited behind his rifle for them to return, the glow of the dead wolf's heat signature slowly dimming in his thermal scope. None came.

Now he squatted down and unbuckled the heavy leather collar from the animal's neck. It had been attached by wolf biologists in the Lamar Valley of Yellowstone Park some eight hundred miles north of here—the land where the wolf had been born. The two-inch collar was lined with stained shearling and held the chunky black box of a GPS unit. Under normal circumstances, the transmitter would emit a mortality signal after remaining immobile for four hours, which would prompt the Interagency Field Team to deploy to the site, investigate the animal's death, and recover the device.

However, 997 had outlived the batteries in his unit. He was twelve years old, meaning he'd survived twice as long as an average wolf in the wild. The animals tended to die early of injury, disease, hunters, or other wolves. Short and brutal lives, like those of warriors or pioneers. When 997's tracking unit quit transmitting a year ago, the field team had decided not to replace the batteries, which would require darting and capturing the old wolf for the third time in his long life—they decided to leave him alone.

Still, Murdoch stowed the collar in a Faraday case, a heavy sleeve lined with a layered metallic material that blocked all wireless signals in or out. He carried his own phone inside such a sleeve at all times on assignment. Then he strapped his rifle to his pack, took the wolf by the hind legs, and began to drag the carcass toward the woods. His heart was chugging as he hauled the ninety-pound body through the trees.

He was into his fifth decade, but his body, weathered with hard use, was slow to age. His night vision was still good, the forest quite clear around him, and he enjoyed the pounding chest and coursing veins of such manual work. It brought up a prickly sweat in whose afterglow he always slept better. Though Murdoch slept quite well for a man who'd done the things he had.

He chose a spot where the spiky, leafless crown of a lightning-killed ponderosa let down a dim silver glow. The moon would help his work tonight, and come spring the sun would spur plenty of understory growth at this spot, speeding the body's decomposition. He checked his GPS watch. Five hundred and eight meters north-northeast of the kill site.

He set his pack against the tree, got out his camera, and took photographs of the carcass for the men of The Ranch. The images were stored on an encrypted SD card, impossible to access without two-factor authentication. Then he slipped the sheath from his entrenching tool, unfolded the handle, and got down on his knees. Since the collar wasn't active, the procedure was simple: Shoot, shovel, and shut up.

Murdoch had just driven the blade into the ground when the wolves began to howl. He put them at a distance of three to four miles, east, their howls scarcely audible given the range and terrain—at least to the human ear. He kept digging, remembering a story from his childhood, a fairytale of sorts. A young couple was driving a horse-drawn sleigh through a dark forest, headed for the next village on a winter night. They'd been warned not to travel after nightfall, as wolves were plaguing the land. But they went anyway, taking their baby with them. A little boy, swaddled tight on the seat between them.

When they were deep in the forest, they heard the howling of wolves over the skirling runners and clinking traces. The horse, spooked, redoubled its speed, but it was too slow. A black wing of wolves came ravening from the trees, yipping and smoking, and set upon the sleigh. The husband turned his whip to the beasts, cracking blood from their backs, knocking some of them tumbling and yelping through the snow, but they were too many. Wolves ganged the horse and snapped at the sleighers' boots; some tried to leap over the armrests into the couple's laps, teeth bared for their throats.

When the sleigh broke from the trees, it was mobbed with the animals, a fury of hot breath and snapping fangs and sharp hackles. The lights of the village came into sight. But there were too many wolves, too close, the hot cloud of their breath spuming across the faces of the young husband and wife. Their sleeves and boots were torn bloody. They'd never make it. They looked into each other's eyes. Without a word, they took up their baby boy and hurled him to the wolves. They thought the sacrifice would satisfy the beasts, divert them long enough they could reach the village gates.

It didn't.

The couple and their horse were killed. The sleigh overturned, the bodies ravaged. But when the villagers arrived, driving off the wolfpack with hayforks and firebrands, they found the baby lying unharmed in a little pocket of snow, still swaddled in his blankets. The orphan would grow up with special powers, the ability to bend the will of animals to his own, directing whole packs of wolves with a raised arm or guttural command.

It was a popular tale in the orphanage where Murdoch was sent after his mother and grandmother passed—his only remaining family. He was fifteen at the time. Too old for the stories of such a place. He escaped the next week and enlisted in the rebel militia, which didn't question the age of boys who could shoot as well as he could.

Of course, Murdoch's own grandfather had told him the same story as a boy, fishing for carp beside the old stone bridge. Back then, the ending was not the same. In his grandfather's story, everyone died, both the parents and the babe.

"You will think it a dark story," his grandfather told him. "But it has grown softer with age. In the time of my own *deda*, the young husband and wife survived to live with what they'd done. No one would so much as look at them for the rest of their days, let alone speak to them. They were silenced in every village across the land. The story haunted their every minute, awake and asleep. Even the lowliest drunk spat at their feet. Sometimes, death is a mercy."

When the grave was two feet deep, Murdoch sat back on his heels and rested. The standard of six feet deep was a remnant of the Great Plague, he knew, when the lord mayor of London decreed all graves should be at least this depth. Most states of America, however, only required eighteen inches for a casket, twenty-four for a naked corpse.

Once he'd hydrated and eaten another energy bar, Murdoch laid the animal in the grave and reburied it, tamping the earth when he was done and covering the site in brush until no trace of the wolf was left. Nature would do the rest.

CHAPTER 26

Trace woke before dawn. He was zipped to the chin in his cocoon bag, his breath steaming inside the dim tent. He ached inside, in a way he hadn't for a long time. His nerves sharper. His heart a raw thing in his chest, throbbing.

The wolves had howled all night, over and over again for hours. It had to be the most lonesome sound in the world, high and haunting and wild, like an old blues song or mountain ballad. Muddy Waters or Lightnin' Hopkins, Bill Monroe or Hank Williams. The sound of being close to someone you loved, someone who brought light to life's darkness, warmth to cold, and then being torn apart from them, your heart plucked from your chest—that was the sound, and it cut him to the quick.

It was more than just the howling. He'd felt a deep, sweet warmth with Imogen around the fire, the pair of them scraping chili from the same pot—a warmth he hadn't felt in so long he'd forgotten it existed. They'd been so close for a few seconds. Breath overlapping in the night, chests heaving. So close to something new—until the howls shattered the night. Everything turned darker at her leaving, double cold.

Trace glanced at Sourmug hanging from a wooden tentpole, snaggle-toothed and grim. "Quit my damn sulking, I know, I know." He rose, made a thermos of coffee, fed and watered Camo, and rode onto a low rise near the camp. As the sun cracked the horizon, Trace lay glassing the landscape, watching the pale tide of light creep over the floodplain. Mist fumed from the creeks.

He didn't need to be a wolf biologist to reckon something serious was amiss with the Dark Canyons. Never had he heard such frequent, strident howls. The latest telemetry data was more than twelve hours old. It showed them headed due west from the pasture where he'd seen them yesterday, and the howls seemed to carry down from that direction.

The herd was his priority. The cattle. But he felt a deep tug to investigate just what was going on with the pack. He raised the Cruz Ranch on the radio. "Base, this is RRP One, come back."

A crackle of static and Imogen answered. "Up early, Range Rider. Not the *chili con pavo*, I hope. Over."

"No, ma'am. Most surely not. And I want to thank you again for that. Sometimes you don't know how much you need something till you get it. Over."

"Just trying to give you a little taste of home out there in the field, Range Rider. Over."

Trace smiled. "Well, I'm gonna head a bit farther afield today, west, possibly outside of radio range. Those wolves we heard when you were leaving? They howled all night like that. On and off for hours. Something's up. The more I can learn about the pack, the better I can protect the herd. Over."

"Ten-four, Range Rider. Check in when you can. And be careful out there. Forecast for snow tonight, at least at the higher elevations. Over."

"Yes, ma'am, will do. Over and out."

An hour later, he and Camo reached the old fire tower on the western edge of the Cruz lease. It had been decommissioned years ago—aircraft and drones were replacing the old fire lookouts. The barbwire was loose, rusty. He tied off Camo to graze and fished out the old saddle blanket he'd stashed in the hollow of a nearby tree. He slung it over the rusty wire, scaled the perimeter fence, and lowered himself carefully on the other side, favoring his bad leg.

He climbed the several flights of metal stairs to the view shed. The lock was jiggered, the door slightly ajar—just as he'd left the place. Inside, the alidade table stood in the center of the room with an old Osborne Fire-Finder on top: a circular map of the area, glass-topped, with a pair of brass sighting apertures that swung around the outer rim on a narrow track. If the lookout on duty sighted a fire, they'd line up the crosshairs of the two apertures on the distant smoke, which gave a bearing they could report to dispatchers or fire crews.

Trace cranked open one of the west-facing casement windows and set up his spotting scope. The rising sun was coming through the crazed glass panes behind him, making the little sky-cabin glow with dusty gold light.

Last summer, he'd hiked here with a young woman he met at one of the park campgrounds. A kind of date. She'd just graduated from a university creative writing program and was on a long solo van trip around the country, visiting as many national parks as she could. She'd sat just where he was sitting now, cradling her chin in her hands. "I always thought of being a fire lookout as one of my dream jobs," she said. "You could sit up here all day, just you and your own thoughts, good books and the soughing of the wind, the shifting moods of the land beneath you. You know?"

Trace had nodded at the time, just to be polite, but it sounded like Grade-A Hell to him. Sitting in the same spot day after day, month after month, watching the world move at its own pace. He had to be out on the move, working, sweating, or something bad built up in his blood.

He'd felt it in the weeks he lay in the back of his truck, recovering from the trap-wound. Like a scream inside him. A need to be outside, in the field.

Before him, the fall landscape looked like a dark, rugged sea with troughs deep enough to swallow ships whole. He wasn't sure what he was looking for out there. Some sign.

He squinted into the scope, scanning the ridgelines, holding his breath as if it might make his vision keener. When his satellite phone rang, he jumped. He pulled it from its pouch and looked at the number.

"Hey, Mama," he said. "Happy Thanksgiving."

"That was yesterday. And you ain't called. Tried your regular cell number and it went straight to voicemail."

"I'm sorry, Mama. I been off the grid a bit. Honestly, I didn't realize it was Thanksgiving yesterday till it was too late to call."

She sniffed. "Hell, I was up. What's got you off the grid?"

"I got a job at the Cruz Ranch."

"Cowboying?"

"Something like that."

"I heard Imogen come home to run it."

"What else you heard?"

"Nothing that nice, but it was a bunch of small-brained peckerwoods saying it, men that couldn't ranch forty acres with fifty cowhands. Ranching's never been easy for no man, let alone a woman." Trace heard the snick of her cigarette lighter. "You been out with her yet?"

"Out with her? She's my boss now."

"Cowboying don't pay shit, it ought to have benefits."

"Jesus Christ, Mama, I can't listen to this."

"Calm down, God. I'm just rilin' you. This here is what you get, you don't call on Thanksgiving. Or did you think you'd escape the ration of shit you had coming?"

Trace smiled despite himself. "Naw, I knew better than that. Where you at, anyway?"

"Home."

"*Home*, home?"

"Bank might've taken back the place, but they ain't changed the locks. Your mama's back in high cotton at the moment."

"How long you planning to stay?"

"Not sure yet. I got back in touch with my sponsor. He's got me into an outpatient rehab program. Just staying here till I can find a room in town."

"I know that's a hard thing to swallow, going into a program. But it takes guts, too. I'm proud of you, Mama."

"Well, I just want to thank you for not giving up on me since your dad passed. I think I near about gave up on myself. And I know I ain't been there for you like I want to be. Though you can't be too bad off if you're hired on at the Cruz Ranch. Better than that damn mine."

"That's the truth." Trace thought of the vast gouge of the Chino terraced deep into the earth, smoking and thundering, not a green thing in sight. "I should have a free day or two coming up. I'll drive over to see you."

"Well, don't go out your way. But I'd like that."

"Me, too."

He'd been scanning the ridges and folds of the terrain as they spoke, slowly working the pan lever of the spotting scope. Now, above a distant ridge, he spied a dark whirling of carrion birds. Ravens like black feathers floating.

He cocked the phone back to his mouth. "Mama, I best be getting back to work. But I look forward to seeing you soon. I really do."

"You, too, boy."

After they hung up, Trace went to the fire-finder and lined up the column of carrion birds between the apertures to receive a bearing. He estimated their range at four to five miles. Tracing the tabletop map, that put them deep inside the Gila Wilderness, around a high valley known for big elk this time of year. Right in the heart of Dark Canyon territory.

"Bingo."

He descended the tower, remounted, and swung the horse toward the Wilderness.

CHAPTER 27

One-Eleven had kept the pack moving all night and most of the morning. Now she had them sheltered beneath a reddish cutbank on the Middle Fork of the river. A low, dark, damp place, like she sought whenever a Thunderbird came hounding across the sky. She stepped out from beneath the ledge and raised her nose to the wind skating down the narrow canyon. Full in her nose, a roundish sting. Snow coming. She saw it paw-deep on the mountains tonight, enough to muffle some sounds and sharpen others. Not enough to touch the dry country of the valley floors and tablelands, but the higher slopes would be powdered white.

The pups mewled behind her, missing Graynose. Deer-killer, father wolf. One of them stepped toward her, out of cover, and One-Eleven bared her fangs. He nearly tripped on his own paws whirling back to his siblings. Still they roiled and panted behind her. The taste of elk had frenzied them. Their first meat in days, but scant. Now they were blood-dizzy, wanting more. Five moons ago, they'd still been eating what she and Graynose and Dozer disgorged for them—meat from distant caches or kills, carried to the den in their bellies.

Now Graynose was gone and she had to get the pack to safe territory. She'd take them high into the burned-over forest. Fire had ravaged the place last summer, bright flames stampeding across the mesas and over the rivers, roaring, blasting trees apart. The rivers ran black with char and the sun turned red with smoke. They could starve in such burned country, but they'd have it to themselves. No elk, no hunters. Little place for men to hide. She knew a cave up there, an old den, where she could see for miles.

Now another littermate—Little Paw this time—stepped from the shadows. One-Eleven was about to growl him back, to nip his flanks or neck, when she saw his small black nose lift sharply over the riverbank, twitching and flaring. A scent. One-Eleven raised her own nose. Nothing at first. Then it hit her, heady and potent, raking the guard hair high from her shoulders. Another bull elk, and close. A thread of power streaming down the canyon. The rest of the pack caught the scent. They jerked still, eyes wide, nostrils flared. They lowered their heads and folded their ears, crouching behind her. They were downwind of the elk or it would've winded them already.

Strange. A large bull low along the river this time of season, far from the protection of the mountains. One-Eleven waited. The pups stood rigid, hackles puffed out like antennae. Hooves sounded along the stony bank, heard over the rattle of winter cattails and brown birches. A wounded bull, lame. She could hear it, the irregular sound of his gait. Now the tang of blood in the air. Slaver jetted from the corners of her jaws, wetting her teeth. The animal rounded the bend upstream. Antlers curly and barbed, big as tree limbs, and a broken hind leg. A red jag of bone jutted from the hock. His breath smoked from a dry nose, loud and irregular. He'd fallen down the canyon side and couldn't climb out.

When the bull winded them, he stamped a front hoof and raised his head, chin high. One dark eye found them beneath the cutbank. The Dark Canyons stood in ragged formation, a state of violent fixation. Muscles tensed, hackles raised, hearts quickened. One-Eleven slowly lowered her head. Her shoulder blades grew high and sharp from her back, cocked. Her snout lengthened, taking aim. She'd never chanced a bull this size, not without Graynose at her side. But the pack needed meat for the hardship to come.

One-Eleven shot across the river, boring through the cold crash of the current. The elk swung its spiked antlers toward her.

CHAPTER 28

Whenever Trace crossed into the Gila Wilderness, he felt he was stepping into another time, a distant past or future. No cell towers, no cars or four-wheelers. Horses and mules the only means of transportation permitted besides one's own feet. Outfitters led bear, elk, and muley hunts here, but they had their favorite canyons and mesas, their honey holes.

Most of the backcountry was still isolated, remote from civilization. Hikers went missing inside the Gila every year. Years ago, a South Carolina woman had been found after forty days alone in the wilderness—the same as Christ—trapped on the far side of a snow-swollen river, discovered by two brothers miles from the nearest road. She was too weak to hike out, so the backpackers left her food, water, and a crime novel—Michael Connelly's *Chasing the Dime*—then rucked out twenty miles, hitchhiked another forty, and alerted the authorities, who found her with a helicopter, night-vision goggles, and a survey map.

The Gila was the first federal wilderness in the country, established in the 1920s with the help of a ranger named Aldo Leopold.

He'd written a book, an almanac which Trace had been assigned in high school but never read. His name graced a neighboring wilderness carved out of the original Gila tract, so the two federal wildernesses—the Gila and the Aldo Leopold—sat side by side inside the greater national forest.

Trace and Camo entered the Gila on a marked trail. The wooden sign at the trailhead was flame-blacked from an old burn, a charred list of hot springs, canyons, and junctions deep inside the Wilderness. The distances to each landmark all but unreadable, but no matter—Trace knew the area by heart.

The territory of the Dark Canyons loosely overlapped the boundaries of the Gila Wilderness, whose western border ran near the San Francisco River, five miles from the Arizona state line. Past that, the Whitewater pack reigned, a clan of Arizona-born wolves infamous for their aggression, known to hunt down and kill any lone wolves in their territory.

Trace reckoned the carrion birds were assembling over a valley at the foot of Ravenfeather Mountain, a high haven for late-season bulls. Few outfitters led trophy hunts there. Many of their clients weren't but once-a-year horsemen, and the trails were too crumbly and narrow up on the mountain. Some seemed to cling midair to the cliff faces, laced with silty washes that streamed down hundreds of feet to gulches too narrow for helicopters to reach. *Doctor-killers*, Old Temple used to call these washouts. *Lawyer-eaters*. Old Temple had taken pride in the fact he hadn't gone to see a doctor for sixty years after leaving the service. Maybe that's why he'd had to see so many of them in his final years.

Trace turned Camo up a dry creek that ran off the main trail, picking their way through fallen limbs and loose rocks and eroded roots to the top of a small mesa of juniper and pinyon pine. On one end, it rose into jagged spires of welded volcanic tuff that looked like some strange medieval castle, the mountaintop refuge of a sorcerer or witch-king. They took a small game trail that zigzagged between the towered rocks, skirting the spine of Raven Creek, climbing until the riffling stream wasn't but a dark thread beneath one stirrup. Stray stones skipped and whizzed down the slope, but Camo trod sure-hoofed, unfazed.

The path climbed finally into a thick forest of ponderosa pine that grew nearly sideways from the reddish slopes. By early afternoon, the creek gave onto the valley hidden beneath Ravenfeather Mountain, whose broad upper shoulders were covered in evergreen spires of spruce and quaking aspen.

Trace sat the horse on a small overlook amid the trees. A little fold of heaven down there, storied for bronze bulls the size of moose. He thumbed up the brim of his battered hat and crossed his hands on the saddle horn, leaning forward, enjoying the view. He hadn't been up here since his father passed. Since the wolf. He squinted across the valley, looking for what had drawn the ravens.

A hot sting in his left hip. He yelped and wheeled, slapping at his rump, trying to kill the offending hornet or scorpion or spider. Instead he found the wolfman standing behind him, grinning in a friendly way, holding what appeared to be a long spear.

"You!" Trace threw his hand to the revolver on his hip.

The bearded man tucked the spear into the crook of his arm. A jabstick like the kind used for dosing cows, a hypodermic needle at the pointy end.

"What the hell, man. You just shoot me up with something?"

"Just a little dose to sweeten your dreams."

Trace looked down at his own right hand, frowning, watching his fingers fumble at the hammer strap of his holster. The digits weren't working right. "Sumbish." He frowned at himself, the slurred word. "Sumbish," he said again, trying to get the word right. "Fuh."

His faculties were running out on him, turning to mush. The horizon tilting. He was sliding off Camo's back. He tried to hold on, grasping at the pommel and cantle and gullet, but everything was turning liquid on him, slippery, as if the whole world had been coated in baby oil. He managed to get his boots underneath him, hugging Camo to keep himself upright. His legs hung loose as ropes from his hips.

He looked at the wolfman. “Fug you done to me?”

He melted to the ground beside the horse, cross-legged, holding the reins in his lap. The wild man stood over him in his beard and camouflage. Trace closed his eyes, hard, then opened them. Now the man wore the skin of a Mexican wolf. Swept ears and yellow eyes crowned his forehead. His face protruded from beneath the fanged jaws, smiling.

Then Trace was lying on his side, sinking down into the earth.

The dark earth.

Sinking.

Gone.

CHAPTER 29

One-Eleven lunged beneath the bull's antlers and sank her teeth into the animal's throat. The wounded elk stumbled back on its broken leg, hooves skittering, wrenching its head violently this way and that, trying to sling her free. His leg collapsed and the pair of them crashed down into the river. One-Eleven underwater, holding fast so the bull couldn't gore her. She came curling out of the shallows on top of the capsized hulk, blowing slaver from the corners of her mouth as Dozer leapt down into the stream and tore into the animal's flanks.

One-Eleven's fangs cut the fat vein of the neck. Blood exploded into her throat. She nearly choked, thick bubbles crackling through her teeth as the bull screamed and thrashed and threw his antlers back and forth, trying to rake her belly or flanks. It took him several minutes to die, the cold water swirling red around them. One-Eleven waited, setting her teeth even deeper. Dozer took hold of one of the bull's legs, subduing his final thrashings. The pups hopped and yipped on the bank, hardly able to contain themselves. Finally Little Paw splashed down to help and the others followed.

Still wary of the bull's antlers, One-Eleven waited until the life had fully burned out of the animal before removing her teeth. She stood red-jawed, panting. Elk-slayer, mother wolf. Dozer and the others looked at her. Waiting. Holding limbs in their teeth. When she dipped her head, they dove in to feast.

They ate and ate, filling their bellies with the heavy power of the bull, a sea of muscle and blood. It smoked from their jaws. Soon the pups were meat-drunk, fat as ticks. One-Eleven led them belly-sloshing into the shadow of a small cave blackened from the smoke of ancient campfires. She circled twice and lay down. The others curled up against her, already dozing. All but Little Paw, who sat staring out at the river, tail swishing slowly. Sentinel pup. Watch wolf. Same as Graynose.

One-Eleven's eyes grew heavy. She couldn't keep them open. So much flight and blood and loss. Beside her, Dozer rolled onto his back and pushed one big forepaw into the air, eyes squinted shut. One-Eleven stretched out on her side, two pups coiled against her belly and the third watching out.

She twitched and whined in her sleep, dreaming. She and Graynose were running side by side, chasing a glowing elk. They followed the animal down a dark canyon that went sidewinding through the earth, fast and crooked and sharp, the elk's antlers trailing long ribbons of flame that illumined the craggy walls. Then Graynose was outpacing her, running faster than he ever had, faster than she ever could. Her shoulders surging in her sleep, breath roaring, lungs burning as she turned a rocky corner and Graynose was gone.

All the canyon howled in sudden darkness.

CHAPTER 30

Trace woke with a start. He reached for his face. A cold gobbet of slobber on his chin.

"Ugh." He wiped his mouth with the back of his hand. Head cloudy, thoughts like mud. His surroundings began to seep in. Small cave, camouflage netting over the mouth. Jerry can beside him, bundle of kindling, a tamperproof bear box labeled DRY BEANS. Someone's backcountry cache or hideaway.

He felt his hip. No pistol or knife. He looked around, found his hat hanging on an iron peg above his head. At least he wasn't dealing with a complete barbarian. The nicker of a horse outside. Trace crawled up to the netting. The wolfman stood outside with Camo, rubbing her neck as she grazed.

"You're up," said the man. He wore heavy canvas overalls, well stained and worn, and a wool sweater with a roll collar like a schooner captain might wear. Over that, the same chest rig he had on during their last encounter, now with an armor plate carrier. He'd taken off his gloves to pet the painted mare.

Trace crawled out from the cave on all fours, dragging his limbs like sacks of dry concrete. "You son of a bitch. You hurt that horse, I'll kill you."

The wolfman glanced at him. "I'd hurt you a hundred times before I hurt this animal. And look at you, fit as a flea."

"The fuck I am. Steel-trapping me wasn't enough, you had to tranq me, too? You could've killed me in that canyon. I still ain't right."

"They say you have to break something to heal it."

"Oh, is that what they say. Here I thought it was: *Don't fix it if it ain't broke.*"

The bearded man found the curry comb in an outer pocket of one of the waterproof saddlebags. Camo quivered with pleasure, one round eye watching him slide the black rubber brush across her shoulder. "A thing that's never been broken has never been properly tested. Won't never be as strong as it could."

"Ain't you a fucking delight to talk to." Trace eyed his pack, pistol, and shotgun propped against a nearby boulder. "I think I'll submit me a review, comparing this conversation to your other tortures." He shook his head. "I might've died in that trap because of you."

"No."

"No? What do you mean, no?"

"I was watching over you the whole time."

"Bullshit."

The wolfman worked the comb in a circular motion across the muscled terrain of the mare's shoulders. Combing with the grain, picking up dander and scurf. Camo leaned toward him, batting her long eyelashes. The bearded man glanced over his shoulder. "How you think the drag hook got unstuck when you were hanging off the side of that slope?"

Trace opened his mouth, closed it. A flash memory of a silhouette atop the ridge. He shook his head. "Just who the fuck do you think you are?"

The wolfman looked at him. "I'm the man who just saved your life."

"Just saved my life? How the hell you figure you saved *my* life? You been throwing *my* life on the got-damn rocks every single chance you get."

The man shrugged. "The Zen masters say we're all thrown off a cliff at birth and we're falling down a rocky slope every second of our lives."

"The Zen masters."

"That's right."

"Well, that don't mean you ought to give a man a shove."

"I think you'll find I gave you just the opposite."

A maddening balance to the bearded man, a live-wire calmness. He hardly looked at Trace as he combed the horse, but always kept him in his peripheral vision. Trace had no doubt the man would spring into action if necessary, cutting him off before he could get halfway to the shotgun leaning against the tree.

"Enlighten me," he said. "How it is you just saved my life?"

The wolfman had gently coaxed Camo in a circle, giving him access to the other side of her coat. When he finished, he cleaned and stowed the comb, rubbed the mare a last time, then turned and sat down on a flat rock in front of Trace. He crossed his legs like a yogi, feet on top of opposite thighs, and pulled a hemp sack from somewhere on his person. He held it out. Inside, what looked like little clods of dirt.

"Chokecherry?" He popped one of the dried berries into his mouth.

Trace held up one hand. "All choked out, thank you."

The bearded man shrugged, chewing for what seemed an overly long time before spitting out the pit. "You lied to me."

"I thought you were going to tell me how you saved my life."

"This first."

"Well, I might've misspoke at some point. When in particular are you talking about?"

"The last time we talked, you said you were going after wolves on your own initiative."

Trace nodded. "Well, I quit after what happened. Actually started range riding. You can take a look at that scattergun. It ain't loaded but with rubber bullets, hazing rounds."

"I already know that. But someone has taken up your old assignment."

Trace straightened. "Who?"

"Cut his trail this morning. Size ten Vibram sole. Walks well, no limp or gait pathology. I'd say a healthy male weighing about 150 pounds. Given the trajectory of the shot, he took down a bull from the western butte, from over five hundred yards, then waited for the Dark Canyons to turn up."

"Did he get one of the wolves?"

"You sound concerned."

"Listen, ranching's been part of this territory since the days of the conquistadors. Ain't going nowhere, no matter how many damn vegans we got in this country. Least I'm out here trying to help wolves and cows coexist while all the greenies and longhair crunchy types just piss and moan in their granola bowls."

The man held out the bag of dried berries again. "Sure you don't want a chokecherry? Might improve your mood."

"This ain't a mood. It's my personality."

"He took M997. One-Eleven's mate."

"I know which one he is. With the gray face."

"That's right. He might be alive if you'd told me who you were working for."

"Yeah, and I might be dead."

The wolfman shrugged. "Day ain't over."

"Listen, I don't know who you think you are, but you got a real inflated notion of yourself if you think you can go up against these guys. It's gonna take more than a scary knife."

"Who are they?"

"I might as well cut my own throat as tell you that."

"If they're so bad, you really think they're gonna let you keep walking around upright, knowing what you know?"

"They already come to see me, and here I am."

"They hadn't sent in your replacement yet. Whoever he is, he's almost surely still watching that valley, waiting to see who or what shows up next. And you were gonna ride right up along the ridgeline, just asking for a bullet in the head."

Trace sniffed. The man had a point. He'd figured if they were going to do anything to him, they would've done it the day they came to take their money back. He'd quit worrying about it after that. But it made a lot of sense for them to task their new shooter with the job. Out here in the Wilderness, his body would be easy to hide.

"I ain't really looked at it from that particular angle."

The wolfman spat out another pit. "You best look at all the angles, friend, you don't want to end up buried under a rock out here."

"Don't call me that. Friends don't let friends step in steel traps."

The bearded man leaned closer. "Hell, Temple, you ain't even an endangered species, not like the lobos. Side with me, you might have a fighting chance out here."

"*Side* with you? Man, you are some kind of crazy. You nearly killed me and scarred me for life, and you want me to side with you? You ought to be my mortal enemy. I can't think of one good reason even to consider it. Truly I can't."

The man held out his hand to the mountains and canyons and caves that surrounded them. Three million acres of federal land. "Who else you got?"

"I don't need no help from some half-crazed, wolf-loving hippie Tarzan living out here homeless on public land. If I had to come up with the exact *opposite* of somebody I'd want to team up with, he'd look a lot like you. Hell, I don't even know your name."

The man stepped off the rock, crouched on one knee in front of Trace, and held out his hand. "I'm Horn."

CHAPTER 31

Murdoch lay in his hide, watching the valley through his spotting scope. The elk carcass had become a feast for mobs of ravens, buzzards, and coyotes, who bickered and hissed around the bloody wreck. He doubted the Dark Canyons would return to the kill—the she-wolf was too smart for that. But he wanted to watch for any activity on his back-trail. Rangers, hunters, hikers—any witnesses to handle.

Since the alpha male's tracking unit was no longer active, the Interagency Field Team had no way of knowing the wolf had been killed—not until Murdoch or the old men of The Ranch saw fit to tip them off. They'd light off a wildfire in the media, fueling conflict between wolf-haters and advocates, outfitters and environmentalists, local populace and federal government. The old men saw it as a way to draw support to their cause, building the base of their organization. The Free West. Show how they were pushing back against the feds. Murdoch, however, had motives of his own.

At noon, he took his lunch from his pack. He'd transferred all of his foodstuffs into sealed, silent EVA bags. A meal of jerky, nuts, and dried figs. Afterward, he got out his sat phone and called The Ranch's operations center on an encrypted line.

A woman's voice. "Ops Center."

"Ops Center, this is Alpha One."

"Authentication?"

He gave her his alphanumeric identifier. He had several alternatives memorized, which could be used to inform the support team if he were compromised, arrested, or under duress.

"Confirmed, Alpha One. Go ahead."

"Field report. One target KIA. Animal M997. Photo confirmation obtained. Disposal complete. Location recorded."

"The old men upstairs will be pleased."

"Any chatter on the comms?"

The woman, a veteran of an unnamed government intelligence agency, would have one of her computer screens dedicated to activity on local police and EMS frequencies, news outlets, and social media, picking up any preprogrammed keywords or scanner codes.

"Negative, Alpha One. Nothing on the streams." She paused. "I do have a direct inquiry here from upstairs. It reads: What is the status of the HVTs?"

Murdoch ground his teeth. He'd been in the field less than a week and already the old men were dogging him about the high-value targets. They could be some kind of pain in the ass. He'd never work for them if they weren't convenient to his own aims.

He sniffed. "HVT 1: Eyes made, continuing to track."

"HVT 2?"

This was Murdoch's predecessor, the son of a local rancher. Murdoch doubted he'd be a difficult target, but the old men seemed antsy to put him down. He gazed out across the valley. He'd had a feeling the rider might turn up, drawn in by howling lobos and dark flurries of carrion birds, but the opposing ridgeline looked clear.

"No update."

After the call, Murdoch returned to his scope. If he were a more emotional creature, the old men of The Ranch would truly exasperate him, make him grind his teeth down to nubs. They were so much of what he hated. They wore their high-dollar silverbelly Stetsons and thought of themselves as men of the country, the farm and ranch, but their hands were clean, uncalloused. Never had they been forced to tear a meal from the land to feed their families, nor had they lived by the gun, though they had whole armories in their homes. Their positions rested on oil and energy, agrichems and overseas manufacturing. On the funds handed down through pedigreed surnames. As the real cowboys said: *All hat and no cattle.*

No matter. The old men of The Ranch were not kings to Murdoch, as they believed themselves. They were pawns.

A vibration in his pocket. The latest public coordinates for the Dark Canyon pack had arrived. Murdoch noted the location, then began to break down his hide.

Time to move higher into the mountains.

CHAPTER 32

The sky was graying, the temperature falling fast. Trace limped down the trail beside Horn, leading Camo, the pair of them cutting for sign. He spoke just above a whisper. "So is Horn your real name?"

The bearded man kept his eyes on the trail. "Depends what you mean by real name."

"The one on your driver's license, for a start."

"Ain't got a driver's license."

"Christ, I should've known."

He shook his head and looked up through the trees, eyeing the sky. The clouds looked thickened, ready to snow. The latest coordinates had arrived, showing the Dark Canyons several miles distant from here, headed higher into the mountains. He and Horn had decided to move, circling the valley to cut the wolver's track while staying in the trees.

"Horn's a family name. People picked at it most of my life."

"I don't mean to pick, it's just a curious name."

"I come from curious people."

Trace waited. "What kind of people?"

Horn squatted down, touching his fingers to a hoofprint on the trail. His movements precise, practiced, as if he did everything according to some pattern or protocol. Customs or rituals Trace couldn't quite recognize.

"My father was a dogman," he said.

"Dogman?"

"He bred and trained dogs."

"Hunting dogs?"

"When my mother was alive, yes. That changed after she passed."

"To what?"

"Fighting dogs."

"Damn. That's a nasty world."

"He was a nasty man." Horn rubbed the back of his neck as he spoke. Trace had noticed a scar there—straight across, like it was made with a rope or chain or leather collar.

"He still around?"

Horn knelt to examine another print. "Far as I know. Lucky to be, too. I about killed him when I was in high school. Last time he ever laid a hand on me. First time I ever got locked up."

"Damn. I'm sorry to hear that."

Horn's teeth showed. "Better than being locked in a dog box."

Trace's mouth fell open. Horn turned and continued down the trail.

The temperature kept falling. A wet bite of snow in the air. Trace could feel it coming in his leg, the once-fractured bone. A dull, pounding ache, like someone tapping his shin with a hammer. He carried the shotgun in the crook of his arm. Horn had only a daypack with a compound bow strapped to one side, a quiver of arrows, and his knives.

Eerie here. Bull elk hiding their bony chandeliers amid the trees, hoping to survive rifle season, and another shooter out here somewhere—one who might be hunting Trace alongside the Dark Canyons, looking to delete everything he knew of the Free West with a single bullet. He licked his chapped lips. An urge to keep talking, whispering, if only to keep fear at bay.

"So how'd you end up a wolf-lover?"

Trace put an edge on the last word, though he didn't mean to. Old habit.

Horn didn't seem to notice. "After juvie, I dropped out and lived in the woods for a time. WMAs and public land, learning to live wild. Off-grid. But I still needed money now and again. Landed back in the system after I got busted in a cage fight. State prison this time. Honestly, it was one of the best things ever happened to me. Because where I was locked up, they had this program where they brought in wolves from a local sanctuary to talk to us about."

He inhaled, swelling his belly. "They brought in this wolf called Uno. He was missing one eye, one ear, and one paw. Still weighed one-sixty dry, one of the biggest full-blood gray wolves ever on record. He looked like something right out of a fairytale. Had this iron-gray coat, you weren't sure if he was a black wolf gone gray or born that color. And he held himself this certain way, like he bore all those missing parts with pride."

A light came into Horn's eyes. "The woman from the sanctuary who brought him in, she told us his story. Said he came from a place called Little America, up there in Yellowstone Park, in one of the few places wolves have full protection, but a hunter killed his mother just outside the park when he was a yearling. He left Yellowstone and ended up making his way all the way down to Mexico. More than one thousand miles across states where he could be shot on sight any time of year without a permit, crossing at least ten thousand paved roads, passing through greater Denver and Albuquerque and Juarez according to the GPS collar on him. Passing like a ghost in the night." Horn brushed a hand before them, as if following the animal across the land.

"Next year, he made his way back to Yellowstone and mated with a female there. They had their own litter, but she was killed outside the park just after the pups quit nursing. Same as his mother. There are sons of bitches who just lay in wait for wolves to step outside the park. Uno raised up those pups on his own, delivering food to the den in his belly, coughing it up for them. The lady told us Uno had lost his ear fighting off a pack of rival wolves raiding his territory, lost his eye defending his pups from a grizzly, and lost his paw to an illegal trap outside the park."

Trace shivered, touched his leg. "That how he ended up in a sanctuary?"

Horn shook his head. "Nope, the rangers didn't even know he'd lost his paw until he was already back in the park, limping around on that bloody nub. He recovered and kept leading the pack, still taking down prey despite that missing foot. He didn't end up in the sanctuary until a big-time stockgrower claimed he took down one of his steers outside the park. Said he saw it happen. But the evidence wasn't conclusive. All the antiwolf folks were calling for lethal control, shooting him, while the wildlife advocates wanted him left alone. Compromise was, they took him out the wild and put him in permanent captivity."

Horn sniffed. "Hearing that, a lot of us in our orange jumpers got real quiet. Hit close to home, you know. The woman was telling us Uno didn't have a second chance, but we did. That we'd been called wolves by people who didn't have the faintest idea what a wolf was, and we should go out and show them what we knew."

Horn shook his head. "But that wasn't what got me. What got me was Uno, the whole time, he wasn't paying one lick of attention to us. No, sir. He had that single eye of his looking out the big, barred windows of the mess hall to the watchtowers and fences and rolls of razor wire out there around the exercise yard. He was looking for his way out."

Horn nodded to himself. "I knew he'd try to find his way back to his pack given half a second's chance. No matter how many miles and fences and roads. No matter his missing eye and ear and paw."

Horn's eyes were blazing now, sparked wild, as if something inside him shone too bright. "He was on the warpath, man. He was still on it. The purity of that." He shook his head. "When I got out, I started adopting wolves and hybrids that needed homes. A rescue. My own little sanctuary. Sometimes we performed as a sideshow, me and the pack howling together at county fairs and such." He had his chin tilted up, basking in the memory, as if he might howl again, right here and now.

"What happened to them?" asked Trace. "Your pack?"

Horn flinched; the light blew out of his eyes. His face became a shield. "I lost them." Before Trace could ask how, Horn stopped in the trail and looked at him.

"Your turn, Temple. Who are we up against?"

CHAPTER 33

Murdoch checked the altimeter on his watch. Seven thousand feet. The first feathers of snow were coming down, falling between the white-and-black-slashed trunks of the aspens. He welcomed this weather. It reminded him of his favorite painting, *Hunters in the Snow.* Pieter Bruegel the Elder. A scene of three hunters with long lances and slumped hounds trudging back into their snow-clad village, a single lean fox draped from one of their shoulders. Their only prize. In the village background, stone bridges stand snow-laden across a frozen river and people play and work on the ice. A sign hangs lopsided from an inn or public house, depicting the patron saint of hunters, Saint Hubert, kneeling before a great black stag. Dark birds have alighted in the trees overhead, one of them swinging long-tailed over the scene, vaguely prehistoric.

Though the painter was from the Netherlands, the scene could have easily been from Murdoch's own homeland before the war. Art critics said the painting showed the futility of man before the hard turning of seasons, the cold crack and lash of winter falling hard on the bent backs of the hunters and hounds. They'd returned thinly laden from the hunt, and Saint Hubert could fall any moment from the inn, his golden halo snuffed out in the snow.

That made Murdoch smile. These Western critics, who knew nothing of war. Such a scene would be a heaven for people whose villages had been reduced to rubble by the bombs of the very nations that birthed such criticisms. What a privilege to have only winter to fight, with unfallen bridges and standing walls. No, *Hunters in the Snow* looked to Murdoch like a paradise—the kind denied him.

He'd spent most of the day waiting for the Dark Canyons to return, though he knew they wouldn't. The she-wolf would know it was better to go hungry than risk a trap or gun, and Murdoch knew of no animal that could live lean like the wolf. Days between meals, their legs still carrying them miles and miles over rough country, more tireless than any machine.

Wolves had been hunted out of his own homeland long before he was born—centuries—but he'd hunted them in Siberia, the Canadian Cordillera, and the Rocky Mountains of Wyoming. He'd shot them from light aircraft and pursued them by snowmobile and dogsled and snowshoe. He'd known the stories and fairytales about them were untrue before he ever hunted them. Modern man had long demonized the other apex predators—a way to feel secure in their dominance, to justify the killing of their competition. Tigers and lions and great white sharks—all had been called cruel and violent. All made the villains of films and books. None so much as the wolf. As if man were not the most beastly animal of all.

In this land, he knew, the Spanish and Mexican governments had offered high bounties for the scalps of Apaches—one hundred silver pesos for a male, fifty for a female, and twenty-five for a child. Thousands of dollars in today's money. The bloody scraps of flesh and hair and skull-bone were paraded on high poles through pueblo streets and tacked to church house walls. The best scalp-hunters had been Americans, who lured the Apaches with promises of peace, fed them mezcal in celebration, and murdered them in the night. Of course, the Apache had been known to tie men to wagon wheels and burn them alive, or stake them open-mouthed on anthills for the tiny marching armies to invade.

Murdoch paused to recheck his GPS unit and reverse his camouflage to a snowy pattern.

It would be much easier to hunt the wolves after they whelped in the spring, when a hunter need only determine the location of their dens and lie in wait while the older animals brought food to the pups. Even in high summer, when the pups were moved to rendezvous sites and left with a yearling or babysitter while the older wolves came and went, hunting. But that type of hunt didn't interest him, and it would be much too easy to be caught. Rangers would know to watch the dens as soon as the first pack was targeted.

But with the spring litter old enough to travel with the pack, the wolves could cover thirty miles a day, making it impossible for the rangers to safeguard them. They were not predictable animals with set patterns of patrol, but Murdoch had closely studied their previous location data to create a picture of runways, circuits, food caches, and boundary lines between territories. A cluster map, color-coded.

According to the latest coordinates, they appeared to be headed upcountry, high toward a burned-over western slope where they might expect few men or elk this time of year. To an old den site, perhaps, where they'd retreated at the opening of rifle season, when the woods were full of shots. Murdoch was headed in the same direction, shortcutting higher up the slope. Periodically, he knelt and tested the VHF receiver to see if they were within radio range.

Hunting out the lobos could take weeks, even months, which he relished. What other excuse would he have to spend so long in the bush, consumed in the chase? It would be hard to imagine a more difficult foe. The wolves were natural guerrilla fighters, operating in small bands with intimate knowledge of the terrain and better ground mobility than any unit of cavalry or dragoons or special operators. Some said Genghis

Khan and his Mongol hordes had learned their battlecraft from the golden grassland wolves of the Mongolian steppe.

Murdoch was targeting One-Eleven first. Not only did he want to take up where the last wolver left off, but the man had hired on at the Cruz Ranch, which had leases in the same territory—two targets at once. Most of the other packs were based across the state line in Arizona or farther north in the Apache National Forest.

One-Eleven was public enemy number one for the old men of The Ranch. The best-known, most beloved wolf in the program. Her disappearance would strike a heavy blow to the feds they hated so much, proving the government couldn't protect the wolves. They believed it would rally the support of like-minded individuals, drawing them to the cause like flies to a carcass.

Murdoch smiled at the rabid infighting of this country, which had already ripped itself apart in one civil war and seemed ever on the brink of another. A nation able to unite against the great foreign powers of world wars, yet still newborn and warlike at home, hardly able to stomach peace. Itching to tear open its own belly again, to battle within its own interior, inside its own towns and wilds.

Murdoch, of course, was happy to help.

When he was learning English, one of his favorite stories was "The Most Dangerous Game." The tale of an American big-game hunter who falls off a yacht in the Caribbean and washes up on the shore of Ship-Trap Island. There he meets General Zaroff, a Cossack aristocrat who escaped the Russian Revolution to his own private island, where he lures ships to wreck upon the treacherous rocks and shoals. He hunts the shipwreck survivors for sport, giving them food, clothing, a knife, and a three-hour head start. The idea is that man is the most dangerous quarry on earth, the most thrilling and difficult to bring down. But Murdoch knew that wasn't strictly true. Most men, unless highly trained and experienced, were relatively easy to kill, much less elusive and cunning than leopards or tigers or wolves.

No, he thought, the greatest game was not man, but nations.

The snow was coming down in curtains now, blanketing the aspens and firs, seeming to rise up out of the ground. Good, it would cover the day's tracks and his snow prints would seem to appear out of nothing when it stopped, as if he'd descended from the sky, beamed down between the aspens.

He rounded a broad knob of exposed rock and looked down at the western side of the slope, where the trees stood like charred black spears from a faint dust of snow.

CHAPTER 34

Trace looked up through the trees, feeling the first flecks of snow on his face.

"They call themselves the Free West," he said. "I didn't know that when they came to me. They just called themselves concerned citizens. Men like my father and grandfather, they said. But I'd heard of those matching silverbelly Stetsons they were wearing. *The men in the pale hats.* That's what people called them. Rumors of meetings at the old auction barn."

"Militia?" asked Horn.

Trace shook his head. "More than that. They never said it direct, but I get the gist they're for state independence."

"Secession?"

Trace nodded. "Looking to make part of Texas and New Mexico its own republic, like it was in the 1800s when Texas was its own sovereign state, independent of the United States or Mexico. They kept saying how the annexation of Texas was illegal. Said, according to recent polls, more than a third of the citizens of the Southwest would prefer their states seceding from the United States. It don't sound so bad to me, honestly. Being apart from the mess of the rest of this country."

"Except them boys in the pale hats will be the ones in charge."

"Well, there's that," said Trace.

Horn paused, squatting down to examine deep prints in the dried mud of a wash. Trace bent over his shoulder. Nothing. Coyotes, badger, a single bear. They kept on.

"And the wolves?" asked Horn.

"A way to fire up support, I think. Show people they're pushing back against the federal government. Draw in all the folks tired of being told by a bunch of DC politicians and big-city voters what they can and can't do on their own land. People tired of government intervention in their lives, crimping their rights. You know well as I do, wolves are a flashpoint for all that. One of the hottest there is."

"So it ain't really about the wolves at all."

Trace sniffed. "It was for me."

Horn nodded. "Reckon that's why they recruited you for the job. They had a true believer on their hands. But let me ask you this. If these Free Westers are so well connected, ain't it occurred to you they might've had a hand in your family's grazing leases getting revoked in the first place?"

"Why would they do that?"

"Turned you into their perfect wolver, didn't it? And fit their narrative of the feds fucking over the locals, too. One of the oldest tricks in a very old book. Bet it pissed off a bunch of folks they wanted pissed off, didn't it?"

Trace thought of the night in the dark auction barn, the speaker telling his family's story. The way it fired up the crowd, made their fists clench and blood boil. The way their wallets widened for membership coins and his own finger found the trigger of a gun.

He licked his lips. "We don't know they had a hand in it."

"No," said Horn. "We don't. And probably won't. But it's a possibility you at least ought to consider. People like me and you, we're the ones scratching around on the actual chessboard of this thing. The ones got real skin in the game, who can actually get knocked off the board. Same as the wolves and coyotes and elk. But we can't forget there's people moving the pieces around us, too. Ghosts in the machine. Most of them with better boots and hats and trucks than you and me ever owned, or will. And they play to different rules."

Trace shook his head. "Well, ain't that a comforting thought, Horn. I really feel better now."

Horned just grinned, his canine teeth perched on his bottom lip.

They cut the wolver's track an hour later. Trace had mounted Camo to spell his throbbing leg; now he climbed down to examine the print. Size ten, Vibram sole, headed uphill. From here they could backtrack to find the shooter's previous bivouac site, possibly even to where he'd buried the wolf. Or they could follow the man's trail as it went winding toward the high slope of Ravenfeather Mountain—the same direction the Dark Canyons were headed.

Trace scratched his chin. "We ought to split up. I could back-follow with Camo, find out what I can, then catch up to you on horseback as you track him. You got a radio?"

Horn shook his head.

"Sat phone?"

Another shake.

"What were you planning to do if you got snake-bit or mauled or fell off a cliff and broke your leg and couldn't get help?"

"Die, I reckon."

"Well, ain't that enlightened of you, Horn."

They were stuck together, it seemed. Trace looked up at the dark mountain shivering against the snow clouds. Harder flurries would already be falling at the higher elevations, covering the wolver's tracks. "One-Eleven had her den up on that western slope two years ago. It's where the big yearling was born. She's gone back there again and again since then. That's my best guess where she's headed, and our shooter, too. Short-cutting through the pass while One-Eleven climbs up out of canyon country."

"Agreed."

Trace touched the ridged imprint of the wolver's sole, then looked up at Horn. "You know, if we stop this guy, they're just gonna send somebody else."

Horn showed his teeth. "We've got to stop him first."

CHAPTER 35

One-Eleven had let the pack sleep, meat-drunk, as the snow started coming down. She'd lain curled up at the edge of the cutbank, ears skimming the air for anything man-sounding—clang, scuff, whisper. The pack had dozed against her, their bellies distended with elkflesh. She'd lashed her tongue across her mouth, tasting the blood dried ragged along her lips. She was born to this, shaped exactly to protect her pack.

Now she had them climbing through the falling snow. It was coming down slanted, a soft white hiss that muffled other sounds. Harder to detect threats, or be detected. The western slope beckoned from the darkness, a dead place but calm. The old den still there, buried in the crater of a fallen aspen. Good sight lines in all directions. Many routes of escape. A good place to survey the terrain farther to the west, where they might have to flee. Land of the Whitewaters—pale-furred wolves, strong and cruel.

She'd rather chance them than men.

The black creek flashed beneath her as she climbed, a dark jag in the snow. Her belly sloshed between her legs. They'd eaten themselves full, which would slow them for several hours. They were vulnerable now, blood-heavy, and the snow was thickening, coming down in drifts. She stopped and looked over her shoulder. She could no longer see the rest of the pack clearly, but she could hear and scent and sense them, shadows in the falling snow. She turned and walked on.

Ravenfeather Mountain stood before them. One-Eleven picked a path over the rough ground, the terrain steepening. A large pack of coyotes had passed through here several days ago, their sign still fresh. The smell of fire-charred fir and aspen drifted from the old burn, and the rutty scent of bighorn rams. They wrecked themselves on the mountain slopes this time of year, crashing their spiraled horns together, crazed to breed. These scents and hundreds more, threading across the night.

When they broke onto a high mesa, One-Eleven stopped dead in her tracks, ears rammed forward, hackles spiked.

Lion.

The ammoniac sting of his scratch pile burned in her nose despite the thin layer of powder. She looped back through the flurried gloom and rounded up the pups, jostling them closer together, telling them not to stray. She bumped Little Paw especially hard. Easy prey for a lion. Snatched and gone before she could even bare her teeth.

She knocked Dozer, too, making sure he was alert, ready to help defend the pack. His mane stood bristled, his eyes wider than usual, staring outward into the snow. One-Eleven turned and led them on, slow now, stopping often, careful of her own footfalls, each step a separate thought. The mesa had burned in the summer and the sparse trees were flame-scarred, dark against the night. They passed a blackened ponderosa and the claw rakings of the lion glowed before them, bright against the bark. Not a day old.

Lion scent was everywhere.

Her guard hairs stood through her undercoat, hard as quills. Her paw pads pounded with blood and her teeth could crack stone. She circled back around the pack again and then started them across the mesa, head low, ears back. Mountain lions would flee wolfpacks of any real size, but only she and Dozer had seen battle. The pups might be growing larger by the day, nearing their adult size, but their age and inexperience would be evident to any lion.

She'd come across the bodies of lone wolves killed for intruding on lion kills, their skulls fang-punctured. Once a pup had been stolen from her den, a single lion print left in the dust. Her breath came fuller, faster, strong through her jaws, whistling with the sharpness of her teeth. She was mother wolf, whelper of pups. A fanged fury, bloody to cross.

Then she saw him, smoke-gray in the gloom, heavy shoulders rolling over giant paws. Long flanks and a lean whip of tail. He was shadowing them through the burned trees and drifting snow. One-Eleven turned and swung across that side of her pack, rubbing her ribs across their snouts as she stared down the lion, bumping them alert. Her snout remained on the lion, aimed there, her body whipping behind it.

The lion went still, lowering his belly to the ground.

CHAPTER 36

Murdoch watched the mesa through his thermal scope. The snowfall had slackened and he could see the pale forms of the animals' heat signatures blazing across the dark field below. One-Eleven was sweeping in front of the smaller wolves, back and forth, while the mountain lion flattened before them, as if to pounce. They were out of effective range; he could only watch.

One-Eleven quit moving. Even from this distance, Murdoch could see her body elongate, tautening, forming into the sharp point of a spear pointed directly at the lion. Her teeth bared, a wicked snarl coming from her throat, visible as breath. A warning. The yearling and one of the spring-born wolves—the smallest, saw Murdoch—came to stand beside the alpha loba, conforming their postures to hers. Their breath smoked in the night.

The high-noon duels of the Wild West were mostly fabrications, he knew—the fancies of dime novelists and Hollywood screenwriters. But here stood two apex predators of the High West squaring off like gunfighters in a spaghetti western, waiting to see who blinked first.

Beasts whose short lives must be some of the most savage and exhilarating on earth. They glowed before him, each calculating the weight and power and temper of the other. Murdoch envied them in a way. Their lives pure, remorseless. They strived to do what their ancestors had done for more than five hundred millennia. To birth and feed and protect their young. To survive. Most of them didn't live a third as long as they would in a cage. Yet none would choose a caged life, surely, if given the choice.

The animals stood fixed, gravid with violence, poised like weapons. Any moment they would explode into a thrashing storm of breath and teeth and claws, their blood spurting white-hot through his scope. Any second now. Then the lion blew out a heavy breath, a visible huff, and slunk off into the charred trees, unwilling to challenge One-Eleven and her pack.

Something welled in Murdoch's belly. A kind of glow, seldom felt, strange for him. Something like love or respect. He'd always experienced such emotions from afar, like distant fires in the night, and it was always animals that stoked or spurred them. Humans were too pitiful, too weak and neurotic, too concerned with their own welfare, as if they were an endangered species. As if they hadn't endangered all the others. It was the other animals that held any truth in the world. At least for Murdoch. That was why he chased them and killed them. To witness a noble beast in the ultimate state.

One-Eleven watched the lion move away, waiting a long time to relax her posture. Finally she turned and moved like a fish through the pack, nosing them each, feeling them with her snout and shoulders. Then she looped back and began to lead them across the mesa. She trotted stiffer-legged than before, the adrenaline coursing visibly through her veins. When the wolves were halfway across the open ground, Murdoch looked back and saw the lion slink out of the juniper and begin to follow behind them, light-footed as a spider, silent in their tracks.

Murdoch shook his head and reached for his pack. "No, my friend. You had your chance. She's mine now."

CHAPTER 37

Trace and Horn crouched at the top of the pass. Midnight. The sky had cleared and the moon come up full and they were looking down on the burned western slope, the charred bristles of fir and aspen standing through a pale layer of snow. A single set of human tracks, faint, wound down the ridge, partially filled before the clouds moved on.

They'd been holding their breath as they watched. Now they ducked back behind the rocks and exhaled through their hands, masking their breath. The wolver could be watching his backtrail, making sure he wasn't followed.

Trace clicked on a red penlight and looked down at his map. "What you think?"

"I think he's set up on this little butte above the old den site." Horn tapped the place on the map. "Prime point of overwatch for the whole slope."

Trace nodded. "If I had a rifle, I could climb up to those rocks there and sight down on him. Unfortunately, somebody saw fit to part me from that particular implement a couple months back. Some got-damn berry-muncher."

"You never went back for it?"

"I did, but I ain't had the funds to replace all the parts you tossed."

"What you got for that shotgun?"

"Not but rubber rounds. Buckshot and a few slugs."

"And the pistol?"

"Four-ten buck. Even shorter range."

"We'll have to stalk him close. You up for that, Temple?"

"Are you?"

"It's my specialty, if you ain't noticed."

Trace bit his lip. "Even so, he's likely a professional of some kind, possibly ex-military. It won't be easy."

"Out here, nothing is."

"That, we can agree on."

They decided to climb high into the hoodoos, then follow a small creek that ran down onto the butte, hoping to flank their quarry. Thirty minutes later, the old trail was a tiny thread beneath them and the wind howled through the sharp teeth of the rocks. Trace had staked Camo in a small copse of evergreens below the pass, setting the stake shallow enough she could pull it free and find her way home if he didn't come back. They hunkered in the lee of a boulder, getting ready to start their descent toward the butte.

Horn dipped his head around the edge of the rock. "If he spots us coming down the creek, that's it." He glanced at Trace. "Said you got a sat phone. Anyone you want to call before we start down?"

Trace thought of his mother sleeping alone in the cold dark of their old house, the gas and power cut off. He thought of Imogen bringing him that meal last night, the spark in her voice on the radio this morning. A warmth in the cold night of his belly, like the first cracklings of a campfire. He shook his head. "I talked to them both today. Don't want to alarm them. But you can use it."

Trace pulled up the flap of his vest's phone pocket, but Horn shook his head. "Thank you, but I can't call the ones I'd like to talk to, not even with satellites."

Trace thought of his old man. "I hear you."

The creek had cut a deep vein in the side of the mountain, a gully that zigzagged steeply down the slope. Soon they were creeping their way down the dry bed, moving on the balls of their feet, careful of every step. Horn led the way, moving in a crouch, hands hovering at his sides, upper body poised over the precise movements of his legs and feet. His boots made no sound—none Trace could detect.

Trace knew himself to be one of the best trackers in the area—that's why the men in the pale hats had hired him—but Horn moved with an animal grace, like some older, wilder ancestor of the species. Easy to imagine him stalking a mastodon or giant sloth, holding a spear with a point hand-chipped from jasper or obsidian. There was a difference between doing a thing well, and doing it to survive.

But no matter how well they tracked and moved, they were outgunned. Horn had no firearm—just the curved knives sheathed at the small of his back and the bow strapped to his pack. The shooter down there would have a rifle accurate to one thousand yards or more, and know how to use it. Someone who knew better than to assume his own security, who didn't just watch his six but three o'clock and nine o'clock and every other hour of the watch, all the time. Someone very, very tough to surprise.

Then again, Horn had got the jump on Trace. Twice.

The bearded man stopped, head cocked, then melted back into movement. Trace knew, if the shooter down there spotted them, he wouldn't even hear the shot. His brains would be blown from his head before the sound arrived. Everything he'd ever known, gone. Same as his old man. Maybe he had a soul—some kind of cloud backup that would beam up to heaven or down to hell—but he didn't much believe that, hadn't for a long time. Too easy to watch how the sun came up or went down over the canyonlands. If this world weren't enough, what was?

If nothing else, the Gila had taught him there was one kind of afterlife everyone could count on. His body would be broken down and spread into thousands of other forms, feeding animals and fungi and bacteria. Some part of him would hang down as vines or sprout up as wildflowers. He would feed a wolf or fox or beetle, and a bear or lion or raven would feed on that. Underground and out again, the oldest story. From Christ to the smallest seed. In that way, he'd rather die out here in the Gila, giving himself to the land rather than rising again as watered green grass in a town cemetery.

When the gully forked, he and Horn looked at each other and nodded, splitting up. Horn went left, Trace right. He kept his head low, cradling the shotgun across his chest like a balancing pole, fox-walking on the outer edges of his boot soles like Old Temple had taught him as a boy—an old stalking technique, testing the ground with the outside of his foot before he rolled his weight inward onto the ball and big toe, slowly compressing leaves and twigs and duff. On Saturday mornings, the old cowboy would sit backward on the porch with his morning paper and coffee and a twenty-dollar bill tucked under a rock on the side table—Trace's if he could sneak up and snatch it. Often he could.

An airliner rumbled high overhead, headed west toward Phoenix or Los Angeles—the passengers' lives far removed from what was happening down here in the deep dark of these mountains. He and Horn might as well be the strange fish at the bottom of the sea.

The full moon shone bright on the snow. At a turn in the creek, Trace eased up the head-high bank and surveyed the snowy butte, looking for any sign of the wolver. Any tracks or movement, the pale dome of a Stetson or dark rod of a rifle barrel. He scanned back and forth, gridding out his field of vision into ten different sectors. The first pass, he just tried to see if anything struck him, anything obvious or odd. Nothing. On the second, he spent longer on each sector, examining each window for subtler signs.

There. He'd seen something. Movement. A shift in one tiny pixel of his vision. Perhaps a hundred fifty yards. He focused there, turning his eyes slightly askance for better night vision—another old trick his grandfather had taught him. Again, a tiny flutter. Not breaking his gaze, Trace slowly pulled his binoculars from their chest pouch, memorizing the pattern of the surrounding trees before he raised them to his eyes. A good pair of eight by forty-two Steiners designed for low light. He found the spot and worked the center focus wheel.

A puff of steam. Below it, rendered like a ghost from the snow, the shape of a man clad all in white—a snowsuit. He was lying prone behind a rifle, the entire weapon vined and leafed like a wizard's staff. Trace zoomed in as much as he could. The shooter's hand lay pale against the gun, ungloved, his index finger extended straight across the receiver. Trace saw it move down to the trigger, ready to fire.

He raised the shotgun with one hand, high like a spear, and pulled the trigger.

CHAPTER 38

Murdoch's sight picture shattered. He twisted fast out of the scope and rolled up on one knee, firing three rounds back in the direction of the shotgun blast. Then pressed himself against a nearby tree, tucked his shoulder against the bark, and edged his head around the trunk. High on one side, then low on the other.

Nothing. No return fire.

He pulled back and waited, listening. He deepened his breathing, trying to curb the spike of adrenaline in his blood, the jets of frustration. He'd been so close to taking his primary target. Tracking the she-wolf through the crosshairs of his scope, watching as she led the pack across a small meadow below the butte. He had her ranged, his sight picture clear. His finger had moved to the trigger, ready to send the round that would take down the alpha female of the Dark Canyon pack—a shot that would ignite a firestorm in the press, on social media, over dinner tables. Destabilization, as he'd been trained. Support dissidents, inflame tensions, divide communities.

Now Murdoch ducked his head out again, hoping to draw a clumsy shot—a muzzle flash that would pinpoint the shooter's location.

Silence.

He guessed the shooter was crouched in the gully a hundred fifty yards away. He brought up his rifle and scanned the area through the thermal scope, looking for a heat signature. According to the dossier, the range rider carried a twelve-gauge shotgun for predator control, which matched the sound of the shot. Surely Murdoch hadn't let some yokel get the drop on him.

On the Eurasian steppe, he'd watched wolfpacks work in tandem, one group creating a diversion, rollicking on the edge of the field while another stalked the rapt antelope from the other direction, downwind. He'd used the same strategy in war zones, distracting an enemy patrol with distant artillery or structure fires while he crept into position, setting up his hide in a bombed-out apartment building or dilapidated factory, ready to take down the distracted fighters.

In a surge Murdoch realized what was happening. He twisted in place to see the shadowy figure of a man moving toward him through the trees, crouched low for stealth. Murdoch tilted his rifle slightly, transitioning to the offset reflex sight intended for short-range engagement, and fired two rounds to the target's chest, center mass.

The man went down and Murdoch, not knowing how many more fighters might be part of the ambush, swept an arm through his pack and sprinted toward the edge of the butte. He went scrambling and sliding down the slope, careful of rocks jutting from the fresh snow, and moved into the thicker cover of trees at the bottom of the decline.

In the crater of a fallen aspen, he began to build a *refugio*—a temporary fortress of rock and timber like the Apache war parties would devise during a pursuit. In mere minutes, they could turn any ridge or summit or arroyo into a fortified position, repelling the flying columns of Spanish or American cavalry sent to hunt them.

Soon Murdoch was lying in his newly built refuge, waiting.

Whoever was after him, they were out of their depth. No, not even the old men of The Ranch knew what masters he truly served, what foreign directorate had recruited him from those militia ranks when he was little more than a boy, trained him in secret, and sent him around the world like a precision-guided weapon. Subversion, escalation, assassination. In latter years, a dream assignment: to build his reputation as a renowned big-game guide, a Great White Hunter like those of the old Hemingway stories, who could work his way into the favor of influential men of the West—old men like those of The Ranch, headquarters of the Free West.

For years he'd been crawling his way into this position, inch by inch, preparing to strike deep into the heart of this nation. No cowboys or wildlife agents were going to stand in his way.

In seven hours the sun would begin to rise. Murdoch's tracks would disappear with the melting snow and he would decide what to hunt first, wolves or men.

CHAPTER 39

One-Eleven leapt straight up at the sound of the first shot, stiff-legged like a mule deer, up with the moon. Then she was flying for the cover of the trees, full speed over the snow, pulling the Dark Canyons behind her. More shots in the distance. She led them through the black trees of the old burn, into creeks and out again to disrupt their tracks and scent. Across a stony flat where their prints would melt fast and down a steep ravine that would slow any pursuers, heading west.

She did not understand what was hunting them. Only that they had to keep moving, distancing themselves from the danger. She looked over her shoulder to see Dozer and the three smaller wolves strung out in a line, jaws slack, mouths steaming. Little Paw at the rear of the pack, trailing slightly but keeping pace. He had to. One-Eleven couldn't slow the pack, not now. Not for one pup. She turned and looked ahead, westward into the night.

Soon they'd be nearing the edge of Dark Canyon territory, west of the Mogollon peaks. Already the stones and earth seemed to quicken around her, resonating at a higher frequency—a rising hum she sensed in her bones. *Danger. Whitewater wolves.* But they couldn't stop or turn around. They had lions and men on their tails. They had to press on, no matter what danger lay before them.

CHAPTER 40

Trace knelt over Horn. The man looked like he was choking. His tongue bulged high in his mouth and veins stood out from his neck like strangling vines. His lips were pale and he had his hands curled up strangely over his chest, hiding where he'd been hit.

"Let me see." Trace gently pulled them aside.

Two dark stars in the center of his vest, closely spaced, where the rounds had torn through the outer fabric and struck the armor plate inside. He slipped his hand down the front of the plate carrier, flat against the man's chest—no blood.

"I don't think they penetrated." Still, he knew the impact could cause internal damage, even stop a person's heart. Horn's mouth was fixed open; he was heaving for air, his hands seemingly clawed up. The shock might have done something to his nervous system—stunned or overwhelmed it—but they couldn't stay here in the open. Trace looked up, eyes sweeping the landscape. He'd seen the shooter flee over the edge of the butte. A long way down. They had time, but not forever. "We gotta find cover in case he circles back."

Trace slung his shotgun over his shoulder and began to drag Horn by the shoulder straps of his vest. Horn moaned and cast his arm toward his bow lying in the snow a few steps away.

"We'll come back for it," said Trace.

Horn growled and tried to reached for the bow with one clawlike hand.

"Christ, all right." Trace picked up the bow and set it across Horn's chest, where the man cradled it in his arms. That seemed to calm him and Trace kept dragging him through the snow. He thought of trying the fireman's carry like he'd learned in the wilderness first aid courses he'd taken for guiding, but he didn't want to stop moving. Not now, not when they were at their most vulnerable, outside cover and unable to defend themselves.

He was breathing hard and loud, his breath spewing in wet clouds from his mouth as he dragged Horn over the side of the gully. Together they crumpled down into the stony bed, safe in cover. Trace set the man beside him, unclasped the side straps of the plate carrier, and lifted the heavy front flap over the man's head. Then he lifted up Horn's shirt, bunching it under his chin.

"Jesus," he whispered.

It looked like someone had hit him square in the chest with a sledgehammer. A nasty contusion was forming below his sternum, a double-eyed hurricane of bruising. Blood was pooling beneath the skin, fuller and darker, shot through with red jags of broken capillaries. Kevlar vests, like what police wore on patrol, couldn't stop rifle rounds, shotgun slugs, or even arrowheads—most anything encountered out here in the Gila. Only hard armor like what Horn had been wearing. Trace shook his head. "I thought you were crazy lugging them damn plates through the woods."

Horn heeled Trace's arm with one hand and showed his teeth—that canine smile. "Who's . . . crazy . . . now?"

"Let's not go that far."

Horn heeled his arm again. "Almost . . . got . . . him."

Trace had brought his shotgun back across his knees. “Almost got your ass killed, is what you almost got.”

“Night . . . ain’t . . . over.”

“No,” said Trace, looking out at the dark woods. “I reckon not.”

Soon Horn was sitting upright, drinking water from his canteen and eating some kind of dried herbs or mushrooms out of a sack. He began to fill his canteen straight from the thin burble of the creek.

“You ain’t afraid of giardia or something?” whispered Trace.

“Already had it. Got the antibodies now.”

“Hmmm.”

“Those purification pills will give you cancer anyhow.”

“Is that right?”

“That’s right.” Horn gulped a few hard swallows of creek water. “You keeping hydrated?”

“Sure.”

“When’s the last time you peed?”

“Wouldn’t you like to know.”

Horn waited. It actually wasn’t a bad question out here.

“Before the pass,” whispered Trace.

“What color was it?”

“Neon. Day-Glo, you might call it.”

“You’re dehydrated,” said Horn. “You need to drink.”

“Not too dehydrated to drag your ass out the open.”

Horn pulled a small separate canteen from the far side of his vest and held it out. “My backup bottle. Filled from the water pump at the visitor’s center a couple days ago.”

Trace took the canteen. His own had run dry hours back and he hadn’t exactly had time to pump more creek water through his purifier. The water tasted delicious, familiar—groundwater pumped straight out of the Gila.

“Visitor center,” said Trace, voice low. “Surprised you creep that close to civilization.”

“Mainly at night. I don’t like crowds.”

"Crowds?" Trace had never seen more than a few campers' worth of folks at the Wilderness visitor center, which was two hours deep inside the national forest, at the end of a steep and winding road. "You know they had some Bigfoot sightings around that area in the last few months, enough the local papers covered it. You sure you ain't that shaggy-ass North American Sasquatch everybody wants to find?"

Horn shrugged. "If I was, would I know it my own self?"

"Christ." Trace shook his head and raised up slightly to look over the edge of the bank, holding his breath. He dropped back down. "We ought not to stay here much longer. That shooter's liable to circle back and finish the job."

Horn nodded and stashed the sack of dried herbs. "I know a place."

Trace began to get out his map. When he looked up, Horn had already begun moving up the creek, so quiet Trace hadn't noticed.

CHAPTER 41

Murdoch had studied the history of this land well—so short compared to that of Europe, Africa, Asia. The first nomads had likely crossed the land bridge between Siberia and Alaska no more than twenty thousand years ago, when the ice-age glaciers made the sea levels low enough to connect the two continents. There had been the Mogollon and Mimbres peoples in this region, who built cliff palaces and ancient trade roads, and the Apache after them—nomadic hunters and raiders whose tongue was related to that of the Dene and other First Nations peoples who remained thousands of miles to the north, up in Alaska and Canada.

Spain, Mexico, and the United States had all clashed with the Apache. The American military had been forced to divide the land into fixed districts of operation, each with its own command of troops who guarded the watering holes and maintained scouting parties throughout the area. Otherwise the Apache could easily escape into the rugged country they knew so well, splitting up and thwarting the cavalry and dragoons sent after them.

It had taken nefarious and deceptive strategies on the part of the U.S. Cavalry to kill or subdue the great Apache chiefs. Mangas Coloradas—Red Sleeves—was lured into an army encampment under a flag of truce. There he was taken prisoner, awoken in the night with red-hot bayonets, and shot while chained to the floor—*killed while attempting to escape*, read the official report. His son, Cochise, who'd already escaped a similar ambush by cutting his way out of a headquarters tent at Apache Pass, would continue his guerrilla war against the Americans for another decade. Geronimo himself, named for the storied wails of stricken Mexican soldiers who cried out to *San Jerónimo* in their death throes, remained at large until 1886, evading some nine thousand U.S. and Mexican troops for months with a band of just thirty-seven Chiricahua—the last free members of his people. In the end, he who once *moved about like the wind* agreed to a peace treaty whose terms were never honored. Geronimo's surrender was reported as unconditional.

Murdoch was glad he wouldn't have to resort to such strategies. He slipped a small pill between his teeth. A nootropic, which would keep him alert for the duration of the night without the rapid heart rate and trembling hands of the crude amphetamines he'd taken in years past. The mist of fatigue would soon clear from his head and his senses would remain sharp all night, as if he had a web of trip wires laid out in the forest around him. He hoped his pursuers would try to creep down the slope of the butte or circle wide to flank him. If they did, he could dispatch them quickly and get back on the trail of the Dark Canyon pack.

He doubted they were rangers or law enforcement. They had no air support, didn't identify themselves, and The Ranch's operations center would've alerted him of radio chatter on their scanners. It was also unlikely the range rider had stumbled across his trail—Murdoch was well into the Wilderness, where cattle didn't graze, and he doubted the man had the skills or inclination to pursue him this far.

He had heard of the outlander camps in some of the national forests and federal wilderness areas—small communities where people were living completely off-grid, prepping for an environmental apocalypse.

More likely would be the collapse of their own nation, he thought. Of course, that would seem like the end of the world to them, because Americans thought they were the linchpin of the entire globe. If their nation crumbled, they assumed the rest of the world would fall into havoc and burn.

They didn't realize the world was already burning. It had been burning the whole time—they just didn't want to see it. They saw only what they wanted to see, what their news channels and pundits and leaders told them. His own homeland had burned and no one had taken notice. They'd seen his people only in one light—as villains and war criminals. So a villain he'd given them.

The next location update arrived. The Dark Canyons were headed west—if they kept going that way, they'd soon enter Whitewater territory, which might spell their doom. Murdoch couldn't let that happen. If the famous she-wolf died of natural causes, the men in the pale hats couldn't claim her death as their victory, helping to strengthen and expand their base—just what Murdoch wanted. After all, the wolves were just the beginning. Practice for people who stood in the way of their aims. Judges, activists, statesmen. Perhaps even the governor. Murdoch's true mission was less to kill than to divide, and the Free West was working toward the greatest rift of all.

No, it wouldn't do to have One-Eleven dying on his watch—not until he pulled the trigger himself. Slowly, he slipped his pack back onto his shoulders, retracted the rifle from the makeshift emplacement of rocks and fallen timber, and folded up the bipod. He'd memorized the entire map of the Gila Wilderness before this operation, spending hours poring over the various layers—terrain, weather, etc. He remembered something strange he'd noticed on the satellite images of this area. Something gleaming beneath the sun, metallic.

A section of wing.

North of here was Aeroplane Mesa. Legend was, Claire Chennault, leader of the famous Flying Tigers of World War II, had once crashed there on a cross-country flight, and Army mail pilots had been known to land there as well, hiking down to the Middle Fork of the Gila River for the trout fishing.

In the 1960s, cargo planes out of Colombia and Mexico were rumored to alight on the mesa in the dead of night, unloading their contraband under cover of darkness. A few of them had crashed into the surrounding mountains, the wreckage not found sometimes for months, even years.

Murdoch began to make his way through the darkness, stepping carefully through the scree field at the bottom of the butte. He had a good idea where his pursuers might hole up for the rest of the night.

CHAPTER 42

Trace looked down at the scorched aluminum tube of the fuselage, beached on a slope of fire-blacked aspens. It was an old Douglas DC-3, a World War II–era cargo plane. What Old Temple used to call a *gooney bird*. One of the wings had sheared off in the crash and lay farther down the slope, while the detached tail section stood nearby, planted on the side of the mountain like some kind of arcane totem. Trace and Horn lay in a hide of rocks about sixty yards above the site, completely hidden when they slipped back from the edge.

"When's the last time you were here?" asked Horn.

"Not in years. Story was, a couple hikers stumbled on it not long after the crash back in the '60s, got rich hauling out all the bales of marijuana and selling them in California. Only a few folks know about it."

"Let's hope our shooter does."

The cockpit and passenger windows were all busted out, and an eerie red light shone faintly in some of the hollows. They'd left Horn's headlamp inside, switched on and hanging from a string, shining its dim red map light. They hoped it would lure the shooter, who'd think they were inside nursing their wounds, planning their next move.

A trap.

"You think this'll work?" asked Trace.

"Better trap than the one that worked on you."

Trace sniffed. "Fair enough."

He lay back and set his hat over his eyes. They'd decided to take turns on watch and Horn volunteered to go first. From beneath his hat brim, Trace noticed Horn squeezing and kneading his thigh where his claw scars were. "You never did tell me how you managed to survive a mountain lion attack."

"You're supposed to be resting."

"I'm reclined, ain't I?"

"It wasn't a mountain lion."

"You said it was a lion."

"An African lion."

Trace put his hand on his hat. "You got to be shitting me, Horn."

"Nope."

"What were you, in the circus?"

"Not at the time."

"Not at the time."

"At the time I was at my sanctuary."

"I thought you had wolves at your sanctuary."

"A tiger and a lion, too."

"Christ, the fucking Tiger King."

Horn looked at him sharply. "Don't you call me that."

Trace held up his hands. "My bad, I won't. So what happened?"

"They got loose."

"Loose?"

"Well, somebody let them out."

"Who the fuck would let them out?"

"I'd taken the idea of a wildlife rescue pretty literal."

"You kidnapped them cats, Horn, didn't you?"

"I took them out of bad situations."

"Uh-huh. Bet somebody came after them, too."

Horn nodded. "The lion was a mascot for this big truck stop. There was a reward and everything. I thought that's who it was, bounty hunters."

"Who was it?"

"People not too different from me. They were trying to get an animal out of a bad situation." He grimaced. "They thought that situation was me."

"Well, there's a head-twister. I hazard to guess you ain't took too kindly to intruders on your property, and the cat got out the bag in the process."

Horn nodded. "I was standing in the way when he bolted from the enclosure. The authorities weren't far behind."

"I bet."

"I lost everything. My home, my pack. Barely escaped with my life."

"How you'd get away?"

"I swam."

"*Swam*?"

"I don't much remember it. I was caretaker of this little barrier island off the coast, the site of a beach resort that went bust. Mainly they had me there to keep out poachers, meth labs, moonshiners—didn't care what else I did. It was two miles across rivers and creeks and marshes."

"This was gator country?"

"And sharks, too. First thing I really remember is pulling myself up a boat ramp on the mainland, dragging my mauled leg. Thought I'd die from that or the heartbreak."

"But here you are."

"Part of me."

"What happened to all the animals?"

"They got rounded up and sent to other sanctuaries and rescues. Most of them, anyway. That truck-stop lion never turned up in any official report, despite the reward."

"And the tiger?"

Horn's teeth showed. "People say, when the moon's right, you can hear a roar coming from the island, even though it's two miles out."

"Reckon they don't need a caretaker out there no more to discourage the outlaws."

"I reckon not."

"And you done traded that island of yours for the country's first federal wilderness."

"Something like that."

Trace lay back again, tipping his hat over his eyes. "I'll say this for you, Horn. You ain't boring to know."

Trace crossed his arms over his chest. He doubted he'd be able to relax—not with his leg throbbing, Tarzan crouched beside him, and a cowboy assassin somewhere out there in the night. But closing his eyes turned out to be like poking holes in a dam; exhaustion came flooding over him, heavy and fast.

Soon he was drifting, sinking back into lost hours, seeing things again in that dusky dreamland of memory. An interior country where memories enacted themselves again and again, evolving with time. He went back to the campfire with Imogen, the glowing aura of warmth and light. The warmth inside his own belly, which he'd carried all day. He felt it brighten inside him, like a blown ember. A longing welled up in his lungs, big as a howl.

Then he was in the saddle again, on Camo's back, looking at One-Eleven across the pasture. She seemed less a wolf now than a fellow traveler, the chieftess of a nation smaller and less powerful than his own, yet storied for fierceness. A warrior culture. Then he drifted further back, riding with his mother on the back of her Harley-Davidson. Just a boy. She'd won a race in the desert and taken him out on the victory lap, circling the speedway in a halo of swirling red dust, the checkered flag snapping over their heads. His mother wide and strong and fearless in the saddle, clad in her battered leather suit. No steel rod in her thigh, no opiates in her blood. The thunder of the big Milwaukee engine beneath them.

Then he fell deeper, dropping down through the mountain into darkness. The ground gone and a windless shaft sucking him down, plunging him beneath the surface, and he feared he'd never get out, never see anyone again, not his mother or Imogen, not One-Eleven or even Horn. He was helpless as a baby, unable to grasp anything to stop his fall like the time on the cliffside with the world rolling around him and the grapnel screaming behind him, ready to gouge and bludgeon him. *We are falling every second of our lives . . .*

A hand on his arm.

Trace jolted awake. Horn was bent over him, a finger over his lips. He tapped his ear and pointed up—he'd heard something. Trace nodded. The dream still had its claws in him, its threads in his mind. He tried to push it all away. Horn pointed down toward the wrecked fuselage.

Trace nodded and rolled slowly over, taking up the shotgun. His heart was hammering inside him but it felt distant, too, buried deep, still tumbling inside its own dream. He edged up to the rocks and looked down. The wind rolled up the slope, carrying distant sounds and scents their way. He'd heard that was why wolves and elk always sought such overlooks—not for the beauty of the view, but for the scents and sounds that came rustling up the slope, giving them a bigger story of a particular valley or canyon or mountainside. Their own kind of picture.

Trace watched the darkness, eyes wide.

If the shooter knew about this crash site, then he was either local—likely someone Trace knew personally—or else he'd studied the area with fearsome detail.

A crackle in the darkness. Dry grass, crunch of snow. Not necessarily a man. It could be an animal of some kind: bighorn, elk, bear.

Again the sound, closer, creeping toward the wreckage.

Trace squeezed the shotgun with both hands. He had a shell already chambered—a less-lethal rubber slug effective to sixty yards. Horn's bow would have about the same range.

Another crunch, closer now. A shift in the darkness, a movement. Horn had seen it, too. Trace waited for the white-cloaked shooter to step into view, holding the fat muzzle of his rifle before him, probing the darkness, aimed for the light inside the empty fuselage.

Instead, a long sleek shape emerged from the black aspens, ash-gray, creeping like a ghost in the snow. A mountain lion. It stopped near the wreckage and sniffed at their tracks, then looked out into the night. Shoulders burled and faceted with power. Flanks long and lean. The fat whip of tail. The cat lingered a moment, jaws open, tongue slightly out, huffing air into the scent organ at the roof of its mouth.

Then it exhaled, a great plume of steam, and moved on, its great paws stamping through the thin layer of snow. In seconds it was gone, vanishing into the night like smoke.

"Damn," whispered Trace. "Thought we had him."

"Go back to sleep," said Horn. "I'll keep watch."

"You'll wake me when it's my turn?"

"I'll wake you."

Trace lay back and set his hat over his eyes. Sleep had never fully left him, as if the lion had passed through his own dream. Soon he was sinking back into that inner duskland. His mother was still there and Imogen and they were racing across a meadow of tiny yellow wildflowers. For hours he was running in step with them, bounding and ranging, their mouths slashed wide at times with blood, and the distant mountains rose aching in his throat. He felt he could run across the whole face of this world.

CHAPTER 43

Horn sits cross-legged in the snow of the hide, stripped to the waist. He has his hands on his belly, feeling it expand and contract with his breath. Inside this orb, he pictures a fire burning, pulsing behind his navel. As he breathes in through his nose, the oxygen feeds this inner fire, making the flames burn brighter. He pulls back his shoulder blades as he inhales and begins to hold the air longer inside him, compressing it between diaphragm and pelvic floor, like the combustion chamber of an engine, and the fire burns higher, hotter. His out-breaths are long and pressurized, pluming slowly from pursed lips.

His eyes are closed, his ears open, attuned to the night.

Soon the fire is spreading beyond his belly, seeping through dark channels of his spirit-body, oozing through tubes and branches and ducts, as through the radiator pipes of a heated building. The fire warms the seven centers of power, from root to heart to crown, so they glow like wild blossoms. Soon seeds of sweat rise on his skin despite the cold and his shoulders begin to steam faintly in the night air. His lips have pinkened. His fingertips. The craggy tip of his nose. As if his blood runs redder beneath his skin, hotter.

Now he directs the fire toward his chest, the thunderclouds of bruise there.

He lets the fire sit with the storm, warming and brightening. Like he did so often in the wake of the mauling, lying on a mattress in an abandoned motel, sending neon tubes of light to the bloody canyons in his thigh, which oozed and jellied and gaped with pain. Sending them the heat to cauterize, to knit themselves back together, keeping some part of the lion inside him.

Now, as he flares his nostrils, he sees the lion charging again from its enclosure, a golden beast with a black mane, and Horn himself standing before the animal, trying to protect the woman who'd opened the gate, and the lion swatting him away, raking the flesh from his thigh in a single blow. Just missing his groin, the artery there. He sees the tigress, too, a tongue of flame crackling off into the bush, never seen again, and his old pack singing beneath the moon, the pale fire of their howls, a ghost-mountain of song. Horn rocks back on his in-breath and asks them for help, these creatures. He asks the lion for strength, the tiger for stealth, the wolf for heart, sucking each of these entreaties into his lungs. These are his prayers.

He shuts his eyes tighter, sucks deeper, and the flames burn yet brighter. Soon he is full of the palest fire—the pale of breath, of ghosts—and he has nearly disappeared inside the blaze. It has risen all through him, filling him to the very limits of his flesh, burning at the edge of every cell and membrane, and the fire is passing beyond him now, breaking free of his skin.

He sees the flames rising from his shoulders, horns and whips of white fire crackling and whirling like the blazes of immolated monks, the churning flesh-fires of witches and saints burned at the stake. He might be burned up in such a blaze, turned to ash, blown away in the first puff of wind through the rocks.

Trace woke with a start, coated in sweat. He'd overslept—he knew it at once. He bolted upright, breathing hard, his hat falling into his lap. The world dim, the sky striped with the first rays of dawn. He looked around in the shivering darkness. A circle of melted snow where Horn had sat watch. He was alone, he realized.

Horn was gone.

CHAPTER 44

Dawn glowed in the trees. It had not yet reached the ground, where One-Eleven and the rest of the pack lay in remnant shreds of night, curled up amid the cold roots of the trees. The younger wolves began yawning and rolling about, already bumping and grappling one another, eyes half open. Rising like stoked flames. The pack had come west through the mountains in the night. No snow had fallen on this side of the Mogollons and the land lay brittle and dry around them, full of dust and dead brush and crackling leaves—a thirsty country, ready to announce their presence with every step.

At first the pups didn't remember Graynose was gone. As always, the bigger siblings began bullying Little Paw. Knocking him around with their hips, slapping their paws down on his back, nipping at his heels and ears. The little wolf wheeled and bared his teeth with such a snarl they leapt back wide-eyed.

Little Paw had not forgotten Graynose.

He sat on his haunches and threw back his head and his mouth became a small dark O. He howled. The others lifted their snouts and joined in, calling over this strange country for Graynose. One-Eleven leapt among them, working her body between them, bumping them hard enough to disrupt their howls.

They looked at her, confused. They didn't know where they were, how dangerous it was. One-Eleven knew. She'd led them to the western edge of the mountains, near the border of Whitewater territory. Perilous ground, especially for young wolves. They'd have to travel in silence, leaving little trace. No marking, no howling. To survive here, they'd need to remain invisible.

But Little Paw was stubborn. His mother had knocked him off-balance, disrupting his call. Now he sat back on his haunches, rigid as a stump, and threw back his head to howl once more. This time One-Eleven whirled and lashed him with her teeth, sending him down into the dirt. Little Paw didn't squeal but rose and shook out his coat. His siblings started in at him, balking when he bared his fangs.

One-Eleven moved among them again, running her ribs along their flanks, alerting them to danger, then turned and started through the trees. She felt the tug of them behind her, as if she drew them by invisible cords. They moved in a loose wing through the forest, stopping often to scent what they found, acquainting themselves with this new realm.

More mule deer here than elk. Some antelope. Javelina. The wolf sign was old. One-Eleven had marked in this borderland with Graynose in late summer, signaling the outermost edge of their territory. Whitewater wolves had come through since then, slashing over each of the scent posts with hiked legs. A pair of males, powerful by their scent, but their marks were at least two moons old. Only the lack of rain had preserved them, kept them bright in her nose.

The pack climbed up along a ridge, where One-Eleven could see the vast coyote-colored plains to the west. The juniper stood gray-brittle, shivering in the wind. White washes of silt ran choked and crooked. Along the horizon, the slow gleam of glass and metal—a distant highway. She turned and led them north, toward a narrow box canyon where the water ran year-round, churning over the rocks. They stayed high in the trees along the ridges, moving in shadow, careful to avoid the stock tanks and hunting blinds that dotted this rugged borderland.

One-Eleven felt exposed. There were too many paths here, too many roads and trails laced with the tracks of horses, vehicles, men—spreading outward from the distant highway. Over generations, the Whitewaters had learned to survive here. They were man-wise, capable of avoiding detection. They crossed that tarmac highway all the time, ruling the forests on the far side. They killed any wolf that intruded on their territory.

One-Eleven stopped and scented. A dry wind from far out of the west, carrying faint threads of smoke. A wildfire in distant lands. No danger to them, but the haze would thicken as the day wore on. The sun would set red tonight.

CHAPTER 45

Panic hissed in Trace's ears. He'd been had, he thought. Yet again. He could see where Horn's tracks went off through the snow, curling down toward the crash site.

"Got-dammit," he said through his teeth. "Got-damn feral-ass dirtbag motherfucker."

He checked his gear to make sure the man hadn't stolen anything and began to stand up. Pain shrieked through his teeth, a stifled shout. He dropped to one knee and yanked up his trouser leg. The trap-wound was swollen and angry this morning, inflamed by the previous day on the trail. All the hiking, scrambling, stalking. It wasn't up to such punishment, not yet.

Trace dug into his pack for his bottle of ibuprofen, took three of the small brown pills, then loosened his bootlaces. He was about to try hefting his pack to his shoulders when he heard a noise on the slope above him. He dropped behind the rocks, then slowly raised his eyes. A rider came into sight, wending down through the trees. Horn. He was riding aback Camo, his tan combat boots spread wide in the stirrups.

When he got to Trace, he swung one leg over the saddle horn and leapt down like a trick rider, then held out the reins. "Figured your leg might be smarting this morning. So I brought you your transportation."

"Done thought you'd run out on me." Trace snapped up the reins. "If this is some kind of apology, it ain't sufficient."

"You're welcome," said Horn.

"How come you didn't wake me for my turn on watch?"

Horn began squatting up and down in place, fingertips steepled before him. He looked like he might be warming up for a morning run.

"Didn't need to wake you. I was in a trance."

"A what?"

Horn kept squatting, dropping lower each time, so low his knees nearly rubbed his ears.

"Yogic inner fire meditation."

"Yoga what?"

"To supercharge my immune system, help my body heal from the chest trauma."

"You got to be shittin' me, Horn."

"Tibetan monks use it to stay out all night in the snow, near naked. It's called *tummo*."

"What if somebody crept up on us while you were all tranced out, what then?"

"My senses remain on high alert in such a state." Horn was still doing his squats. "Besides, you farted in your sleep enough to alert the whole mountain of our presence."

"Oh, bull fucking shit."

"Yes, sir, farted and whimpered all night, just like a dreaming dog." He looked up at Trace as he dropped into another squat. "Or wolf."

Trace thought of the dreams he'd had, running across mountain meadows. Horn finished his squats and began a set of side bends. "I'm gonna cut wide for sign, see if anybody visited us last night from a distance. Maybe I can pick up his trail."

"What about me?"

"Let's be honest, Temple. You ain't in a fit state for this job."

"The hell I ain't."

"You had one good day in that leg. We both know it. Now you're a handicap."

"Horseshit."

"All right, then. Let's see you heft your pack and walk to that tree. Without limping."

"I ain't got to walk if I got the horse."

"This job's gonna get done on foot before it's over. Going where a horse can't."

Trace sniffed and looped the reins over a branch and hitched his pack to his shoulder, balancing on his good leg. Then he snaked his arm through the opposite strap, steadied himself, and stepped toward the tree. It was ten paces away. Sweat broke out on his brow. A fine, cold film. He was five steps in, halfway there, when his bad leg buckled and his knee smacked the ground and he fell hard on his side in the dirt, gasping like a landed fish.

Horn stood over him. "Like I said, you ain't fit for this job."

"Yeah, and whose fault is that? You're the one set that trap on me."

Horn shrugged. "Could've cut your throat instead."

"Fuck you, nature boy. I hope you choke on one of your cherries."

"I understand your anger. I do. And I don't hold it against you."

"You are such a pain in the ass."

"I forgive you."

Trace sat up. "Got-dammit, Horn, what am I supposed to do? I can't just up and leave you to handle this on your own."

Horn unlooped Camo's reins from the branch and held them out to Trace. "You ain't got a choice, Temple. I'm leaving you."

"The hell I don't. I'll just tail your ass. Follow the stink of heathen Sasquatch."

"It won't take me half a mile to lose you."

Trace snatched the reins. "Thank you for your confidence."

"Think about it, Temple. Even if you were in fighting trim, it's likely this shooter is looking for you. Got your name and description, probably a whole file on you. He'll know what you look like, your hat, your shoe size, your boot sole, maybe even your horse. Me, he's gonna think I'm just another hiker or hunter, an outlander at worst. No big threat. Besides which, you aren't provisioned for what could be a multiday stalk, and I don't have the resources to provide for you. I'm living lean in case you ain't noticed."

"Oh, I noticed."

"It's best for both of us if you head back to the Cruz Ranch for now." Horn kicked himself into a headstand against a tree and began a set of inverted push-ups. His face purpled, weird veins springing from his forehead and throat. He paused at the end of his set. "Besides which, I don't want witnesses for what I got coming to this poacher when I find him."

Trace squeezed the reins, denting the leather with his thumbnail. "It don't sit right with me, Horn, leaving you out here with him."

Horn kicked himself upright. "It's why I'm here, Temple. What a preacher might say was a calling." He cracked his oversize knuckles. "But it's mine. I don't want nobody else brought down in that."

"What about the people he works for?"

"If they send two of you that come up empty, they might just learn their lesson, leave this place alone."

"Don't bet on it. These are some stubborn types, Horn. That much I know. They might just keep on coming."

Horn squinted out at the land beyond the small shelter of rocks. "Then they'll come. And I'll be waiting for them."

Trace hauled himself up. "Listen, I'll check in at the ranch, put the leg on ice, then gear up and meet you back out here as soon as I can. Say, three days. I might not can scramble around good as you, but I can watch your back and provide cover. Something."

"How we gonna find each other?"

Trace pulled out his sat phone. "There's a number written on the back. My regular cell."

Horn took the phone and held it slightly apart from himself, looking at the thick black fob of the antenna with suspicion. "Can't nobody track me with this thing, can they?"

"It ain't a damn radio collar, Horn."

"What if something happens to me? The authorities might find it on my person. Track it back to you."

"I'll say I lost it." Trace put his hand on the other man's shoulder. "Besides which, if this shooter is any good at his job, ain't nobody finding you out here."

He meant it as a joke, but Horn didn't seem to take it that way. He just nodded, face serious. Then looked back at the phone, sort of cradling it in his hands. "Thank you for this."

"Of course." Trace set his good foot in the stirrup and hauled himself up into the saddle with a wince, pulling the reins to his sternum. "Best keep the phone off to preserve the battery. Turn it on for an hour every day at noon, and I'll call when I'm headed back out. But you can reach me anytime if need be."

"Okay."

Trace took off his riding glove and leaned from the saddle. "Good luck out there. I'll see you in a few days." He held out his hand.

Horn's eyes went round. A man with few friends, maybe. Of his own species, at least. He started to extend his hand, then tugged it back and plucked off his glove. It was the first time Trace had seen the man seem hurried, off-balance.

He shook Trace's hand. "Good luck," he said, making eye contact.

His hand felt hard and dry, calloused like stone. The hand of someone who lived outside, under a bridge or in a cave. The fingers bullet-like, capable of picking hot coals from a fire or tying shoelaces on a subzero morning.

Awkward then, little else to say. Horn just stood there. He seemed slightly mystified, bewitched. Trace nodded to him, then hupped the horse. As he and Camo rounded the first corner of the trail, Trace looked back over his shoulder, but the man was gone.

Trace raised the ranch on the radio as soon as he was back in range. Imogen answered. She sounded breathless, though it was hard to tell for sure through the static. "Roger, Range Rider, this is Base. Good to hear from you. We were getting a little worried here. You all good, got some snow up there? Over."

Trace sat the horse and looked back the way he'd come, toward Ravenfeather Mountain. The snow was already melting off, the slopes darkening. New Mexico's fire season had been officially changed to year-round a few years ago, and the first heavy snowfall seemed to come later and later each year. This one had been lighter than expected, only hitting the higher elevations.

"Range Rider?"

Trace held the mic back to his mouth and thumbed the button. "All good, Base. Snow was light. Say, can I come up to the house tonight? Need to talk to you about something. Over."

A brief pause. "Why don't I come out there. Been stuck in the office all day. Same spot? Over."

Trace nodded. "Yes, ma'am. Same time? Over."

"Ten-four, Range Rider. See you about dark. Supper's on you this time. Over and out."

Trace hooked the radio back to the shoulder of his vest. A stir in his belly, warm. The thought of her coming out to camp again. Just the two of them, the fire, a pot on the grate. A flickering glow in all that darkness, the vast blind country on every side.

He shook his head and patted Camo on the neck.

"Quit dreaming."

CHAPTER 46

Murdoch had been watching the crash site when the lion came slinking through the thermal field of his scope, pale as a ghost. He watched the animal pause before the wreckage and make a look of seeming disgust, opening his jaws and sticking out his tongue. Wafting a scent picture of the area to the sensitive roof of his mouth. The Jacobson's organ. The animal had detected something strange or alien here—men, likely—but didn't appear alarmed.

So Murdoch knew no one was holed up inside the fuselage, not at the moment. He could thank the lion for telling him as much. Likely the red light glowing through the windows was a trap, something akin to the glowing lure of a deep-sea anglerfish. His pursuers must be posted somewhere in the rocks above the crash site, hoping he'd approach.

Smarter than he anticipated.

It would take too long to circle to a point where he'd have a clear line of fire, so he decided to move on. Let them wait the rest of the night while he put miles of distance between them, carrying on his mission. He would deal with them soon enough.

Come dawn, he was crossing a saddle to the west of the ten-thousand-foot peaks of the Mogollon Mountains, walking beneath fir trees as the rising sun came crackling through the branches. There was better access in this part of the Wilderness. A few trails and primitive campsites. A paved road just three miles to the north. He'd look like just another hunter to anyone who crossed his path.

He watered at a spring he'd marked on his map, filled his canteens, and continued on, passing a slanted trail sign. The Dark Canyons would be harder to intercept as they moved west. He'd marked the caches, rendezvous sites, and runways of their home range, but now they were moving toward the territory of the Whitewater pack, which he didn't have well mapped.

Still, an elation hummed just beneath his skin. There was little in the world he could say he loved. The emotion was foreign to him, glimpsed mainly from afar, like a distant cabin in the night, the windows aglow. It had died with the bombs that fell on his village, his family, his grandfather—if it ever was there. But what he felt now was something close. Love for the chase. His prey out there in the wild, elusive as mist or spirit, and the rare knowledge he was not just the hunter this time but the quarry, too. He was being tracked, pursued, hunted—it heightened his senses, honed them. His hair felt like tiny antennae on his skin. His ears felt sharper, eyes clearer.

He lived for this.

By noon, he was crossing the next spine of mountains, slightly smaller than the last, hiking down a western slope. It had not snowed here last night and the country was still dry. The late-summer monsoons had been light this year and the old-growth evergreens had a yellow cast to them, parched. He stopped, dropped his gear, and reversed his outer suit, shifting from the white snow pattern back to the high-desert camouflage.

He was starting to feel willowy in his limbs. Low glycogen, he knew. Time to eat. He climbed out onto a forested thrust of rock with a broad view in three directions, set down his pack, and pulled out two packets of meal replacement powder—a lightweight solution that provided five hundred calories of protein, carbohydrates, and fatty acids per serving. He emptied the packets into a thermoplastic bottle, added water, and shook the formula into a thick vanilla shake.

He lay on his belly among the rocks, slurping from the bottle as he inventoried the landscape. He'd been all over the world pursuing game and men, and this old country of the Apache was the most rugged he'd known. Not even the naked, contorted jags of Afghanistan could compare, where he'd arranged bounties on the heads of Green Berets, nor the green-dark mazes of West Virginia coal country, where whistleblowers and witnesses sometimes disappeared on their morning walks through the woods.

A harsh country here, no mercy for the weak. A land of forest fire and flash flood, sheer cliffs and loose stone. A violent terrain, made as if with a god's claws and teeth. A land where the cougar and wolf still laid claim, and it took someone like Murdoch to combat the natives.

A glint down his backtrail.

He licked the frothy mustache from his upper lip and brought up the binoculars, never letting his eyes deviate from the spot. It jumped into view, focused. A squiggle of trail. He looked farther up the track and saw movement again. He tried to follow it, but there was too much cover. Strangely, in the flashes he caught, it looked more like an animal moving along his trail than a man, though it had to be the latter. It walked on two legs.

Murdoch watched as long as he could. It moved like his own shadow, sliding smoothly along his trail, catching up to him. A strange thrill at the sight.

He got up and moved on. Throughout the day, the smoke of wildfires blew in from California and the sun began to sink red in the west, burning like Mars in the brown-gray haze. Like they'd been transported onto an alien planet, or into the future of this one—a world burning without end. A long red dusk. As darkness fell, Murdoch found a bivouac site.

Tonight, he'd set a trap of his own.

CHAPTER 47

Still a bloody red glow in the west when Imogen's silhouette came bobbing along the trail, raising faint curls of dust. She'd come on horseback this time—a black mare with a russet mane that nickered happily at the sight of Camo staked out to graze. Imogen swung down from the saddle in her black gambler hat and coat, her dark hair pooled in the collar like a shawl. A pair of silver spangles jingled on her wrist. Something seemed different about her—Trace couldn't say what. But when they hugged, he sensed a warmth radiating from her, as if her flesh glowed beneath the layers of clothing.

She set her hands on her hips. "So, what's for supper?"

Trace had just dumped a flavor packet into a bowl of macaroni noodles. "Temple Camp Special. Something I like to call Mack Truck and Cheese."

Imogen sat down on the stump next to him, set her hat on her knee, and shook out her hair, scratching her nails down to the scalp. He looked at the symbols tattooed on her fingers, moons and birds and lashed eyes.

"I believe I could eat a dump truck's worth of supper," she said. "So I hope that means there's a lot of it."

"Enough for a saunter of cowboys."

"A whole saunter, huh?"

"Old Temple used to say a 'saunter' was the official word for a group of cowboys."

"A *stagger* of cowboys sounds more like it, you ask me."

Trace grinned. "The old man would've liked that one. He used to say the only thing that could drink more whiskey than a cowboy was a hole in the ground." Trace began spooning out helpings into a pair of metal bowls. "Mack Truck and Cheese is two boxes of grocery-store macaroni and cheese, a can of tomato sauce, diced tomatoes, pinto beans, and green chilis. My family ate it at least once a week my entire life, and it was a staple anytime we camped out on the range. Hunting, scouting, working cattle."

Imogen tucked in with gusto, holding her bowl in one hand and eating overhand with the other. She wore an old revolver on her belt, the holster tucked toward the back of her hip, the Cruz Ranch brand pokerworked into the skinny wooden grip. After a while she leaned up on her hip and took a small silver flask from her back pocket. "Have a taste of that."

Trace turned up the flask. Mezcal, hot and wild, like smoked lightning on the tongue.

"*Espadín*," he said. The word meant *sword*. "Damn, you broke out the good stuff."

She smiled and took a swig of her own. "Thought you might could use it. You sounded serious on the radio. What did you want to talk to me about?"

Trace set down his bowl and rubbed his hands on his thighs. "I wanted to tell you, if something ever happens to me out here, if I was to go missing or there's an accident of some kind, I'd like you to please push the rangers to investigate it. Tell them I said something could happen to me, that I said they ought to call in the ISB."

"Investigative Services Branch?"

The special agents of the National Park Service, who investigated high crime on NPS land. Trace nodded and pulled a folded envelope from his hip pocket. "Give them this. There's a note in there for my mama, too."

Imogen set the flask aside and took the envelope. She turned it over, seeing it was sealed. "What kind of trouble are you in, Trace?"

"Honestly, it's better you don't know."

"Drugs?"

Trace shook his head. "It ain't that."

"You still don't know why I hired you, do you?" She cocked her head as she said it, looking at him in a way that made him uncomfortable. Like he was big in her eyes, or glowed. Like he was something he wasn't.

"You mean, besides the way I saunter?"

She smiled. "Besides that. The fact is, we don't get to trust very many people in this world, not even our own families sometimes. Not even ourselves. But you and me, we go way back, all the way. To Garrison and before. To the time we could hardly reach a stirrup or doorknob." She put the envelope in the interior pocket of her ranch coat, then set her hand on his knee. "I can trust you, Trace. I know I can. You don't have to tell me what's going on. But you can, I want you to know that. You can talk to me."

Trace stared at her hand on his knee. He felt that strange unreality of things, as if his outer world had crossed with that dusky dreamland inside him. The fire beating on their cheeks, the sweet pangs knifing through his ribs. When he looked up, her face was close to his, flame-licked. Every word stuck in his throat. He kissed her.

She smiled. "Been a while."

"Since behind that big tree on the playground."

"You remember that, do you?"

"A boy don't forget kissing the prettiest girl in school."

"What was that, second grade?"

"Second for me, third for you." He paused. It hadn't been but a play-kiss, a mimicking of what they'd seen on daytime soap operas, but it had swollen up Trace's heart like an elk's. He wasn't sure it had ever gone back down to its right size. Not in her presence. "I was about ready to carve our names in that tree after that."

Imogen leaned close, cocking her chin to whisper in his ear. "*Still could.*"

She kissed him. Soon her tongue found his. Her hands on his face, in his hair. He kissed her neck and throat, tasting the salt of her skin. His hands slid under her coat, feeling her ribs, the bunched terrain of her back. Then their hats were off and their coats and they were on the ground, on the saddle blanket by the fire, shedding their shirts and boots and socks, clawing and grappling like they wanted to kill and devour each other.

Trace set his teeth to her neck as her nails raked the backs of his arms. She pushed him down her belly, unbuckling her concho belt and slithering out of her jeans and lifting her hips to him, his teeth and tongue, holding the back of his head with both hands. After a time, she reached down and pulled him into her, the hot seal there, spurring him with her heels. Hot copper and the smoke of their common breath. Their bodies raveled into knots and out again. They groaned and panted and rocked, wrecking themselves on each other.

CHAPTER 48

Murdoch lay inside his sleeping bag. His hands were laced over his chest, holding a silenced semiautomatic pistol, the barrel tucked under his left arm so it wouldn't imprint against the downy nylon cocoon. He'd left the bag unzipped so he could throw it open if necessary, and he'd chosen this spot precisely—the base of an uprooted fir. The snarl of roots would act like a headboard, protecting his flank, and the crater made for a natural foxhole.

He'd strung a perimeter of trip wire around his tiny camp. The polygon of fine black filament would alert him if tripped, vibrating a fob around his neck. He breathed in and out slowly, finding a state of steady vigilance. Calm but alert. He planned to stay awake, waiting for his shadow to show up. His pursuer. He would send him down, back into darkness, as he'd done so many times before. Men weren't very hard to kill, in his experience. Though he did seem to have a special affinity for the task.

He'd killed his first when he was thirteen. It was the winter after their village had been bombed and Murdoch had spent the day hunting the lean snowy woods for game, trying to concentrate in spite of the shivering cold. He was returning home with only a single thin hare stretched over his shoulder. When he came to the charred rubble of the old Roman bridge, he found an ogre sitting there on a stool, a short-barreled AK-47 in his lap. The village truck mechanic. A fat man, twenty stone, his dark-stubbled neck pocked with white nicks of razor scar. He sat blocking the bridge, a jar propped on his knee.

"Boy, I am the new tollman."

"I don't remember any old one."

The man smiled, showing dark teeth. He cast a hand back at the scorched pilings Murdoch had to scramble across to get home. "A bridge like this? There have been many, many tollmen before me. All manner of tolls paid. All manner. That hare will do nice."

"It's for my family, for supper."

The fat man leaned forward on his stool, almost close enough to snatch Murdoch by the front of his shirt. His jowled face had an oily sheen, like a glazed pastry in a shop window. Murdoch could smell the rotgut vodka radiating from his pores. The man shifted the automatic rifle slightly from his lap, showing the lump stretched against the groin of his boilersuit. "There are other ways the toll can be paid."

Murdoch stepped back. "I got something you'll like even better. Let me go fetch it."

He walked back up the path and into the woods, deep enough the man could no longer see him. He squatted there, breathing hard, trying to decide what to do. The river was too cold this time of year to ford—he'd freeze to death before he reached home. The next bridge, kilometers distant, was guarded by militia at least as dangerous as this troll.

He circled to a range of one hundred meters and lay prone, watching the man stroke and talk to himself. Murdoch steadied his breath and took aim, trying to remember a man was only an animal. Another beast of the field. Little different from the polecats and pine martens he hunted, the deer and wild boar. A man was lower, he decided. A creature capable of evil.

Still, a strange vibration ran through his teenage fingers, as if someone had reached down and plucked his body's strings. Chords of fear or reluctance rang in his veins, unsteadying his aim, making his breath plume like a sleigh horse's.

He fired.

Missed.

The tollman rose from his stool, his face twisting into a hammy red fist. He swung his AK to his hip and began clapping shots through the trees. Murdoch worked the bolt and fired again. A violent pink nimbus flickered about the man's head, quick and gone, and he staggered back onto the stool and fell off one side, heavy as a sack of potatoes.

When Murdoch searched the body, he found other tolls. A few crumpled dinar, an old wristwatch, a perfume bottle of homemade vodka. A locket with the picture of a girl he recognized from school. The pewter smudged with greasy fingerprints. A girl gone missing.

He resisted the urge to shoot the man again.

Instead, he dragged the body down to the cold dark shallows of the river and shoved it off, watching the humped form float downstream. Corpses turned up all the time, snagged along the banks or wedged in the rubble. Bloated remnants of one faction or another. The tollman's passing would make no headlines, spark no investigation—not in a land where people were machine-gunned into mass graves and thrown from helicopters. No, the dead man would have no recourse but to return as an angry spirit to haunt his killer. But a person had to believe in ghosts to be haunted by them, and Murdoch had chosen not to believe—or rather, he'd chosen to become a ghost himself. A thing to be feared.

He left the tolls on the stool. Offerings for the living or dead. Then he slung the man's Kalashnikov over his shoulder and crossed the bridge without looking back.

Now he lay in his cocoon, waiting, feeling that same strange thrill run through his fingers and along his ribs, as if he'd touched a tuning fork. *Fear*, which he didn't feel often. He let himself savor this rare sensation, knowing it would keep him alert, his senses sharp. The fallen fir had left an opening in the canopy and he stared up at the night sky. It was a known area for stargazers, he knew. Cosmic Campground, a few miles away, was one of the only dark sky sanctuaries on the continent—an area devoid of light pollution. But smoke from California fires had moved in from the west. The stars were few, the night smeared dark as pine pitch.

Around 3:00 AM he began to fatigue. He'd not taken another one of the nootropic pills to stay awake—consecutive days on the medication made him lethargic—and he was no stranger to long nights with little sleep. Still, he always seemed to get tired this time of night. The witching hour, as the old village crones used to call it. Mean hags with hooked noses who told tales that kept children up at night. It was the hour when ghouls and spirits were said to be about, when skeletons danced and shapeshifters performed devilries.

Sometimes Murdoch wished he believed in such superstitions, as they might keep him awake at this hour when the very world seemed to grind to a halt for a few brief moments. His lids fluttered, his eyes threatening to roll back in his head. He pulled a coffee packet from his sundries pouch and emptied the dry grounds into his mouth, packing them into his lip like smokeless tobacco. At the same time, he began to increase his breathing, faster and deeper, telling his body it was no time for sleep.

He invited visions of *vampiri* and *vukodlaci*—werewolves—and other demons of his Slavic childhood. The *psoglav*, said to have a horse's legs and a dog's head filled with iron teeth, and the *zwodziasz*, which came sometimes in the form of a nightjar, leading men into wastelands. This demonology of crones. He thought of a cougar pouncing on him in the night, tearing out his throat, or his pursuer standing above him, driving a stake into his heart. Still, his eyelids continued to disobey him, as if possessed of their own will, and he began to wonder if some part of him wanted to die.

Murdoch jolted awake, grasping the fob vibrating in the well of his neck. Had he fallen asleep? He slid quietly out of the cocoon bag and brought up his pistol, looking over the edge of the crater. Nothing. No movement in the trees. No sound. Not even a swaying of branches, a crackle of leaves. False alarms had to be expected—any small animal could trip a wire.

He knew better than to emerge from cover to investigate. Instead he reset the alarm and remained in position, knowing it was likely a small mammal on some nocturnal errand. If nothing else, he should thank the animal for waking him, bringing him back to the surface.

An hour later, he'd settled back into an almost meditative state, imagining himself no more than a log lying in the earth, a natural part of the landscape over which the sounds, scents, and shadows of the night drifted. He was nothing. Nowhere. Invisible. His breaths long and infrequent, like a man in hibernation.

The fob went off again.

Again he came up out of the bag, ready for intruders.

Again, nothing.

He got on his rifle and ran a patterned scan of the area through the thermal scope. A gray and black ghostland, glowing only with a perched owl and a distant trundling skunk. Murdoch settled back into the bag, battling annoyance, irritation. That was not where his mind should be. He had to stay alert, focused, centered. He had to smooth over these breaks in his rhythm, keep himself anchored.

It was nearing dawn when the wire tripped a third time. Murdoch was sorely tempted this time to investigate. But his mind proved too strong, strangling the desire. It was bad fieldcraft. Too exposed. He would not be pried from his hole.

Dawn broke across the upper sky in stripes. The smoke had lingered and there was a heavy yellow tinge to the air. Murdoch emerged from the root crater and watched the light seep across the ground, illuminating boot prints inside the perimeter. Someone had been here, nearly close enough to touch him.

Murdoch felt a weird twitch in the back of his head, like he'd felt when One-Eleven had turned to look directly at him from five hundred yards. Something that should not be, yet was. A glitch in the code of the world. A sudden shift in levels, when you realized your reality was not what you'd thought. The ground was less sure beneath you and there were things in the world you had not yet seen. The footprints were a message, he knew, sure as if they'd been written in stone.

I am here. I can touch you.

CHAPTER 49

"It was me," said Trace. "I was the one they hired first for the job. I wanted to get back at whoever and whatever took our ranch and my old man along with it, and the lobos seemed a sure enough target. When I had a change of heart, they sent somebody in my place."

They were sitting in front of the fire, warming the kettle for coffee. Dawn a dull knife along the horizon, the sun yet to rise. The land lay dark around them, hazed with smoke. Imogen sat on the stump beside him wearing his sleeping bag like a quilt.

He could hardly believe she'd stayed the night. He'd spent half the time staring up at the domed ceiling of the tent, full of awe for the place he found himself and the creature nestled beside him. The blood and muscle of her, the spirit and heat. She was a wonder. The thing that hit you like a semitruck, so hard you'd never be the same again. It seemed crazy, but that's exactly what falling for someone was. Crazy. Just like everybody said, but you didn't know the truth of it till it hit you like a thunderbolt and split you clean through. You no longer felt like one tree but two, and they were your other half. It sounded cliché, but like Old Temple used to say: *Nothing's cliché when you're the one it happens to.*

Trace held his hands out to the fire. "I could make excuses. Like how hunters kill them all the time up north, legal. Wyoming, Montana, Idaho. Collared wolves, too. Any that step out of Yellowstone or protected areas. Only difference down here is the law, not the act. That's what I told myself."

Trace looked at the fire, the flames whirling around the bottom of the pot. "Truth is, I did think it was wrong. Hell, I think I wanted to do it just for that reason. Just to punch back at something bigger than me. To show I still had power in the face of everything that happened to my family—to hurt the very things I blamed for taking what we had. It took nearly dying to realize I didn't want to live that way."

Imogen's breath smoked beside him. "And now?"

"I might still be lost, but I'm looking for a better path."

"Range riding?"

"Maybe. I'm in thick now."

"What do you know about the men that hired you?"

"I'd rather not say, for your own protection."

"There's danger in ignorance and danger in knowledge. I prefer the latter. Especially if they're operating on land that's home to my people and stock."

Trace shook his head. "All I'm comfortable saying is they're some kind of separatist movement."

Imogen reached out and clamped his knee. "The Free West?"

"You know them?"

She stared into the small fire. "Oh, I know them all right. My old man, after he got sick, he seemed to turn some corner in his personality. He was angry all the time, just bitter. Everything was someone else's fault. Blamed the government, the immigrants, the libs, the lobos. Had him a scapegoat for every last frustration and disappointment you could imagine, and then some."

She pushed her chin out. "A man's entitled to his opinions, sure, but he'd just shovel this shit all over us, all the time. Family dinner was a real treat, let me tell you. The old man high on cancer drugs, bourbon, and meanness, just railing at the world at large. Pretty much anything that didn't look, talk, and walk like he did, and some that did. Pretty soon he found his way to the Free West, and what they were selling was just what he was buying. It was like he'd found religion.

"He'd tell me how he found some people out there willing to stand up against tyranny. How there were still heroes in the world, acting undercover, just beneath the surface of the world we saw, working to split us apart from the mess. A couple of them came to our house, dressed neat as Jehovah's Witnesses but with silverbelly hats and Colt .45s. A couple of real John Waynes. Week later, my mom got their bank statement in the mail. The old man had given them half their entire life savings.

"I just felt bad for my mama, most of all. She'd lost her husband of fifty years to this anger, this vision she couldn't care one iota of a goddamn about. She only cared about him."

Imogen shook her head. She still had her hand on Trace's knee. She squeezed, looking at him. "I'm proud of you for breaking from them."

Trace looked out toward the Wilderness. "Problem is, I ain't so sure they're done with me."

CHAPTER 50

The Dark Canyons were on the move, trotting beneath the haze-choked sun in loose formation—a flying wing that One-Eleven had to keep in constant check. The pups were crazed with interest in this new territory, inspecting every last log hollow, cleft of rock, and half-buried set of bones. One-Eleven kept them moving, sweeping back to prod and nip their hindquarters. They were safest on their feet, on the move.

In the night, they'd passed downwind of a dark encampment of circled vehicles with no fires, lanterns, or lights—just shadows moving on a dark plain. The men had their heads bent to great tubes pointed to the sky. Along the distant highway, headlights moved slowly through the night, rising into view and disappearing again, dropping into swales or river bottoms.

It was nearing noon and the sun hovered amid rags of smoke, a reddish orb. The shadows lay stunted and the air was dry, buzzing with heat. They climbed the spine of a ridge and were descending the other side, working their way down a steep slope of loose rock, when One-Eleven looked back and saw a pup missing.

Little Paw.

She turned and bolted back up the slope, switchbacking along narrow game trails and dropping down into the trees on the far side. She had her nose to the ground, tracking her missing whelp, threading together shreds of sign. He couldn't be far.

In a flash she knew where he was, what temptation would prove too great for his curious mind. She came down on the site from above. A steaming place in the earth, a hot spring that gurgled day and night. Bright algae flourished beneath the surface and a sulfurous scent bubbled out, born from the hot bowels of the land. The place attracted hikers. Their boot prints everywhere, circling the spring, and there was Little Paw raising his head at her from the edge of the pool, tongue out—proud of what he'd found.

Voices on the approach trail. One-Eleven gathered her body into a knot and exploded into a run, bounding straight down the slope even as the hikers' heads bobbed through the understory, their boots crackling on the dry path, nearing. Little Paw stood planted on wide legs, rigid with pride. Too big now to whip away by the nape of his neck. So she ducked her head and swept her ears back and flashed through the clearing at speed. Her legs struck like lightning across the edge of the steaming spring and the rest of the pack was brought to a dead run behind her, rolling past Little Paw with such force he couldn't help but bolt after them, jerked by his deepest instinct: to run with the pack.

One-Eleven pulled the Dark Canyons back up the slope, turning to see the hikers standing slack-jawed at the foot of the spring. She towed the pack over the spine of the ridge and they slid and tumbled down the far side, rifling into the cover of the trees. They kept on and on, running like fire through the dry brush, weaving and darting between the pines. One-Eleven led them over broken slate paths to mask their trail and across creeks again and again. They passed old mines square-mouthed in the mountainsides and corroded equipment as the hoodoos towered over them, shadowless beneath the noon sun.

They flushed a band of coyotes that yipped and squealed, shouting up a terrible racket as they fled. Finally the pack emerged onto a broad forested rim. One-Eleven's shoulders and hindquarters were searing. The force of her breath blew slaver through her teeth and every tongue in the pack flopped out. She stood at the edge of the rim. A broad desert plain of sage and cheatgrass sloped away before them, westward toward Whitewater country. She could hear the coyotes still yipping in the distance, sounding the alarm.

Now she caught sight of something on the plain. Two small clouds of dust rising from the ground, curling in the wind like dust devils. Her body tensed.

Whitewater wolves.

Two of them racing this way, ears back, pale shoulders churning with power. One-Eleven couldn't turn the pack and retreat. They were too fatigued to outrun pursuers. They would be hunted down and torn apart, one after the next. She looked back at them. Her pack. Her flesh on fire, lungs searing. Strings of saliva dripping from her chin.

The pack stared back at her, open-mouthed. Her heart doubled.

One-Eleven turned and looked at the Whitewater wolves. She stood her ground, planted high on the rim. She was alpha loba, wolf-mother of the Dark Canyons. She threw back her head and howled, loud and long, like she might raise a whole army from the Gila, lifting the buried bones of ten thousand dead. Then she charged down the slope to meet the wolves on the plain.

CHAPTER 51

Murdoch watched the distant vectors of dust curling up from the coyote grass, racing head-on, converging. Like two trains speeding toward destruction. He was high on a blasted slope, lying prone behind his rifle in the caving powderhouse of an abandoned silver mine.

He'd marked these ruins as a possible point of overwatch on his map back at The Ranch. This morning, he'd followed an ancient set of narrow-gauge tracks to reach it, the rails running rusty and twisted around the mountainside, past ancient iron carts with seized wheels and shattered supply sheds until they reached the deserted mine. The place had remained untouched since the 1940s. The rickety headframe and sheave wheel stood like a skeletal watchtower over the basin. Buildings of corrugated tin and tumbling stone sat in various states of implosion. Down the slope lay the old tailings coughed out of the place, a concrete-colored glacier of sulfide and pyrite and other minerals whose crystalline dust had been known to kill miners in just two to three years of working the place, burying itself in their lungs.

Murdoch had come to watch for wolf movement in the basin.

The latest GPS coordinates put both the Dark Canyons in this area and a pair of collared Whitewater wolves—M665 "Rio" and M666 "Luche"—brothers who'd earned reputations among the wolf-watching community as two of the most formidable animals on record. Mexican gray wolves tended to be smaller than the gray wolves of the Yukon, Alaska, and Northern Rockies, but these lobos weighed more than 120 pounds each—fearless fighters who'd killed lone wolves caught inside their territory.

The powderhouse where he'd set up his shooting position had once stored the dynamite and blasting powder for the mine. The structure was recessed slightly into the mountainside to dampen the blast of an accidental explosion. There were no windows in the mortared stone walls and the heavy rafters were still in place, latticing the sky—the rest of the roof had caved in long ago.

He'd planned to stay here no longer than noon, not giving his pursuer enough time to catch up, but he'd glimpsed movement along the basin rim just before twelve o'clock. In no time Murdoch was on his gun, finding One-Eleven and her pack as they emerged from the pines and trotted high along the distant tree line. They looked hangdog, fatigued, their tongues hanging long and pink from slack jaws. Even the she-wolf appeared weary, prodded ever farther from the heart of her territory, facing threat after threat.

Then he saw the plume of dust rising off the plain. Two pale wolves, moving at speed. Murdoch swung his scope back to the Dark Canyons. His heart alive in his chest, beating like it rarely did. He ranged them: 712 yards. He'd made plenty of kills from this range with this load. He began to calculate a firing solution. Windage, elevation, Coriolis effect. Slowing his breaths, steadying his sight picture. Leading One-Eleven as she trotted along at the head of the pack.

When she paused, he had her laced in his crosshairs, pegged broadside on the basin rim—a perfect shot. The sheave wheel creaked high over the mine and his finger lay on the trigger, ready to send the round. His curiosity stayed him a moment. He wanted to see what she would do. Whether she could make his hair stand on end again, that eerie tickle at the back of his head. She threw back her head and howled high over the plain, the sound still rolling across the expanse as she charged down the slope to meet the Whitewater wolves.

Murdoch's scalp prickled. *Some wolf.*

Now the plumes of dust sped ever closer to collision. He thought he noticed a slight hitch in the step of the Whitewater brothers, a fraction's hesitation. Perhaps they feared an animal willing to meet them in a head-on charge—a lobo so bold.

Still the brothers rumbled onward, their gaits stiffening as they urged themselves on and on, driven like soldiers toward some new and unknown weapon. One-Eleven showed no hesitation, streaking across the plain of brown grass and sage with long, hound-like strides, as if shot from a sling, a curly pennant of dust hanging in her wake. In seconds they would meet, a violent intersection of teeth and blood and fur. Five, four, three—

Murdoch shrieked as something ripped through the back of his leg. He felt it punch through his hamstring and glance his femur, the click of steel on bone. He scrambled to the nearest corner and twisted to look. An arrow, the long shaft jutting from the back of his right leg. A bloody broadhead poked through the thigh of his trousers. He looked up through the roof timbers and no one was there, just the yellowish sky. Then another arrow sang down and smacked into the wall, wedging itself between the stones, as if hurled down from the heavens.

In a flash, Murdoch knew his mistake. Arrows could be lofted from the top of the headframe, arcing down on his position. Anger shot up inside him at the oversight. At the world for taking advantage of the slightest chink in whatever wall or guard or hide he tried to construct.

"*Majka Hristova*," he hissed. Mother of Christ.

The first time in years he'd broken into his mother tongue.

Murdoch dragged himself to the door of the powderhouse and pulled himself outside, lying on one shoulder as he raised the long barrel of the rifle to the top of the headframe. He sighted down the side of the gun at the figure perched on the upper platform, crouched behind the iron wheel of the sheave—a giant pulley holding a braided steel cable that ran down to the winch house.

Murdoch fired three times. The rounds sparked off the wheel spokes as the figure ducked behind an iron plate—a makeshift shield he must have dragged up there with him. No matter. Murdoch had him trapped. The climb down was too exposed, an array of ancient ladders and catwalks and scaffolding that hung creaking in the wind—easy as shooting a bird from a wire.

Murdoch waited to see what his enemy would do. The man couldn't raise up to draw his bow again without exposing himself. Then again, Murdoch couldn't wait forever. The broadhead hadn't nicked an artery or he'd already be dead, bled out inside the powderhouse—but he was losing blood fast. The more he lost, the weaker he'd become. He fired five more rounds into the iron shield, hoping it might rattle the bowman into making a mistake, a desperate attempt to climb down or raise up to return fire. Nothing.

Not taking his eyes from the tower, Murdoch dragged over his pack and set up behind it, resting the rifle barrel on top, aimed at the headframe. Then he took a clotting agent from his med kit, tore off the top of the packet with his teeth, and poured the granulate into the wound to help slow the bleeding.

When he looked up, he saw something fly off one side of the platform, whirling and flashing. His eyes tracked it like a flushed bird. By the time he realized it was only a canteen—a diversion—the bowman had thrown a strap over the braided steel cable of the sheave and leapt from the far side of the platform. He slid down the cable like a zipline, legs straight and feet out, straight down toward the winch house, out of sight before Murdoch could get off a single shot.

"*Hristova.*"

Murdoch moved quickly now. He opened his tool roll, took out a small pair of lock-cutters, and snipped off the exposed arrow shaft on either side of his leg. The shaft itself would have to remain in place until a surgeon removed it; otherwise he risked hemorrhage. He repacked the entry and exit wounds with the rest of the quick-clot, then unclipped a coil of synthetic rope from his pack and spooled one end around the stump of an old fencepost, knotting it tight. He clipped the other end to a reinforced D-ring on his pack and began to crawl away from the powderhouse, dragging himself toward the edge of the mine. He was compromised, no match for an enemy in close quarters. Not in this condition. He needed distance and time to arrange a defense or extraction.

An avalanche of tailings ran down the mountainside, a wide channel blasted down through the trees for hundreds of feet, steeper than a ski run. Murdoch hurled his pack over the side, the rope singing past him as the bulk of his gear went tumbling down the mineral slope. Then he clipped himself into the line, strapped his rifle across his chest, and shoved himself over the edge.

CHAPTER 52

One-Eleven stood stiff-legged on the plain, watching the Whitewater wolves flee before her. Her breath poured hot through her jaws and the dust of her own trail was just catching up to her. She licked her bloody fangs, feeling the grit coat her teeth and tongue.

Just before she and the enemy wolves collided, rifle shots had cracked the sky, several in rapid succession, as if thunder and lightning followed with her, brought down fast and hard on the plain. Storm-bringer. Death-giver. Lightning wolf.

The Whitewaters had never learned to tell if shots were aimed in their direction, as One-Eleven had. They'd never been hunted, their mates killed. Her head-on charge had awed them and the gunshots struck them boneless with fear. They were like pups when she hit them. She tore a chunk from the flanks of one brother as she passed, a red banner that made him squeal and twist, and then she whirled to face the second wolf, slinging blood from her teeth. The two Whitewater wolves turned and ran, looking back wild-eyed at her, like she had two heads or fangs the size of sabers—a creature unknown to them.

Dozer and Little Paw were first to catch up with her, the smallest wolf outrunning his siblings despite his size. He'd run his heart out, trying to keep pace with his big brother. Now they stood beside her in the whirling dust of the plain, chests high, legs stiff, watching the Whitewaters flee before their mother. Then they ran their muzzles along her sides, leaving webs of slaver in her coat. Little Paw threw back his head to howl.

He howled alpha loba, mother of wolves. The others arrived and raised their own voices beneath the blood-red sun. Their harmonies rose high over the plain, strange and wild. Voices piercing and diverging, wheeling to their own ends and merging into higher, keener crescendos. Peaks of sound raised against the sky, as if calling out to sun and moon.

One-Eleven let them sing. She raised her own head, laid back her ears, and sang with the pack. Her voice above and beneath them, apart and beside them. She felt them all around her, their bodies and breath, muscle and blood. She lost herself in their howling, the rally of flesh and fur and sound. She sang Graynose. Meat-getter, sire wolf. She sang land and water, elk and sheep. She sang Little Paw and Dozer and all her whelps, raised on milk and meat. And she sang herself. Pup-bearer. Wolf-maker. Elk-killer. Battle-wolf. Let the Whitewaters know. Let the elk and antelope, the raven and coyote. Let all the Gila, every bird and stone. Let them know she was One-Eleven, alpha loba of the Mogollon Mountains, born to fight and die.

When they finished, she turned and led the pack back the way they'd come, weaving a trail through the sage. The juniper shivered around them, parched gray. The sun had tipped past the noon apex, balling westward, reddening, flashing the plain with bloody panes of light. One-Eleven would lead the pack south, toward a deep stone canyon she recalled from another time. Whitewater Canyon, site of the original den of the Whitewater pack. An old haven, which still roared with power.

She turned at the edge of the trees and looked back the way they'd come. Out there, far across the plain, the two Whitewater brothers stood broadside, watching her. Sentinel wolves, guardians of the pack. The smaller one shone bloody in the sun, but did not pant. No display of pain or fear.

One-Eleven stared back at them a long time. Then she turned and moved on.

CHAPTER 53

Trace drove through the dusty haze of late afternoon, thumping the steering wheel with his thumbs. Old honky-tonk voices crooned over the airwaves. Hank Williams and Lefty Frizzell, whose big six-strings swung wide from their hips as their gullets quivered.

He was headed home. The Temple Ranch. The first time since the bank seized it. More than two years. He couldn't help but feel a twitch of nerves at the prospect. But then, he had plenty to make him twitchy. Poachers and outlanders and the prettiest rancher in all of New Mexico. Nerve endings and synapses were firing all over him, in parts of him lost and forgotten, in territories just discovered. Fear and awe in equal measure, thrill and terror.

His mother had messaged him that morning as he sat aback Camo watching the herd. She asked if he might want to come out to the house for supper. She wrote: Mack Truck n Cheese, your favorite.

Trace couldn't help but grin. Two nights in a row—he couldn't argue with such luck. He told her he'd come.

It felt strange to be behind the wheel of the truck after so much time in the saddle. Stranger still to be headed home. He still thought of it as that: home. No matter he'd slept in the back of this truck nearly every night for the last two years. Either there, inside his tent, or laid out beneath an open sky, the stars close enough to touch. Last night, with Imogen.

His belly warmed at the thought of her, but he was haunted, too. He couldn't help thinking of Horn out there beneath this same red-smoked sky, alone. Trace reckoned he'd be in a damn dark place if it wasn't for Horn and Imogen, and a person ought to be grateful for the good things that came their way. For the people in their life. Maybe that's why he decided to come this evening. To strengthen another strained bridge. And he knew Horn wouldn't want him back until his leg had time to recover.

The wheels rattled over the cattle grate. The tires made that familiar crackle on the dirt and crushed stone of the drive. The herd and equipment had been sold at auction, but the bank had had trouble selling the homestead itself with no grazing leases to accompany the property. The fence was down in places, barbwire snaking through the scrub. He was sure the wells were blocked or spoiled, the gates unlatched. The trails of poachers and dirt bikers crisscrossed the old pastures. It hurt him to see. Like looking death in the face, or the slow wheel of time.

It reminded him of something. A poem he remembered from high school. He'd never been much of a student, never read much of what he'd been assigned. The books lay forever stacked inside his backpack while he was out on the range, riding fences or inoculating heifers. But this poem had been on one of the standardized tests. The whole thing printed right there, unavoidable, which you had to read and answer questions about.

It was in Egypt, he remembered. Or seemed to be. An *antique land*, the poet said. A stone head the size of a boulder lay half buried at the feet of a statue. A King of Kings, decapitated by the slow march of centuries. His face sneering from the sand, his words still etched into the base of the statue. Trace remembered the inscription: *Look on my Works, ye Mighty, and despair!* And nothing but level sands in all directions. His great works toppled and buried, vanished back into the sands from which they'd been raised.

Trace had read the poem again and again. The time had rung for pencils down and he was still bent over it. He hadn't answered any of the questions in the section. Hadn't even looked at them. The poem had done something to him. Shifted his world, deep as a tectonic plate. Made him see everything like he never had before. That was poetry, he thought. That was a fucking poem. He'd learned more from that one test than he'd ever learned in a class.

He crested the first rise in the drive and saw the old ranch house in the distance. The windows all boarded like a dust storm was coming and tiles missing from the roof—the first time in the life of the place. No Temple ancestor would let a single tile remain missing for more than a day—a matter of pride. When he'd built the place, Old Temple had left a whole roof's worth of clay tiles ricked behind the workshop, planning for the cracked and wind-thrown ones to come. No one now to replace them, and nature never slept.

Then he was parking, walking to the door. The same big slab of oak he'd pushed open every day after school, walking the mile-long drive from the highway where the bus dropped him. Unless it was one of those surprise days when his mother was waiting there on her motorcycle, the engine beating up a plume of dust. Her tan, muscular arms spread wide between the chrome horns of the handlebars, the tattoo of a Milwaukee V-twin on one shoulder. The baddest mama in the whole state, if not the world.

Trace was about to knock when he heard footsteps coming down the front hall. Hard-heeled cowboy boots, like what his mother wore—*and the men in the pale hats*. A vision flashed in his mind: three men in silverbellies and exotic boots coming toward the door, sidearms drawn, and his mother tied up in a kitchen chair, forced to summon him here.

A pause behind the thick slab of door. Trace was breathing fast. He put his hand to his hip, felt the pocketknife he carried there. As if that would help. He heard the metallic clack of the deadbolt. The door groaned open and there stood his mother, hollow-cheeked but beaming, her face wrinkled like a hundred extra smiles.

"Hey, Mama," he said. He was flushed, on the edge of tears.

She stepped out and took him in her arms.

CHAPTER 54

Murdoch had picked up a walking stick left against a trailhead sign. A twisted length of juniper, dried pale and hard, like the staff of a wizard or warlock. A figure of old tales. It was customary for returning hikers to leave such sticks for the next person who happened along the path, hours or days or weeks later. Murdoch used it to help him hobble straight-legged along the trail.

There was an old mining village ahead. A ghost town. A place that died out around the same time as the surrounding mines, all but abandoned when the silver was no longer being blasted and picked out of the ground. Plenty of places to hide, to set up a defensive position while he waited for extraction.

He stepped off the trail to check the wound, leaning against a tree and pulling down his pants to reveal the bloody mess of his thigh. He'd repacked the wounds with hemostatic kaolin gauze, which became sticky and gelatinous when exposed to blood, helping to stanch the bleeding. Even so, fresh blood continued to bloom from the gauze and crawl down his leg.

Murdoch cursed under his breath. The arrow had missed the big femoral artery on the interior of his thigh, but he feared it had clipped one of the descending branches, causing a leakage of bright arterial blood with every heartbeat.

He needed an extraction, and soon.

He took the tourniquet from his med kit, looped the band above the wound, and twisted the windlass until he'd cinched off the blood flow. Then he pulled up his pants and stepped farther off the trail, down the banks of a stream that purled and flashed with shallow water. Down the way, on the opposite bank, an old miner's shack sat back in the trees. Windows papered over, foundation stones tumbling loose. It appeared abandoned, but when the wind turned, Murdoch caught a powerful odor like cat urine. The telltale scent of a meth lab—ammonia, acetone, paint thinner, and other chemicals used to cook the drug.

Murdoch had no way of going around, not in his condition. He eased down beside the water, set the spout of his canteen into the stream, and dialed the operations center at The Ranch. It took three rings longer than expected for someone to pick up.

"Ops Center."

"Ops Center, this is Alpha One." He gave his authentication code. "Casualty incurred. Extraction needed. Level-two care required in-flight."

"Location?"

He referred to his GPS unit. "Rendezvous 33.39133 north by 108.7898 west. Town of Mogollon. Recommend rooftop extraction, structure TBA."

"Hold for confirmation."

Murdoch recognized the woman's voice on the other end, but her tone seemed colder than normal, harder. As if someone were standing at her shoulder.

He was waiting, his canteen bubbling up with cold stream water, when he heard a scrape of feet and someone lurched from the cabin just downstream. A man in shambled corduroys and flannel shirt-jacket and knee-high rubber boots, the clothes draped like scarecrow rags from his wiry frame. He was jerking his head in silence, wearing a pair of over-the-ear headphones and laboratory goggles. He pawed open his button fly and began to piss in the creek, swaying slightly in his over-large boots, the neon yellow stream pulsing in time to his jerking head.

Murdoch lay still. He'd muted the phone. The man leaned back and looked upward. A smoky yellow sky, tiger-striped with red streamers of falling sun like the atmosphere of some alien planet. Then he looked upstream, right at Murdoch. An abrupt hitch in the arc of urine.

Murdoch had eased down onto his side, his rifle pointed generally in the man's direction. Not aimed at him, but close. Only a small adjustment needed. He stared back at the man and slowly shook his head.

The man nodded, swallowed, and tucked himself back into his pants. He retreated up the bank to his cabin, hands held out to his sides. When he was inside, Murdoch climbed back onto the trail and unmuted the phone.

"Ops Center, I repeat: Request confirmation."

A brief pause.

"Alpha One, this is Ops Center. Aviation reports visibility concerns. Smoke should clear by 0600 hours tomorrow. Can extraction wait?"

Murdoch's lip curled into a sneer. He'd waited on a lot of birds in his time—a lot of pilots who demanded perfect flying conditions to leave the ground. It was even worse in the private sector, where aircrews could simply refuse orders, not wanting to extend their necks for mercenaries or contractors. But the pilots at The Ranch were airborne cowboys accustomed to flying low, herding cattle and scouting hunts from the air—they lived for operations like this one. More likely, the old men didn't want to risk one of their million-dollar helicopters on an emergency extraction under less-than-perfect conditions.

"Ops Center, extraction cannot wait."

"Alpha One, Command requests update on mission objective."

"No change from last update. One target neutralized. Tell Command to scramble that helo or this asset will be going offline."

"Roger, Alpha One. Will forward. Call back in twenty for confirmation."

The line went dead.

"Sons of bitches." If they didn't scramble soon, it would get dark before they could make it here. He stowed the phone, set a nineteen-minute timer on his watch, and continued on.

He watched the old miner's shack as he passed, though a lone tweaker didn't concern him much. He'd have shot the man, but it was too messy. An obvious sign of his passage lying brainless in the stream. He couldn't allow it on principle. If the man decided he didn't want somebody knowing where his lab was, then Murdoch would have no trouble dispatching him.

No sign of movement behind the papered windows. He hobbled along with his juniper staff. He had non-opiate painkillers in his kit but hadn't taken them yet. His mind was so full of data streaming in, working so hard to calculate a way out of this scenario, the pain hadn't registered like it normally would.

Soon he was limping down through a cemetery on the ridge above the old mining town. Creosote fence posts canted and broken, fencing rusted out. The gravestones were varied: great stone monuments that lurched lopsided from the reddish earth alongside rough-cut tombstones thin as ironing boards, the chiseled names and dates too time-worn to read. The bones all but identical underneath, told apart only by forensic minutiae. The shattered and crumbling roofs of the ghost town came into view below.

Murdoch redialed The Ranch.

"Alpha One, requesting extraction confirmation."

Clicking keys on the other end of the line. He pictured the woman sitting there at her desk with three wide computer panels arrayed before her.

"Hold, Alpha One."

It was one of the most advanced private TOCs he'd seen, a tactical operations center staffed by U.S. intelligence veterans with experience running black operations in foreign environments, but whose loyalties were closer to home. State independence.

Patriots, as they thought themselves.

Murdoch, of course, cared nothing for their cause beyond the rifts it could open, the further destabilization of the nation. Cracks zigzagging through the heart of America. The crumbling of a superpower he'd hated since those bombs had dropped on his village. The old men of The Ranch thought he was Austrian, a descendant of the great Prussian hussars and boar-hunters. How little they knew. Still, it didn't escape him that his true comrades weren't here to help. He had infrequent contact with his handler from the SVR—the modern incarnation of the Russian KGB—and the man could do little to help him on U.S. soil.

He was alone.

"Alpha One, extraction is a go. Helo scrambling now. ETA 1700 hours at given coordinates." A pause. "No in-flight level-two medical assets available."

Murdoch sniffed. If he'd succeeding in killing One-Eleven, they would've uprooted an entire trauma unit and sent it his way on rotor blades. But he'd known who he was working for when he took this assignment. After proving his bona fides in Africa, Murdoch had started as chief guide and tracker for the exotic big-game hunts they ran on The Ranch, which allowed him to work his way into the covert interests of the organization. The Free West. The old men spoke a lot about values and loyalty, but he knew they wouldn't stretch out their necks for him a single inch farther than they had to—maybe not even that inch.

He held the phone close to his mouth. "Rendezvous reached. Reconfirm at 1600. Out."

He stood on the last switchback over the ghost town. It was set inside a narrow valley, only a single line of buildings on each side of the main street. General store and coach stop, hotel and smithy and various houses slowly crumbling into the dust, already snaked over with vines. A dry creek ran down a deep, bricked canal beside the street, which had flooded more than once in the town's history, nearly wiping it from the map. Small footbridges crossed the canal to buildings on the far side. Many of the spans were rotting and twisted, missing boards. The creek no more than a trickle, clotted with dry brush and debris.

He waited ten minutes in cover, watching for activity and checking the tourniquet. Then he descended the rest of the way down the hillside, hobbling down through the dry brown grass with the twisted length of juniper, heading toward the single main street. It had been paved after one of the flash floods but lay covered in dust, only a few tire tracks visible since the last rain—days old. A remote location for photographers and explorers deep inside the Gila.

He peered through the windows of a former stage stop full of old junk, surprisingly undisturbed over the years. Beside it a general store that looked straight out of the 1800s, built from a hodgepodge of timber and stone and corrugated tin panels so rusted they'd bled down the walls. There was an old hotel and theater farther down, two-story buildings that might serve for a rooftop extraction. He limped past the rusted hulk of a Ford Model T roadster with weeds and wildflowers sprung all through the engineless chassis. A line of mine carts sat on a length of narrow-gauge track, each marked with petroglyphic faces and potshot rounds. Then he stepped out into the street.

The sun hung red and smoldering before him, perched above a high tower of rock at the end of town. Murdoch started down the road between the flat-faced buildings, shuffling toward the old theater with its pale adobe walls and second-story balcony. Someone stepped out of an alley and faced him in the street.

Fifty yards. The man had a compound bow.

Murdoch let go of the walking staff and whipped his rifle around on its sling, raising the weapon as the man turned sideways in the road and drew the bow. Murdoch had just shouldered the gun when the arrow hit him in the chest. He staggered back a step and his rifle jerked skyward. Toward the red sun, the tower of rock. The arrow's fletching shivered from his chest. Then he brought the gun down and fired again and again, five or six rounds as the other man darted out of the road and over the edge of the bricked canal. A long drop, at least ten feet.

Murdoch fell down in the street and began dragging himself toward the theater, crawling on his side. He went up the front steps and pushed through the creaking door and began fighting his way up the stairs. His bloody handprints smeared the curling paisley wallpaper. He was thinking of the second floor. The roof. Blood everywhere. He looked at his arm. The broadhead had torn across his bicep before hitting his chest. A red mess of muscle and tendon. The arrow shaft protruded at a slight angle from his chest.

He had to get upstairs. The staircase moaned beneath him. Blood scalded his chest, his stomach. It ran down his pants, bathed his groin. He reached the upper darkness of the theater balcony, still crawling. Patches of fiery sky through the broken ceiling. He looked at the glowing dial of his watch. 16:27. Thirty minutes to extraction.

He had to make the roof.

Rows of theater seats. He hauled himself upright and used their backrests for support, struggling from one to the next. A cargo pallet stood propped like a ladder against the far wall, leading to a hole in the ceiling.

When he looked up, a wave of weakness rolled through him. He swooned. So easy to sit on the floor. Bleed out in the darkness. Murdoch blinked. He thought of how far he'd seen stags run with bullets blown through their chests, lungs full of blood. As long as they could. He dropped his pack, let his rifle hang loose on its sling, and began to haul himself up the makeshift ladder. Slat by slat, twisted sideways, tasting his own blood in his mouth.

CHAPTER 55

Trace's mother had pulled down the plywood boards from the back windows of the house. The sky was turning the color of fire, a ruddy glow that filled the room. They were sitting at the same giant table where they'd eaten dinner hundreds of times, thousands. The old burn scars and knife nicks and coffee rings like cave art to Trace—a language of home. They'd put most of the heirlooms and furniture in storage, but some were just too big to fit.

Trace slid his palms across the varnished surface, feeling the familiar irregularities in the wood and polish. "Surprised they didn't take this out and sell it at auction. Didn't Old Temple bring it up from Mexico?"

His mother grinned over her bowl of Mack Truck and Cheese. "That he did. Some famous estancia in Chihuahua. Way he told it, he put it here first and built the whole house around it. Reckon you'd have to take off the roof and lift it out with a helicopter, you wanted it out of here."

Trace smiled. She looked and sounded better than she had since they'd lost the ranch. She'd been going to an outpatient rehab program and was waiting on financing approval for an inpatient slot—her brother up in Durango had agreed to cosign. It seemed to give her a jolt of positive energy to be back here, even if she was squatting in her own home, sleeping with the front windows boarded up and cooking on a portable gas stove. None of it seemed to bother her. He could see she was making progress, moving toward some kind of light.

She reached out and squeezed Trace's arm. "We ain't talked about you, honey. How's my boy doing?"

Trace cocked his head. "You ever feel like you're being tugged between something good and something bad, and you're just running back and forth in your head all the time between the two, wearing yourself thin?"

His mother nodded big. "Oh, that's life, son. That's living. Sometimes it's hell even when it's good, and sometimes it's good even when it's hell. I can't explain it. I do know there's a lot of people they go through their whole life in a daze and don't ever feel much of one way or another. Too timid or too comfortable, or else they just go and numb themselves, like I done. It's like they're riding in a car and you're out on a horse, out in the wind and weather. Sometimes you just got to hope the damn thing don't throw you to the wolves."

"That's pretty good advice, Mama."

"That's the thing about advice. Hell of a lot easier to give it than take it."

Trace nodded and spooned himself another bite of Mack Truck. "Though I'd rather be thrown to the wolves than some of these sons of bitches out in this world."

"Amen, son."

Trace was putting the dishes in the sink when his phone vibrated on the counter. He recognized the number with a jolt: the satellite phone he'd given Horn. It could have fallen into other hands, so he hit the button to accept the call and said only: "Hello?"

"Trace?" Horn's voice, crackly through the line.

"Yeah, it's me, man." Trace moved to the corner of the kitchen, lowering his voice. "You all right?"

"Been better, I won't lie."

"What happened?"

"Our friend in the pale hat." Horn's voice sounded thick, strained. "Me and him caught up with each other. He's wounded, bad, but he ain't done. I'm about to go after him, but I'm hurt myself. I want you to know, if you don't hear from me, he's still out there. You better get yours and go far."

"Where are you?"

"Don't come. It's too dangerous."

"Well, where should I avoid going?"

"Mogollon area. The old ghost town." A slight pause. "I have to hurry, friend. I have to go."

"I'm on my way," said Trace. The line was already dead.

CHAPTER 56

One-Eleven heard the sound first. A faint pummeling of air, nearing.

Thunderbird.

Headed toward them, louder by the second, coming out of the eastern sky at speed. They had to get low, down between the high walls of a narrow canyon or gulch. She rallied the pack and urged them down a steep wash she'd avoided for the dust it would raise. They kicked up a billowing plume as they descended, locking their hind legs at times, skidding down the pale silt of the slope on wide paws, turning sideways to slow themselves and wheeling downward again, bounding like bighorns or ibex in flight.

They crossed a dirt double-track at a run and the terrain leveled slightly and then dipped again. They dropped in and out of shadow, across the red flare of western faces and through the purple murk beneath the trees. One-Eleven thought of nothing but the refuge of Whitewater Canyon, too deep for the Thunderbird to reach them.

They ran down through the ruins at the confluence of Whitewater Creek. Exposed pillars, stairs, catwalks to nowhere. An old powerhouse. Then lower, dropping into the canyon itself, and the Thunderbird was nearly on top of them. One-Eleven could feel the violence of the machine in her paw pads, earth and stone trembling. The pack splashed down into the creek just as the machine crossed overhead with a flash and roar, red-blazed and gone, racketing westward.

One-Eleven didn't wait for it to return. She led the pack on and on, deeper into the narrow canyon where the water gushed and roared. She turned to rest in the shelter of an undercut, the pack gathering around her. Only then did she realize.

Little Paw was missing again.

One-Eleven raised her snout to the sky and howled.

CHAPTER 57

Murdoch lay on the theater roof. The red haze of dusk above him. Nightfall coming fast, rolling in like an army. He could hear his extraction speeding inbound, racing the falling sun. A turbine thunder, faint, like cavalry pounding toward him.

It wouldn't save him. He knew that now. He was too badly wounded, had lost too much blood. He wouldn't survive the flight home. The old men would have his body cremated, the ashes spread across some remote section of The Ranch. A few rote words to their Christian God, in which he pretended to believe.

The only God he'd known was out here, under such a sky. The red-shot stone and shivering trees. The animals moving horned and antlered across the landscape, shadowed by the clawed and fanged creatures that hunted them. Here was the only place the world seemed to contain any logic, where its underlying code could be glimpsed. Where cruelty was less common a sight than on any street in any major city on the planet, and the mechanisms were bent toward sustenance, not domination. The wilderness was the true church of this nation, though few seemed to see it.

The sound of the helicopter pounded closer. It would be one of The Ranch's "little birds"—light machines that raced around the sky like dragonflies. Beneath him, inside the theater, he heard a thump, or thought he did. Perhaps his pursuer, whoever he was, was coming for him. His shadow, as he thought of him. Murdoch inched back the bolt of his rifle, catching the brass glint of a chambered round.

He did not feel very afraid. He'd seen so many men and animals die in his trade, so many by his own hand. Death held little wonder for him. What screamed inside him now, building like the sound of a machine, was not pain or fear but rage. At his own failure. A kind of madness. He'd set out to strike a deep blow to this land and its people, to open wounds and widen rifts. To hurt this nation he hated, that had taken his childhood from him. His family. That crushed his village with bombs, just to kill a passing militia unit.

He had failed. If he died on the floor of that helicopter, in a lake of his own blood, he would have achieved nothing. No vengeance. All those years of single-minded effort, will, and highly developed craft. All for nothing. Wrath blew through him, red and terrible. Another idea began to form in his mind. He checked his rifle again, though he'd done it just a few seconds ago.

Another thump in the building beneath him, closer this time. His shadow on the theater balcony, the floor right beneath him. No matter. He needed only a minute or two longer.

The sound of the helo dropped out a moment, blocked by a mountain or ridge. Murdoch's eyes closed. His chin dropped. Darkness coming, taking him. Then rose the howl of the she-wolf, inside his mind or out, and he jerked awake. The sound of the helicopter came barreling back, redoubled. He watched the machine leap over the tower rock on the far heights of the mining village and come down like a whirlwind on the place, kicking up a red storm of dust. The roof timbers rattled beneath him.

At the same time, a shadowy figure rose from the hole in the roof across from him. A man-wolf in the dusk. *Vukodlak.* A creature of the old tales. Moving slowly. Wounded, too. Still pursuing his prey.

With great effort, Murdoch lifted the heavy muzzle of his rifle. Not toward the creature crawling toward him, knife in teeth. Heavenward. Toward the rotorcraft pulling into a hover over the roof. He knew right where to aim.

If this wilderness were the national church, Murdoch would set it alight. Let the old men of The Ranch roll in the flames.

His shadow cried out: "No!"

Murdoch pulled the trigger.

CHAPTER 58

One-Eleven jerked still at the sound of shots in the distance. Never so many at once. She'd climbed to the top of Whitewater Canyon to look for Little Paw, to howl him down. Now the Thunderbird came arcing out of the sun, whirling and smoking across the sky, as if summoned.

It flashed and shrieked through the dusk, balling into flame. One-Eleven's hairs stood on end, raised like antennae. The fireball tumbled behind a distant ridge. A flash in the lower strata of haze, a tremor in the earth. Then silence.

She waited, listening. All the Gila did. Every cow elk and antlered bull, every bighorn and black bear and mule deer. Every mountain lion and jackrabbit, ringtail cat and wood rat. Eyes unblinking, ears erect. Awaiting ash clouds or incineration, earthquake or fire or flood.

One-Eleven raised her head to the darkening heavens and howled high on her forepaws, as if to call the very stars to earth.

CHAPTER 59

Trace heard the piercing cry of a wolf rise from the canyons, high and long, like the first wail of a great siren.

"Jesus."

He was on the old highway just below Mogollon, saddling a horse.

As soon as he'd gotten off the call with Horn, he'd kissed his mother, jumped into his truck, and roared toward the Gila at top speed, flashers blinking, heading for the narrow highway that climbed switch-backing toward the heights of the old Mogollon ghost town. The spring rains, he knew, had washed out the road several miles short of town.

He called Imogen from the truck. "You know anybody in Reserve or Alma might loan out a horse?"

Reserve was thirty minutes from the turnoff. Alma, closer. Two of the nearest towns to where they'd grown up.

"I'm in Alma visiting my aunt. She's got horses. Where do you need them?"

"Only one," said Trace. "At 159 toward Mogollon."

"I'm on my way."

"Imogen, just one."

"I'm on my way."

She showed up with two horses.

"Don't," she said, holding up a finger. "Don't you even try."

He tried to dissuade her the whole time they were unloading the horses. He was still failing at the task when they heard the sound of a helicopter in the distance, then gunshots. No stopping her then. She wasn't about to let him go alone. All he could do was look to the sky and ask God and his old man and even Old Temple to help protect them. They mounted the horses on the narrow shoulder of the road and started up the rocky trail that bypassed the washout.

Soon they were back on the highway, climbing toward town. The horses' hooves clicked on the tar. They passed stone ruins on the hillsides and tin sheds rusted thin, old propane tanks like forgotten bombs. Trace looked up at the high, steep slope to his right. Jags and pinnacles silhouetted like giant dark teeth against the red sky. He checked the time, then looked over to Imogen. "Shouldn't it be full dark by now?"

She looked at her watch, then at the sky, then sniffed the air. "Oh my God."

Now Trace smelled it, too. Their eyes caught, widening.

Fire. As if the setting sun had set the land alight.

Trace turned his horse broadside in the road. "Please, you got to go back."

But even as he said it, he saw she couldn't. The glow was brightest back the way they'd come, the haze pulsing like a heartbeat. Imogen looked that way, then back at him. Eyebrows raised. She didn't even have to say it.

There was only one way they could go.

Minutes later they were riding into town. A single dusty street between buildings slouched with age. Above them to the west, like a lingering sunset, that fiery glow. Soon flecks of ash were falling gently around them like warm gray snow, powdering their hats and shoulders, dusting the manes of the horses. The air began to sting in their nostrils and the animals shuddered and shook their heads.

Trace saw scrapes and gouges and bloody streaks in the dust of the road. The open door of the theater. Above the place, from the rooftop, a strobe flashed against the haze. Trace and Imogen looked at each other, nodded. They dismounted and hitched the horses to the rail. Trace slid his father's .30–30 rifle from the saddle scabbard—the only weapon he'd had in his truck. They crept through the door and saw blood smeared all over the steps and wall. Trace started up the stairs, Imogen just behind him, one hand on the revolver she carried at the back of her hip.

He flicked on his flashlight on the theater balcony and found the pallet ladder propped against the wall, the hole in the ceiling. Blood still wet on the slats. They climbed onto the roof where the ash and smoke were even thicker, swirling in the light of the strobe. Two men lay in seeming embrace. The wolver on his back, dead, his rifle and hat lying beside him. Horn's head rested on the man's chest. He had his hook-blade knife in one hand, but the blade was clean, unbloodied. He was still breathing.

"Horn." Trace knelt and touched his shoulder. "Horn."

The man turned and looked up at him. His eyes were red and tears flashed through the grime on his cheeks.

Trace crouched beside him. "What happened?"

"I couldn't stop him."

"From what? Did he get One-Eleven?"

"No. But what he done might be worse." He shook his head. "I wounded him, bad, but he got away, climbed up here. I followed him but I was hurt. It took me too long. I had to get myself out of that canal. I was just climbing up here when a helicopter come down on us."

"We heard it. Was it Game & Fish?"

Horn shook his head. "Civilian, no markings. He must've called up an extraction, hurt like he was. Only way they could find us so fast." Horn's eyes looked past them, cutting an arc across the sky. "Bird pulled into a hover over us and he just opened up on it with his rifle, I don't know why. Emptied a whole magazine into it. Bird went wheeling off south, spinning like a top, spitting fire. It swung over the ridge and I watched it roll upside down. Must've gone down in that dry timber down there on the western slope, lighting it off." Horn shivered. "I watched him do it. I was just a few feet away and couldn't stop him. Time I got to him, he was all but gone. I tried to ask him why he done it, but he bled out."

"You called it in yet?"

Horn nodded, touching the sat phone strapped to his chest. "I did."

"Good." Trace bent closer to him. "Now where are you hurt?"

"Y'all got to get out in front of the fire. Wind's out the west all night. Head east into the Gila. Get up to the old Ravenfeather scar where there's hardly any fuel left."

"Can you move?"

Horn shook his head. "I'll slow you down too much. Hit my head in the bottom of that creek. Dizzy as hell, vision's doubling. Think I lost consciousness for a while. And there's something wrong in my right leg, can't barely walk on it." He looked to the glow in the sky. "Y'all go. I deserve what comes."

Imogen had been watching the fiery light outlining the ridge. Now she gripped Horn's shoulder and twisted his sweater in her fist, bending to look him in the face. "No way we're leaving you for that fire, hear me? I ain't living with that. So, my new friend, you're coming off this roof, even if we gotta drag your ass off it."

Horn looked from her to Trace, mouth open.

Trace clapped his shoulder. "You heard the lady."

Twenty minutes later they were on the trail above town, riding up through the cemetery. Imogen led. In high school, she'd guided for an outfitter that ran ghost-town tours through the area. She rode the smaller gray mare while Trace followed on the black gelding with Horn squeezed in behind him.

They'd examined him on the porch. He was concussed. Pupils wide and unsteady, blood oozing from the back of his head. He had a large knot in his right shin, which could be a broken bone, and an entry wound in his hip—maybe a ricochet. He'd live, if they could get out of here in time.

The horses wended between the gravestones. The sky behind them glowed brighter every time Trace looked, a reddish glare beating against the night. They were just about to turn out of sight of town when they looked back a final time. In horror they watched the fire top the opposite ridge like a wave. Tongues of flame rocketed high into the air, wheeling and cracking against the upper darkness. The fire came rolling down the slope like an avalanche, a tumbling inferno. Even from this distance, they could feel the heat pressing on their faces.

"Jesus. You think the creek and road will slow it?" asked Trace.

Imogen shook her head. "Not for long."

Still they didn't move, unable to tear their eyes from the flames somersaulting down the far side of the narrow valley. The enormity of it. The horses woke them from the trance, jerking against their bits, shuddering like broncos as the distant flames reeled through their black eyes.

They turned and rode on, following the trail around a broad prow of sandstone. It was immediately darker and cooler in the lee of the rock. But the sky seemed to be radiating, pulsing through the trees. The air thick with ash, a swirling miasma that made it hard to breathe. They could hear the fire now, a dull roar like whitewater on the other side of the ridge. Now and again the high crack of an exploding pine—the sap superheated, blowing like gunpowder from the heart of the tree.

They made their way north, passing through a narrow gap in the next ridgeline. They forded a dark creek with the air crackling behind them and the horses wet to their barrels and climbed onto a new trail. They hadn't gone far when they came upon a tumbledown miner's shack standing in the overgrowth on the far side of the creek, the front door hanging open.

They slowed slightly to look and a man stepped from behind a boulder next to the trail. A scarecrow in an overlarge flannel and rubber boots, eyes wild in a wasted face. He racked a shotgun between his legs.

"Gonna need one a them horses."

CHAPTER 60

Little Paw hadn't answered any of One-Eleven's howls. Every time she started to climb out of the canyon to search for him, the rest of the pack followed her. She tried snarling and barking them back, but the smoke was stinging their noses and the sky flaring and their strongest instinct was to stay with the pack.

A screen of smoke lay over the top of the canyon, throbbing with distant flames. One-Eleven had seen the way a fire could run wild over the land like a stampeding herd, crazed and bright, blowing trees into balls of flame. Nothing could stop it. She sensed they were safest here, deep between steep walls of stone, with whitewater curling and foaming between the rocks. No trees or brush to burn.

But Little Paw. She wanted to search for him. The instinct burned hot inside her. She whined. Graynose could've stayed with the pack while she searched. She raised her head and howled high enough to crack stone, to lift bones from the earth. Little Paw was out there somewhere. Hurt or lost.

She climbed up again, all the way to the ruins at the top of the canyon. Concrete pillars and stairs, rusted iron skeletons, mortared clay bricks. The sky swirling, glowing. The fire close, moving fast. It could barrel over the ridge at any moment, rolling down to blow the flesh from their bones. One-Eleven mounted a lone set of stairs. She looked into the darkness out of which they'd come. The sky undulant with heat, warping and rolling, buzzing with bright flecks of embers.

She looked back at the pack. They were hunchbacked, rubbing shoulders and sides, whining and licking and showing their teeth. Wild with fear, crazed. They wanted to flee, to outrun the flames, but One-Eleven knew they couldn't. The burn could overtake them at the speed of a Thunderbird, leaping from tree to tree, crossing canyons and topping mesas. She raised her snout again and howled. She howled for Little Paw and Graynose, for the elk and deer and antelope. She howled for the whole Gila, already burning. Flee or die.

The rest of the Dark Canyons raised their noses and howled beneath her, voices high and wailsome. Again and again they howled, the sound rising and falling, coming together and apart, sung with such power the wolves bounced on their forepaws as they howled. A song for the end of the world.

Finally One-Eleven came down the stairs and began to lead the pack back into the canyon. The path no more than a small stony ledge against one wall. They were nearly back to the wet dark shoulders of the creek when she froze straight-legged on the narrow trail. Below her stood the Whitewater pack, pale-furred among the stones, seeking shelter in the canyon. They snarled at her, fangs aglow.

CHAPTER 61

The scarecrow man jerked the shotgun again. "Like I said, I'm gonna need one a them horses."

"That ain't no nice way to ask," said Imogen. She took her right hand from the reins and laid it flat on her thigh, closer to the revolver holstered on the back of her hip.

"Ain't asking. And don't you dare move that fucking hand another inch. I see that six-shooter there on your belt."

Trace was sitting his horse next to hers, slightly back. His own rifle lodged in the saddle scabbard, useless. Too fast a move and the man could blow a load of buckshot right through them—impossible to miss at this range. Trace's heart was going fast. Anything seemed possible.

A long howl sounded in the night, now more of them. They echoed through the ridges, high and bodiless, like banshees or lost souls. Everyone went silent, unable not to listen. Even the scarecrow man cocked his head behind the shotgun. Strange to hear wolves so close, for so long. The sound shot straight to the nerve endings, raising invisible hackles along their spines.

Trace felt Horn's ribs swell against his back, as if the howls inflated his chest.

When the sound died away, the scarecrow man spat in the dirt. "There's something I don't mind it burning." He made a lasso in the air with the muzzle of the shotgun, encompassing the horses and their riders, about to pick which one he wanted.

Horn cleared his throat. "You can have my seat, friend. He held out his hands to show he was unarmed and bumped Trace's heel with the toe of his boot, requesting the stirrup.

"I ain't asking for a seat, motherfucker. It's a horse I want."

Horn was already climbing down from the animal, his injured leg held out to one side as he slowly lowered himself to the ground.

"In exchange for my seat, you turn over that shotgun."

"The fuck I will."

"Unload it first," said Horn, hobbling forward on his injured leg. He looked a pitiful creature, back-hunched and visibly wounded, bloodied all over. Drunk-seeming. Like a man just come from a bad night under a bridge.

"You ain't dictating terms." The scarecrow man followed him with the shotgun.

Trace noticed Imogen's hand inching back on her thigh, toward the gun on her hip. But a leather strap ran behind the hammer, securing the piece in place—it was no quick-draw rig.

Horn staggered forward, hopping on his good leg. Maybe five feet from the man. His hair hung down in strands, greasy and twisted around his face. He held out his hands. "It's a fair arrangement, friend. The world rarely offers us such."

"Arrangement? I'm gonna arrange a meeting between you and your maker you step another fucking inch."

"I believe you," said Horn. "But in the time it takes you to shoot me and re-rack that scattergun, my friend back there will draw hers and put you down. I've known that lady maybe an hour, and I know she'll do it. She'll draw and she won't miss and she'll sleep at night because it was the right thing putting you down."

The scarecrow man grinned, sliding the barrel away from Horn's chest. "Then maybe she's the one ought to get it first—"

Horn sprang. The man swung the barrel back toward him. Too late. He didn't know the wolf beneath the rags. Even on one leg, Horn had closed the distance in a flash, moving inside the reach of the gun. His body a living whip, too fast to see, slinging the man to the ground and knotting him there. He locked the shotgun beneath his good leg and latched the man's neck in his right arm. His bicep flexed against the carotid artery, cutting the blood flow to the brain. The man writhed and gurgled, heels scraping in the dirt.

Horn looked up at them, his face bathed in the reddish glow of the sky.

"You want him dead or asleep?"

CHAPTER 62

One-Eleven bared her fangs at the Whitewater wolves, showing them what they faced. Canines long and curved and sharp—twin daggers that cut the tendons of antelope and tore the throats of elk and ripped the flesh from lesser wolves. She licked them, wetting their points for battle.

The Whitewaters churned and growled beneath her, their breath puffing amid the swirling ash and red sky. She was outnumbered, but the trail was too steep and narrow for them to attack in force. They'd have to come at her one by one. One-Eleven lowered her head and snapped her teeth. Come and face the fury of the mother wolf, ready to fight and die for her pack.

The Whitewaters whirled beneath her, spitting slaver, roiling like the creek itself. Among them the lobo she'd slashed on the plain, his side still bloodied from her teeth. A male her age, unpaired—only the alphas could breed. She saw the fear in him, rattling his ribs. The spike of his hackles, the bend of his ears, the stiffness of step. He knew what he faced. Still, while the others strutted and blew, he was the game wolf, the one who stepped first. He came charging up the trail, fangs bared. A pale lobo, white and silver and tan with a lance of rust along his side.

They came together in a flash, weaving and snapping, ripping at each other. One-Eleven tasted his blood and breath, the ash and alkali in his coat. She dipped fast to the inside of the trail and slammed her shoulder into his ribs and knocked him shrieking over the edge, tumbling down the steep slope to the rocks below.

Another Whitewater wolf lunged in and snatched her throat. She squealed and tried to twist free of the jaws. She couldn't breathe. Her windpipe constricted, her breath a whistle. The teeth digging deeper, rending her flesh. Her vision dimmed, her limbs jellied. The smell of her own blood. Then a great snarl shook the canyon and Dozer came barreling down the trail like an angry bear. He struck the enemy wolf with the full force of his weight, a crack of flesh and bone that sent the pair of them somersaulting down the path. One-Eleven came raging down the trail in their wake, snap-snarling with fury, her teeth shining red. She was throat-taker, death-giver. She was One-Eleven, Queen of the Gila.

The Whitewaters turned tail. They fled downstream in a river of fur, their pale backs gushing and capping, shouldering off into the swirling darkness. One-Eleven stood wide-legged on the trail and watched them go. Heart charging, breath ripping in and out of her mouth. She wanted to chase after them, to drench her face in the red scald of their blood, but stayed herself. She lowered her head and ran her nose along Dozer's flanks and back.

The big yearling rose unwounded. She'd never seen him explode with such fury. Meanwhile the young wolves whirled around her, rubbing their faces against her neck, licking the blood from her jaws and throat. They swished their tails around her legs and nipped at her coat, guttering from their throats. Fang-barer, blood-maker. Mother wolf.

One-Eleven stood firm as they roiled around her, watching where the Whitewaters had disappeared into the canyon darkness. Then she and the pack all cocked their heads at once. A whine had issued from the base of the slope.

The wolf she'd knocked from the trail was still alive.

One-Eleven peered over the edge, saw nothing. She picked her way down the loose slope, boulder to boulder. Stones bounced and clattered beneath her as the rest of the pack watched from atop the trail, nervous.

The Whitewater wolf was hopping around in the talus bed at the bottom of the canyon side. He was on three legs, holding one of his hind limbs half-cocked, the paw off the ground. Broken leg or busted hip. They stared at each other. He curled his lips a few times, a flash of teeth, but made no sound.

One-Eleven kept looking at him. He had the bloody mark of her fangs on one side of him, the rusty stripe down the other. She could dart in and take his throat. Or she could leave him among the rocks, alive.

The ash whirled around them, dusting the river.

CHAPTER 63

The scarecrow man pawed at Horn's arm where it cinched his neck. His face was swollen to bursting and wild veins splintered his forehead.

"Asleep," said Imogen.

Horn nodded and palmed the back of the man's head, as if to comfort him. His eyes rolled back and his hands fell away, landing palms up on the ground. They took his shotgun and pulled off his rubber boots, which Imogen strung from the saddle of her horse. Trace scribbled a note on a crumpled gas receipt.

BOOTS UP THE TRAIL. DICK.

They stuck the note under the man's belt buckle and rode on. Ten minutes later, Imogen dropped the boots in the middle of the trail, a water bottle stuck inside one of them.

They kept to the path along the creek, making the best time they could across the stony ground. They forded the creek again and again as the trail crisscrossed from bank to bank, the shallow water swirling around the ankles of the horses. Five hundred feet above them, canyon rocks stood like watchtowers against the red sky.

A giant bone-colored boulder loomed out of the darkness beside the trail, a rugged stone cross mounted on top. A dwarf-size door had been hewn from the base of the rock, the opening crudely mortared over with irregular stones.

Trace shivered. “Place always gives me the willies.”

It was a sepulcher for four silver miners killed nearby, victims of an Apache raid in the 1880s. Their friends had tunneled deep into the boulder and laid the scalped and mutilated remains inside, then walled off the opening.

Horn squeezed Trace’s shoulder, excited. “This is where Earth First! did their first public action, did you know that? In 1980, I think. They put up a plaque commemorating the hundredth anniversary of the raid. In honor of Victorio, the Apache who led the war party, and his efforts to protect these mountains from mining and other destructive acts of the white man.”

Trace nodded. “I did know that. In fact, my grandfather Old Temple was one of the locals who tore down said plaque. Got himself in the newspaper saying if those Earth Firsters kept it up, he’d start his own organization called Shoot First! and see if he could outdo the Apaches’ record in scalps, targeting greenies and their ilk.”

“Don’t he sound like a peach.”

“Sweet as vinegar.” Trace twisted slightly in the saddle, talking over his shoulder. “You know Geronimo used to hide out down in Whitewater Canyon, just south of here, before he surrendered to the Army?”

“Don’t call it a surrender.”

“The man laid down his arms and went to prison, what else would you call it?”

Horn shook his head. “Geronimo agreed to a peace treaty with the United States government, made through a general the President himself sent to negotiate with him. According to that treaty, he and the rest of his people would be given houses, land, cattle, horses, mules, and farming equipment in a land rich in timber, grass, and water. And he and his men would see their captured families within five days. Those were the terms of the treaty made in Skeleton Canyon, as confirmed by Apaches, soldiers, and civilians who were there. That's the only reason Geronimo laid down his arms."

"So?"

"So the government reported it as an unconditional surrender. Geronimo and his warriors were immediately imprisoned and put to hard labor. Didn't see their families for six months. Bunch of Florida businessmen got together and lobbied to have the men sent to Pensacola. Fort Pickens. They made Geronimo a tourist attraction out there, charged fifty cents admission for adults, twenty-five for children. People came from all over the country to gawk, more than four hundred a day sometimes. The Apache families had been split apart, the women and children sent on to Saint Augustine. The terms of the treaty were never upheld."

Trace shook his head. "Little wonder my granddad never trusted a single word from the government."

"Seems like Geronimo and your granddaddy might've had more in common than either one might think."

Trace grunted. "Or admit."

Soon they were riding through the mining camp where the massacre had taken place. At one time there had been a hotel, church, schoolhouse, even a post office. But a flash flood had ripped through the canyon, all but wiping the place from the map. Now just scattered markers. Thin-rusted barrels and stone foundations and roof timbers jutting from canyon walls, left when the waters receded. Everything glowed with a reddish, otherworldly light.

Trace rode up beside Imogen. "You think they'll bring in the hotshots or smoke jumpers?"

Elite crews trained to fight fires in remote wildlands like the Gila. They would cut fire lines and light back-burns, scraping and digging down to the mineral soil to rid the fire of fuel.

Imogen nodded. "They better. Better question is how long till they get here. If they can't contain the burn before it makes a run into the Wilderness, it'll get harder. Only the Forest Supervisor can authorize the use of mechanized equipment in there. Chainsaws, helicopters, bulldozers. But there has to be a threat to life, property, or cultural resources."

"We count as life, right?"

"Likely they'd authorize a helicopter to pull us out."

"What about the horses?"

Imogen shook her head. "They'd make us leave them. And I doubt they'll do an air rescue at night in these conditions. Which means we're on our own at least until dawn, and I wouldn't leave the horses anyway. Our only chance is making the high ground of the old Ravenfeather scar."

She sat her horse and turned slightly in the saddle. She'd switched into some kind of new mode, Trace realized. A side of her he'd sensed but never seen in action. She cocked her head at them and pushed out her jaw. "We're gonna need to be smart, calm, and lucky to get out of this alive, and you two are gonna need to do exactly what I say when the time comes. Think you boys can handle that?"

Trace and Horn looked at each other.

"Yes, ma'am."

"Good."

She turned and rode on.

"Damn," whispered Horn.

"Right?"

When the trail got thick with blowdown, Imogen dismounted and led on foot. Slow going. They entered a narrow gorge with deadfall everywhere, toppled trees and thick brush. The sky was brightening though dawn was still hours distant. The fire, nearing. They knew it but said nothing. Nothing to do but keep going.

Trace recalled a story he'd all but forgotten. They were in middle school and Imogen had just started guiding for her old man's outfit. She was with him on a rifle hunt, which tended to draw a rowdier crowd, hunters who liked to drink whiskey and piss in the woods. It came out that Imogen had shot one of the clients. A man from out of state. He hadn't died and all the adults had kept mum about whatever happened, not even spreading rumors.

But Imogen always seemed different after that. Harder, gaunter. She didn't quit guiding but redoubled her time in the Gila. She'd come to school with red nicks of brush on her face and arms, dressed in muddy boots and trousers, stepping right out of her latest hunt into the classroom. When elk season was over, she and Garrison got together and the two of them delved into even more dangerous pursuits.

It took a long time for the story to get out. A dark patch of woods, a pretty young girl, and a drunken out-of-stater who thought he could get away with a little pawing and groping—and received a bullet for his troubles. Though she didn't look it, Imogen had come up hard. Since her old man's death, she'd had to prove she had the grit and steel to run a ranch day after day, season after season—and had. Through drought, disease, and calamity of every stripe.

Trace watched her. She was sure on her feet despite the darkness and loose terrain. Didn't panic, didn't rush, working through each obstacle on the trail, wading at times through the icy black crash of waist-deep creeks. She had Horn ride her gray mare to spell Trace's gelding while she led on foot.

Around them, everywhere, crackles and crashes in the brush. Animals were fleeing east, trying to keep ahead of the flaming front. Trace heard a thumping of air and looked up to see a string of ravens flying up the gorge at speed, not more than ten feet above his head.

He didn't know if that was a good omen or bad.

Soon an arch of irregular stones appeared in the hillside, mortared into a shallow cave. A charcoal kiln or smelter from the mining days. The horses began to act strange. Trace's gelding folded back his ears and shivered; the mare started stepping sideways on the trail. Imogen felt it in the lead line. She stopped and the three of them looked around. High walls, dark against the sky.

"There." Horn pointed toward the crude grotto. "Something's in there."

Whatever it was, the horses were jumpy. These were veteran mounts, accustomed to backcountry hunts and tours, the scent of blood and fire. Trace slid the rifle from the scabbard and laid it across his knees. Imogen handed off the mare's lead and moved toward the stone arch, bent low, her hand at the back of her hip. It looked like a door in the earth, a tunnel, though it was no more than a few feet deep.

Trace was dismounting when Imogen looked back, her voice a hiss.

"It's a wolf."

CHAPTER 64

One-Eleven whined and paced. Little Paw's loss wailed inside her like a wind, whipping canyon-deep through her belly. It twisted her ribs, torqued her tail. She turned circles and pawed at the dirt. Her tongue slapped wild from her mouth and her eyes burned. She climbed back up to the powerhouse ruins. A whirlwind of smoke and ash roared around her, glowing with racing embers and fiery debris. A hard west wind had come on, lashing the flames high and bright and vast. Trains of fire rumbled along the ridges, driving deeper into the Gila.

One-Eleven heard something and looked up to the ridgeline, hoping to see Little Paw. A lone bull elk streaked from the trees instead. He bore great antlers of flame, whips of smoldering vines and burning brush that lashed his flanks, crazing him. The bull leapt straight off the canyon rim and tumbled through the darkness, wrecking on the rocks beside the stream.

One-Eleven looked back up and saw the glittering eyes of desert bighorn perched high on the canyon sides, standing on invisible ledges between the fire beating above them and the wolves below. The rest of the forest was heading east, deeper into the Gila, trying to outrun the flames.

If the wind kept up, none would.

CHAPTER 65

They stared at the wolf beneath the crude stone arch of the old smelter. Trace turned on his map-light, a dim red glow that wouldn't ruin their night vision. Stone bricks, smoke-blacked, framed the animal on three sides. He was small with a thick dark coat, and his right foreleg was caught in the jaws of a steel trap.

"Christ," said Trace. "He ain't even full grown."

"It's the one they call Little Paw," said Horn. "From the Dark Canyon pack."

Imogen was closest to the animal. She knelt with her hand on the grip of her revolver. "How can you tell?"

Horn walked the mare slightly closer and leaned forward, one hand flat on her neck to calm her. "Look at that back paw. See it's twisted, smaller than the others. Born with what they call a club foot in people."

"His front paws look oversize," said Imogen. "Like he's wearing little boxing gloves."

Trace crouched beside her, holding the animal in the red glow of the flashlight. He'd seen the little wolf while tracking the Dark Canyon pack, his limping gait unmistakable. He was perhaps forty or fifty pounds now, sized between a juvenile and full-size yearling, but looked larger on his own, at night, just feet from them. The trap was a coil-spring model like the one Trace had hauled out of the Gila, but instead of a drag, the chain was bolted to an iron ring driven into one of the foundation stones, locking the animal in place.

The pup's lower foreleg was a bloodied mess, the fur torn down to the red tissue. He yanked and wrenched the limb in the steel teeth of the trap, hurting himself worse, ripping the flesh to the bone. Trace pressed his hand to his mouth at the sight. His throat produced a strange noise, a low whine he didn't remember making before. It vibrated between his fingers.

He touched Imogen's shoulder and crept closer. The young wolf bared his fangs and growled.

Horn clicked his tongue. "It ain't the size of the dog in the fight . . ."

Ash and smoke swirled through the red glow of Trace's flashlight, heavier every second. They weren't safe here. Too much brush and blowdown in this narrow gorge. The fire could come ripping between the high walls like a flash flood.

"We gotta keep moving," said Imogen. "Any ideas?"

Trace looked back at Horn. "You got any tranqs left, or did you shoot 'em all up in the cheek of my ass?"

Imogen raised her eyebrows—she hadn't heard that particular story.

Horn was already slipping off his daypack. "I got something in my med kit, but no jabstick. You're gonna have to rig something up."

He handed the pack down to Trace. "I'll walk you through the first part."

The man's eyes were still glassy and blood had seeped down his thigh from the wound in his hip. Trace knelt with the pack and looked up at the others. "Y'all sure you're okay with this?"

Imogen came over to hold the light for him. "Long as we quit talking and start moving."

"Yes, ma'am." Trace laid the pack in his lap and followed Horn's instructions, removing the med kit from one of the side pockets and finding a glass vial with T-ZOL written on the top. Horn had him draw two milliliters into a syringe.

"How long will he be out?"

"Well, he won't be out, per se. Just immobilized, eyes still open. Shouldn't be more than thirty minutes if we dose him right."

Trace took the flashlight as Imogen expertly lashed the syringe to a small straight stick using a length of paracord from Horn's pack. Then she hitched the smaller stick to the end of a telescoping hiking pole, loose enough so the tip of the pole would slide forward and depress the plunger when they pushed the needle into the wolf.

"In theory," she said.

Trace nodded. "In theory." He looked at Horn. "There enough in here for a second try?"

"Only enough solution made up for one dose. He gets that syringe in his jaws and that's it." The bearded man looked at the smoke billowing up through the steep walls of the gorge. His teeth showed. "No time for a second chance anyway."

Trace crept toward the wolf, the makeshift jabstick tucked under his right arm. Imogen beside him, carrying the flashlight in one hand, turned off. No light now but the glow of the coming fire, dim through the smoke.

"You think it was that tweaker set this trap?"

Trace nodded. "Bet he's got a sideline in skins."

Imogen had her thumb on the button of the flashlight. The head was right-angled so it pointed like a pistol. "Maybe we should've let our buddy Horn choke him to death."

Trace wiped his eyes with the back of his hand. They were teary, stinging with the smoke. "This fire might do it for us."

Without the flashlight, the wolf was just a shadow in the night. His teeth flashing, clicking. Trace knew the animal could see them coming much better than they could see him, his night vision vastly superior to their own. His pupils would be at their widest, capturing every particle of available light to conjure the pair of twilit figures creeping toward him like enemies.

The animal seemed to calm as they neared, motionless inside the dark grotto. Gathering himself, maybe, for the fight of his life.

"Ready?" whispered Imogen.

Trace took the pole in both hands. "Ready."

She held out her arms, aimed, and thumbed the switch. White light blasted from the torch, jacklighting the wolf among the charred stones. Blinding him. Trace lunged and jammed the syringe into Little Paw's hip even as the animal twisted to rip the pole from his hands. Trace leapt back and Imogen cut the light. Darkness rushed back in.

"Did you get him?"

"I don't know."

"How long?"

"Three to five minutes."

An eternity. They waited, he and Imogen crouched shoulder to shoulder while Horn sat the mare behind them. A low roar suffused the gorge. Trace wasn't sure if it was the coming fire or just the creek moving over the stones, echoing between the walls as it had for thousands of years, sawing down through five hundred feet of moonstone and volcanic tuff.

Then a sound in the night, a clatter of hooves. A herd of antelope rounded the bend and ripped through the darkness around them. Shadows bounding over the rough ground, splashing in and out of the creek, bodies and breath and hooves like a single dark presence in the night. Then gone.

"That's not a good sign," said Imogen.

"I reckon not."

The animals were headed upstream, higher into the Gila, at ten times the speed Trace and Imogen and Horn could muster.

"The front's close," whispered Trace.

When they looked back to Little Paw, the young wolf was down, as if asleep. They moved in slowly, using only the red light now, prodding the animal with a long stick before moving inside the radius of the trap chain. The animal's eyes were open but unmoving, reddish gold in the light. Trace was breathing hard. So close to a living wolf. The idea it could awake any second from the trance. Not even a year old, yet plenty big enough to rip him to pieces.

Trace set his boots on the levers of the trap and pressed down with his toes, opening the steel jaws. Imogen moved in with alcohol and swabs from Horn's med kit, cleaning the wound. Her face just inches from the wolf's mouth, those hidden rows of teeth. The animal didn't react, breathing shallow but steady. Eyes open, unblinking. They didn't bother with antiseptic cream or bandaging. The animal would just rip them away, trusting his own tongue to clean the wound.

Imogen sat back. "That's all we can do."

They'd just backed away when another herd came clattering through the gorge behind them. Elk this time, moving fast, branches and vines flying from the antlers of the bull. Some of the cows had bubbled patches of burns on their flanks. An orange glow came licking at their heels, crawling along the gorge walls, pushing through the ashfall like the headlight of an oncoming train. The heat rolled across them, flaring on their faces.

"God, it's here."

CHAPTER 66

This is how you die, thought Trace. A wildfire could still be some distance away, burning on the other side of a distant ridge or wide plain—and then it wasn't. It was right on top of you. The wind strengthened or shifted and the fire made a run. Before you knew what was happening it was too late. You were overrun. Wildland firefighters might have sixty seconds to deploy their personal fire shelters, tucking themselves beneath the thin silver shields like children laid out in sleeping bags. Everyone else could only pray or run.

Without thinking Trace knelt and scooped up the injured wolf and turned toward the creek. A reckless act but something had set like a stone in his mind and wouldn't budge, not unlike the time Old Temple refused to give up the right of way to an impatient driver in town and got knocked off his horse, the animal sent skittering down the sidewalk. Trace cradled the young wolf to his chest like a sick calf, dropping down through the bushes and splashing into the shallows of the creek, churning his way through the knee-deep current. He laid out the animal on the stony midstream shoals, as far as possible from the brush and fuel on either side.

Then he turned and thrashed his way back to the trail. Imogen had slipped his horse's lead and swung into the saddle. Now she kicked her foot from the stirrup and held out her arm and he swung up behind her. She heeled the horse and they punched their way through the night, the animals barreling down the trail. They crashed in and out of the creek as the path ripped from one side of the gorge to the other, climbing and falling, embers and animals racing around them, shooting off into the darkness.

Trace felt the heat on his back, clawing at his jacket. He held tight to Imogen's waist like he had as a boy on the back of his mother's motorcycle and glanced back, eyes squeezed down to slits. Shining blades of fire whirled and twisted up the gorge where they'd just been, wind-crazed, leaping from fuel to fuel, detonating trees into skeletons of furious, balling flame. The animal lay between banks of fire, inside a lone dark eye of heat, the wet shoals steaming beneath him. Trace closed his eyes and sent something to the little wolf, from his mind or heart, whatever he could. Peace, protection, hope—a little piece of himself. All he had. *God be with you, little one.* Then they rounded a bend and Little Paw was gone.

The horses made a sudden turn off the trail, so sharp Trace was nearly thrown, and they began charging upward, climbing a narrow chute in the side of the gorge. The animals plunged through the steep silt of the wash, blowing hard between the stone walls, haunches heaving with power. It was immediately cooler here, darker. Hardly any trees or brush. A narrow defile cut over eons into the volcanic rock, sliced by yearly freshets and storm water—a place sunlight rarely reached.

Soon the flames were licking at the bottom of the wash, igniting the brush down there, looking for more fuel. Smoke barreled up through the narrow walls, carrying embers and flaming splinters over their heads. The horses became harder to control, jerking and shuddering. Imogen shouted for them to pull blankets from the saddlebags and cover the horses' flanks so the embers wouldn't burn them.

Trace tried to remember what to do if the fire overcame them. The radiant heat could be lethal even if you avoided the flames themselves. The superheated air could weld a person's lungs shut, melt the fibers of their clothes to their skin. You were supposed to hold your breath if you tried to run through the flames. Get low to the ground and wrap your face in something thick, a blanket or coat, if the flames surrounded you. Anything so the air couldn't bubble your lungs and throat.

God be with us.

They emerged onto a steep forested slope that hadn't ignited yet but soon would. Fire moved fastest uphill. Any moment the flames could come charging up the slope, an avalanche in reverse. A wall of bare cliffs stood farther up the slope.

Imogen reined the horse. "No way we can outrun this thing to the old Ravenfeather scar. We need another idea."

Horn pulled up alongside them. "Isn't there a fire tower up on Bullwallow Mountain? It ought to be cleared of fuel up there, bare enough to ride it out."

"How far are we?"

Trace got out his GPS, hoping it would still work through the smoke. "Four miles." More than an hour on horseback, assuming they didn't get lost or trapped. He pointed to the ridgeline before them. "If we follow that spine upcountry, we should hit the 4x4 road that runs up to Bullwallow in a mile and a half."

A level-2 road, maintained for high-clearance vehicles.

Imogen nodded. "It's our best shot. That west wind's still kicking. At least we'll be moving perpendicular to the front instead of downwind." She patted the neck of the black gelding and looked back at Trace. "Sable here needs a breather. I want you two on the gray for now." She kicked one boot out of the stirrup for him.

"Yes, ma'am." Trace used the open stirrup to swing down to the ground.

She nodded at Horn. "You ride well but ought to be back-saddle, being concussed."

The bearded man nodded. "Yes'm."

Horn handed the reins to Trace and scooted back onto the horse's rump, leaving the saddle open. Trace mounted and the gray mare sidestepped and twitched beneath the added weight. "Sorry, girl." He rubbed the horse's neck.

Imogen began tying a bandana around her neck to use as a mask. "One last thing. If we get trapped, we'll look for a meadow, creek, or other bare spot to take shelter. When I give the word, I want the two of you on the ground, belly-down, digging a hole for your faces. No arguing. We'll lie shoulder to shoulder, cover ourselves in my wool blanket, plant our faces in the dirt, and say our last words or prayers. Got it?"

The men nodded. "Yes, ma'am."

Trace looked back a moment, watching the gorge flicker and pulse like a volcanic rift. He kept rubbing the gray mare's neck, trying to comfort her. "What's this girl's name?"

Imogen's face softened. The corner of her mouth curled up, a hook in his chest.

"Ash."

She turned and rode on.

CHAPTER 67

One-Eleven stood amid the powerhouse ruins watching the ring of fire tighten. She could smell her own fur burning, flecked with embers. The hills were full of fire on every side, churning with flames that blackened the sky.

She heard a stony crackle and looked over.

Dozer was staring at her from the top of the canyon trail. Head low and ears back as blown coals whipped and swirled around him. The younger wolves huddled behind him, red-eyed from the smoke. One jumped and squealed as an ember singed his nose.

Dozer kept staring at her.

One-Eleven snuffed the ground and came trotting back to them, leading them back down into the canyon. No trees or brush to burn down here and the mist rolling off the rapids doused the live coals caught in their coats. Their refuge, carved bloody out of Whitewater territory.

One-Eleven froze.

The injured Whitewater wolf. He stood broadside on the trail, tongue hanging out. His right hind leg dangled off the ground, kinked slightly where it should be straight. Somehow he'd made it out of the talus field at the bottom of the slope and climbed back to the trail. One-Eleven twisted her head, showing him the tips of her teeth.

The Whitewater wolf just looked at her. He reeled his long tongue between his teeth and stared. Amber eyes. Bold chest and shoulders. Wide jaws arrowing down into a sharp snout. One-Eleven showed him the points of her teeth again. He just kept looking at her, calm despite his state. She came closer, walking sidewise, chest high. Approaching from his weak side, angling. He'd have to wheel hard to catch her with his teeth.

He turned slightly, hopping on his good leg. Just watching her. She could leap in and take his throat. She could knock him back down the slope. He straightened and lifted his head, looking past her. Presenting himself. One-Eleven neared and scented him. Her nose grazed his fur, moving from ears to flanks, down the long stripe of rust on his side and the swollen kink where his hind leg was broken. No blood or exposed bone. The limb might mend.

Few would allow this inspection. Most would turn and snap. He stood rigid as she ran her nose over him, reading him. Standing there on three legs as the forest roared above them and flakes of ash drifted down between the canyon walls, dusting their coats.

One-Eleven made a little hop before him, lifting just off her forepaws, her ears raised like a jackrabbit's. He jerked slightly on his forelegs, hurt but game. One-Eleven skipped to a different angle and did it again, rearing slightly. He turned toward her and bounced again, his shoulders flexing. Now another angle, and another, the wolf hopping on three legs, bold enough to push his sharp chin toward her, making her jump. He clicked his teeth in mock combat.

The pups watched, their heads tucked around Dozer's legs and chest, hidden in the shaggy thicket of his fur. Finally One-Eleven snuffed the ground before the outsider and whipped around on the trail, light on her feet, flashing the underside of her tail, and bounded deeper into the canyon. Dozer and the others scrambled after her, stringing themselves out in a line. The Whitewater wolf turned and limped after them, deeper down into the stony dark.

CHAPTER 68

They rode the dark spine of the ridge. The country to the west roared in the night, sending up a great black forest of smoke. Horn leaned to Trace's ear. "When I was little, they used to burn incense in church sometimes. I asked my mama why. She said the smoke was supposed to lift our prayers to heaven."

Trace looked back at him. Horn's eyes were wide despite the smoke, full of reflected flames, the pupils knocked nearly out of round. He thought of Garrison with a pang, that squared-off pupil of his. Then he looked to the sky. Dark, slowly revolving towers of smoke. "That's a shit-ton of prayers. We best hope some of them are for us."

Horn gripped his shoulder. "All that burning out there, all the trees and animals, they ought to want us dead."

"Don't it seem an inopportune time to start with that end-times shit, Horn?"

Horn ignored him. "Creation ought to want us dead but don't. Keeps giving us beauty and clean air, meat to eat and wolves to hear. Been turning the other cheek for ten thousand years and more."

"Maybe it don't know any better."

"Oh, it knows. Hell, it made us. It just thinks longer than we do. Moves slower. We shoot rockets to space and it cuts the Grand Canyon with a saw blade of snowmelt. Cutting it deeper this very minute. Never stops. Grain to grain. Never worries for itself. Just is. What I hazard to guess might be the sweetest goddamn flint of dust in the whole cosmos and our species all but blind of that fact, digging and blasting and pouring concrete, trying to remake the place in our own image. Ain't fully our fault, of course. It's in our code. Our natural programming, handed down by God or evolution or cosmic accident. Take your pick. But we have the ability to recode. Free will. Freedom. Rope enough to hang ourselves, or else pull our shit together."

Trace shook his head. "I didn't realize that concussion of yours was gonna be such a headache. Might should've left you on that roof."

Horn clapped his arm. "Whatever happens, I'm glad I didn't cut your throat that day in the canyons."

"Hell, Horn, you might've done me a favor. It's better than burning alive."

"Nah." Horn pantomimed the thrust of a knife. "Not the way I do it."

Before Trace could reply, a blast of hot air nearly blew them off the trail. Debris flew across their path and they looked west to see massive boulders of smoke rolling right toward them. The wind had kicked up again, hard.

"Sweet Jesus."

The fire crested the spine of the adjacent ridge and came leaping down the far side, jetting and spitting, crazing down onto the slope behind them to overrun the spot they'd left not thirty minutes ago. They were illuminated in the glare, fire-glazed, eyes forced wide, while the horses wheeled and shivered beneath them.

Imogen turned in the saddle. "Follow me!"

They rode as fast as they dared, dark trees flashing out of the smoke on every side and the sound deafening, embers racing as if on wings. They had to get down off the spur before the fire came charging up the incline. Imogen steered them down a narrow chute on the opposite side from the flames and the horses skidded and clattered down the loose ground. Trace could see more embers streaming over their heads, arcing down like mortars to ignite spot fires on the dark terrain before them. The land rose toward the blunt dark peak of Bullwallow Mountain, paled here and there with thin ledges of remnant snow.

They crashed down into a creek thick with brush, the trees hanging slanted over the water. Imogen turned upstream and then they were out of the creek and driving through branches and thickets, bouncing high from the saddle as the horses hurdled over downed trees and deadfall, the animals' chests and necks raked bloody from brush and blowdown.

Then the road. Somehow. Dark and rutted, hacked rough out of the mountainside. They heeled the horses and rode hard. People said you couldn't outrun a wildfire. The flames moved too fast, faster than any horse. But they had no choice now, nowhere to shelter. They could only flee.

Horn wrapped his arms around Trace's torso and locked his hands, squeezing hard. Hugging him. Another pang in Trace's chest. A boy on the back of his mom's motorcycle, hugging her waist while she wheelied down their dirt drive, showing off for the cows.

He could feel the heat building behind them. They rode at breakneck speed, dodging fallen trees and jumping gravel drainage ditches and swinging past stacks of timber cleared from the road. Spot fires burned on the land around them and at times Trace could barely see Imogen on the dark horse through the smoke.

Trace leaned to the mare's neck, whispering to her. "Sweet Ash. Strong girl. Fast girl. Best horse. Just a little longer now. We're gonna be okay. Just a little longer."

The flames caught them a mile short of the fire tower. The trees along one side of the road ignited. The horses spun walleyed and reared and they had to swing down from the saddles before being thrown.

"Let them go!" yelled Imogen. "Let them run for it."

They let go of the reins and the horses bolted up the road, disappearing into the smoke. The flames jumped the road and they were left inside a tunnel of fire, the walls twisting and cracking around them.

"Give me your hand!" Imogen placed Trace's hand on her belt at the small of her back and motioned for Horn to do the same to Trace. They marched up the middle of the road this way, three in a line, the air rippling around them, weird with heat.

Imogen became a wavering black ghost before him. Trace squeezed his eyes down to slits, wondering how hot it had to be for them to roast inside their sockets. Every breath seemed to scald the insides of his nose and mouth so he clapped his free hand over his face, breathing through the leather fingers of his glove. Anything to take some of the heat before it got inside him, burning his tongue and gums and the ridged roof of his mouth.

He felt skillet handles of heat laid on his cheeks and wanted to shriek. He could feel Horn there behind him, clutching his belt, hobbling on his hurt leg, his face buried in Trace's back. Trace could see Imogen just in front of them, her face thrust into the crook of her arm and her hat jammed low so it wouldn't blow off, the brim glowing with embers. A red halo. Her body bent forward, as if towing them down the road.

Trace imagined their bodies found charred in the road a week from now, curled up in some ultimate agony, their bones all clutched and glued together. The forest filled with blackened forms like theirs. He thought of the horses and the wolf he'd left on the shoals, hoping it would be different for them.

The world gone dark and screaming and Trace held to Imogen's belt like a lifeline. He feared opening his eyes would burn them blind, but he wanted to see her a last time in case there was no hereafter, no chance in the world that came next or didn't. A part of his chest cracked free of his ribs and went through the smoke and heat, flew to her like a bird to a branch.

He opened his eyes.

A darkness before them, a sweet darkness of unburned ground. Black summit earth raked down to mineral soil. Before them rose the steel latticework of the fire tower, glowing. It was like entering a cave. The air must have cooled fifty degrees as they straggled onto the bare summit. The horses were standing near the base of the tower, ears pinned back to their skulls, but they appeared unhurt.

Everything within the immediate radius had been cleared of fuel so the summit couldn't burn. Imogen kicked open the door of a shed to look for supplies. Trace heard a drumming on the tower steps and looked up. The fire lookout descended from the haze above them. She wore a soot-streaked boonie hat and round black eyeglasses and an emergency respirator, the pale filter bulging outward with each breath. In her arms, a bundle of fire blankets for the horses.

They strapped the blankets over the animals, hitched them to the girders, and blindfolded them against the sight of the flames. Then they followed the woman up the thin steel steps, the structure banging and rattling beneath their boots. Inside the corrugated metal view shed, she clapped and stamped out the embers still flecking their shoulders and coats. She sat them down on the floor and took off her hat, an older woman with wild steely hair and deep-furrowed cheeks, kindly weathered. Her eyes were full of tears and she hugged all three of them close, as if she'd been waiting for them.

"Thank God you're here."

CHAPTER 69

Hot winds buffeted the tower. At times, the 12x12 cab rocked and shuddered like it might take flight, rocketing off the mountaintop into darkness. The lookout gave them water and chocolate bars and a respirator to share when one of them started to cough. She was on and off the radio throughout the night, relaying what she saw through her binoculars to the emergency response team. Firelight glowed in violent pulses against the windows and they went down often to check on the horses, watering them and adjusting their fire blankets, doing their best to comfort them.

When the wind pushed the smoke in another direction, Trace stood beside the lookout at the railing. A hellish landscape. Black ridges razorbacked with flames and bright craters of fire throbbing on the hills, as if the land had been firebombed. Flames moved slowly along ridges and slopes, like lava oozing across the distant terrain.

The lookout shook her head. "I been coming up here thirty-five seasons. World's changing. This land is no stranger to fire, but they keep coming later and later in the year, deeper into the fall. You heard of zombie fires?"

Trace shook his head.

The woman was holding a coffee mug against her chest. Her cheeks had deep smile lines, as if carved. She thumbed up the brim of her hat. "Up north they're starting to see them. Siberia, the Arctic. Now Canada and Alaska. Fires that smolder under the snowpack all winter, spreading underground, burning through the peat and leaf litter, only to sprout up in the spring."

"It's like they hibernate."

She nodded. "Course we don't have the right conditions for that here. But fire season is truly year-round now, that's for sure."

Dawn began to fracture the horizon. Fissures yawning open, hazy and strange. The sun a red star in the yellow sky. The fire still going, rolling deeper into the Gila as the mountain smoldered in its wake.

Just after sunrise, the drone of engines. Everyone stepped out onto the catwalk and watched the big twin-engine aircraft rumble overhead, speeding to head off the fire. It circled over Ravenfeather Mountain and a long red ribbon slid from the fuselage door, falling slowly, slithering back and forth in the air—a crepe-paper streamer to read the wind. Soon a line of parachutes bloomed over the mountain, the ram-air canopies striped red, white, and blue.

"Smoke jumpers," said the lookout. "They'll use the old Ravenfeather scar as an anchor point, a natural firebreak."

The radio crackled. "Bullwallow Tower, this is HQ. Over."

The lookout tapped a turquoise ring against the rail, punctuating some thought or prayer, then went inside to answer the call.

The rest of them watched the canopies float down on the mountain. Imogen leaned on the rail. "What are we gonna do about the silverbelly bastards that started all this?"

"We'll push to talk to the regional ISB investigator," said Trace. "Tell her what we know about the men in pale hats."

"You think that'll do any good?"

"I don't know. I doubt it."

Horn stiffened at the mention of a Park Service investigator. He was standing hunched at the rail, gripping it hard. The back of his canvas jacket stretched wide across the shoulders, scorched like a shield at the edges. Trace pictured the man's back underneath the layers, red all over, possibly bubbled in places from the heat.

He cocked his head at Horn. "We'll figure out some way not to mention you-know-who. Don't want the Park Service trying to hunt down our feral friend here."

Imogen winked at Horn. "What friend?"

The lookout stepped back onto the catwalk. "They've dispatched a hotshot crew to fetch us, want us to stay put until they get here. Shouldn't be long."

They nodded. Then Imogen leaned on the rail and looked down at Horn. "Mind checking on the horses one last time?"

His out if he wanted it. His escape route back into the Gila. They could say they met him by chance, crossed paths on the trail. *We never did get his full name . . .*

Horn hugged them both before he descended, as if celebrating their imminent rescue. But his face told a different story. Eyes black-bored, jaws twitching.

Trace's trap-wound throbbed and a hollow place opened in his chest. He hugged Horn back, double-hard. This son of a bitch who'd nearly killed him.

"Thank you. You fucking heathen."

Horn squeezed him tight and turned his mouth to Trace's ear. "I'll find them that done this." His voice cold and low and guttural. "I'll burn them to the ground."

Then he was gone, footsteps pounding down the tower stairs.

Imogen took Trace's hand and they stood at the rail, looking out at the smoking landscape, the fires still churning in the distance. Horn had been gone a little while when a howl rose from the burned country, high and long, like the wailing of the land itself.

CHAPTER 70

One-Eleven's ears shot up. She was standing high above Whitewater Canyon. Beneath her, the creek rushed black and thick with char. Smoke, paler now, rose from both sides of the canyon, churning upward amid the tower rocks. Old iron walkways and steel cables were bolted high into the canyon cliffs and long streaks of rust ran down like blood. She bounded higher onto a ridge above the canyon and looked across a broad slope where the juniper and pinyon were still smoldering, faint blue smoke fuming in the yellow haze.

The rest of the pack had made the climb behind her, even the Whitewater wolf with his injured leg. The terrain hard and broken here, jagged spires and deep folds. But she'd heard the howl and so had the others, their ears tugged sharp and straight. One-Eleven found a broad knob where her voice would carry and raised her head to howl.

Another wolf answered. A weak, guttural sound at the start, cough-laden, like the wolf had something caught in its throat. Smoke or ash or the black dust of charred earth. Then the animal's voice broke through, a howl that rose like a ghostly tower over the terrain, echoing high above the smoke. A voice and a name.

Little Paw.

One-Eleven threw her head to the sky and howled to him, bouncing on her forelegs, her ears swept back like she could take flight. Her mouth formed the small dark O that carried her voice far across the Gila. Now the others joined in, Dozer and the rest. They bounded up onto the stony knob alongside her, their voices rising and falling, piping high over the terrain, calling to the missing member of their pack.

One-Eleven turned and moved through the Dark Canyons, rallying them, spinning up their spirits. She ran her snout right along the Whitewater wolf's jaws, feeling his teeth against her face, pulling him deeper into the pack, making sure he would follow. Then she turned and set off through the smoldering landscape, leading them toward Little Paw.

EPILOGUE

TWO MONTHS LATER

Trace sat Camo on a small rise above the herd. He watched the white and russet cattle move over the cold, brown grass and snow. It had taken three weeks for the Mogollon Fire to be contained. They'd watched spotting planes and fire bombers make pass after pass on the edge of the Wilderness, dropping floods of red retardant into the path of the flames, and more smoke jumpers and wildland crews had traveled in from out of state, cutting fire lines and igniting back-burns. Another snowfall, heavier this time, helped extinguish the last of the flames. For a time the mountains wore ghostly crowns of vaporized snow.

The fire was blamed on a helicopter crash near the western border of the Gila National Forest. The rotorcraft was registered to a hunting ranch and outfitter out of West Texas, Quicksilver Ranch, whose representatives stated their pilots were making a routine flight to pick up one of the ranch's guides—a man who'd been scouting the country for a late-season elk hunt. All of their paperwork was in order, and it seemed several established politicians and high-ranking officials had deep ties to the outfit, having hunted with them for years.

Trace informed the Park Service investigator that he'd been tracking the ranch's guide on suspicion he was targeting wolves, but there was no supporting evidence. Yes, she told him, it appeared a member of the Dark Canyon pack—M997, also known as Graynose—had gone missing since the fire, but the wolf's collar had quit working years ago and there was every reason to suspect the animal had died in the flames or been pushed out of the pack. After all, the Dark Canyons had gained a new alpha male, a former member of the Whitewater pack—a wolf known as Rio, who carried a long belt of rust along his coat.

"Moreover," said the investigator, "the remains of the guide, Mr. Maximillian Murdoch, have yet to be recovered and may never be. Our experts say the heat of the fire could have incinerated the body. Only the remains of a local poacher, already suspected of methamphetamine production, have been found, along with his arsenal of traps and snares. He would be a much better suspect for the disappearance of any wolves. There's simply no evidence to keep this case open."

Trace couldn't say he was surprised. The men in pale hats were ghosts, upstanding members of their communities who knew how to undermine the law without breaking it themselves. How to hire out the wet work and stay clean on paper. They'd had plenty of time to come in and recover the wolver's body from the rooftop after the fire had passed. But Trace knew such ideas sounded to the investigator like the ravings of some cowboy conspiracy theorist, an embittered range rider with a thin connection to reality.

No matter. He was still out here. He hoped the men in pale hats had learned to stay out of the Gila, to pursue their aims elsewhere. If not, he was no longer alone. Imogen had him establishing a mobile base camp to support more range riders. She and his mother had discussed turning the program into a workshop for ranchers and cowhands coming out of rehab, giving them an opportunity to work far out in the country, away from the situations and substances that haunted them.

Not only that. Trace looked toward Ravenfeather Mountain, deeper in the Gila. Somewhere out there, he had a friend. He hadn't seen Horn since the morning at the fire tower, but he sensed his friend was still out there, watching. Footprints in the dirt, fires in the night. A long-haired archangel, in need of a bath. Now and then, Trace would hear a lone howl rise from the land and wonder whether it was a wolf or man.

He radioed Imogen near dusk. "Base, this is RRP One. Returning to Camp Three. Over."

A crackle of static. "Ten-four, Range Rider. You see anything today? Over."

Trace looked out at the landscape, vast badlands flaring beneath the falling sun. "Herd's good. Got one calf I'll put in the report for the hands to come out and check."

"That report of yours," said Imogen. "I was thinking of coming to get it in person tonight."

"You know what, I had that same idea."

They seemed to have the same idea most nights.

On the way back to camp, Trace caught a thin rill of movement along a sun-reddened slope and lifted his binoculars. The Dark Canyons leapt into view. One-Eleven leading, trotting among the rocks, and the new male beside her, limping slightly, that rusty patch down his side. Then came the wolf he liked to see most. Little Paw. Limping, too, but keeping pace. He'd grown, his body catching up with his overlarge forepaws.

One-Eleven stopped and looked right in Trace's direction. The hair prickled at the back of his neck as it always did at such moments. A creature out of storybooks and fairytales, which had gone nearly extinct at the hands of men and returned. Then the she-wolf turned and led her pack down the next swale, out of sight.

ABOUT THE MEXICAN WOLF

The Mexican wolf (*Canis lupus baileyi*), also known as the lobo, is a gray wolf subspecies that ranged the American Southwest and Northern Mexico for thousands of years before those regions carried those names. It is said to be the most "basal" of all New World wolves, and its ancestors were likely some of the first gray wolves to cross the Bering land bridge into North America.

Due to a long and concerted effort to eradicate the species, along with extensive habitat loss, the Mexican wolf was all but extinct by the mid-1970s—just fifty survivors were believed to haunt remote slivers of the old realms. A multi-agency team was assembled to save the species.

Roy T. McBride, a Texan tracker and houndsman who'd spent eleven months pursuing the infamous "outlaw wolf" Las Margaritas through the borderlands of Durango-Zacatecas, boiling his traps in oak leaves and laying them from horseback, captured five surviving Mexican wolves and delivered them to conservation centers in the United States, adding to a pair already in captivity. All wild lobos would be descendants of these wolves.

The Founders.

In 1998, wolves of the "McBride lineage" were reintroduced into remote areas of Arizona and New Mexico, released in small bands to range the lands of their ancestors. The man once trusted to hasten the destruction of the species had helped pull the animal back from the brink of extinction—along with a dedicated group of biologists, advocates, ranchers, wildlife officials, and regular citizens.

Today the Mexican wolf remains on a knife-edge of survival. No more than three hundred members of the species exist in the wild at any given time, spread across a small section of the American Southwest, and they have no shortage of enemies. There are those who still believe wolves should be eradicated from the wild, even if that would eradicate the wild itself.

AUTHOR'S NOTE

Wolvers is a work of fiction. However, I have endeavored to provide a more accurate portrayal of animal behavior than is common in literature or popular media, where apex predators—sharks, lions, tigers, wolves—are often characterized as monsters or villains, and a neglect of basic biology is all too evident. That said, I am no wolf biologist, and I leaned on the work of many authors and experts to render One-Eleven and her pack. This involved not just a great deal of reading from the canon of wolf literature—I've included a bibliography of the most influential books in my research—but going into the field where wolves still live and range, from Yellowstone National Park to the Gila Wilderness itself, and tracking down subject matter experts like Dr. Joanna Lambert, Rick McIntyre, and Dr. Doug Smith, former head of the Yellowstone Wolf Project.

As for the Gila, I tried to remain as true to the landscape as possible. Many of the locations and points of interest are real, though several place names have been changed slightly where license was taken. Still, the knowledgeable reader should be able to connect the dots easily enough and even travel to many of the sites here described.

Trace's story was influenced by the lives of famous wolvers such as Ernest Thompson Seton, Roy T. McBride, Carter Niemeyer, and even Aldo Leopold—men whose views of wolves and/or actions toward the animal changed radically after hunting them. Time and again in my research, I came across such stories of transformation. Perhaps there's something to those old werewolf tales after all . . .

Many real-life wolves inspired this novel, including Wolves 8, 21, 42, and 253 (aka Limpy) of the Yellowstone Wolf Project, as well as OR-7 (aka Journey) of Oregon; Anubis (M2520) and Hope (F2979) of the Mexican Wolf Recovery Program (both killed illegally); and several pre-reintroduction wolves such as Lobo, the Custer Wolf, Rags the Digger, Old Three Toes, and Las Margaritas—"outlaw wolves" of remarkable cunning and endurance, who succeeded in eluding trappers and hunters for years.

As for One-Eleven, she's based on no single she-wolf, but she certainly owes something to O-Six, the former alpha female of Yellowstone's Lamar Canyon pack, who was one of the most capable and beloved wolves on record. A wolf of "indomitable will," known for "her ability to bend a harsh landscape to her own ends, to do what needed to be done to provide for herself and her family every day, without fail" (Nate Blakeslee, *American Wolf*). O-Six was killed legally when she ventured outside the park in 2012—the eighth and final wolf killed in Wyoming that year.

As of 2022, at least 240 Mexican wolves have been killed in Arizona and New Mexico since reintroduction, with 131 of those killings being illegal.

ACKNOWLEDGMENTS

Thank you, first and foremost, to my family and friends who encourage and support me along the often rocky and treacherous path that is the writing life. You are my pack.

Thank you to my editor, George Witte, and my whole team at St. Martin's Press. It seems particularly rare and special in this day and age to have so many novels together—working with you all is a dream.

Thank you to my agent, Julie Stevenson—Montana native and daughter of a smoke jumper—whose boxing gloves hang ever-ready for her writers. I'm fortunate to have such a fighter in my corner.

Thank you to my great friend, collaborator, and freelance editor Jason Frye, who not only lent his insight to this manuscript, but accompanied me to Yellowstone to see wolves in the wild.

A great thanks to wolf experts (and legends) Dr. Joanna Lambert, Rick McIntyre, and Dr. Doug Smith, all of whom were kind enough to speak to me when I tracked them down with questions or just to hear their stories. Rick has more than 100,000 recorded wolf sightings and once spent 6,175 *consecutive* days going out into the field to observe wolves in Yellowstone.

A very special thanks to fire lookout Rázik Majean—a thirty-five-year veteran of the Gila—who let me take shelter on her cabin porch during a thunderstorm after I climbed the 9,970-foot summit of Bearwallow Mountain on my dirt bike. I'll never forget your kindness in showing me around the tower, and the tears in your eyes as you described your own encounter with a Mexican wolf in the wild.

Thank you to all the rangers, outfitters, and locals who shared their stories of the Gila. A special thanks goes out to Trevor Lasick of the National Park Service—a fellow son of South Georgia who gave me just the right trails to take during my first foray into the Gila.

Thank you to all of the wildlife authors and advocates whose work has been instrumental to the reintroduction of the wolf to the wild—this novel would not exist without your tireless, heroic work. I've included a bibliography that highlights some of the books that most significantly informed this novel.

Last of all, I'd like to thank everyone who reads this book and takes an interest in the wild places of our world and the creatures who inhabit them. Without your love and advocacy, the noose around our wildlands will continue to tighten.

BIBLIOGRAPHY

The New Wolves: The Return of the Mexican Wolf to the American Southwest, Rick Bass, UNKNO, 2001

The Ninemile Wolves, Rick Bass, Mariner Books, 1992

Wolfish, Erica Berry, Flatiron Books, 2023

American Wolf, Nate Blakeslee, Crown, 2017

A Woman Among Wolves: My Journey Through Forty Years of Wolf Recovery, Diane K. Boyd, Greystone Books, 2024

The Wolf in the Southwest: The Making of an Endangered Species, David E. Brown (Editor), High-Lonesome Books, 2002

The Last Stand of the Pack: Critical Edition, Arthur Carhart, University Press of Colorado, 2017

Vicious: Wolves and Men in America, Jon T. Coleman, Yale University Press, 2006

Hunt for the Shadow Wolf, Derek Gow, Chelsea Green Publishing, 2024

The Return of the Mexican Gray Wolf: Back to the Blue, Bobbie Holaday, The University of Arizona Press, 2003

A Sand County Almanac, Aldo Leopold, Oxford University Press, 1949

Of Wolves and Men, Barry Lopez, Scribner's, 1979

El Lobo: Readings on the Mexican Gray Wolf, Tom Lynch (Editor), University of Utah Press, 2005

The Mexican Wolf: A Historical Review and Observations on Its Status and Distribution, Roy T. McBride, U.S. Fish and Wildlife Service, 1980

The Alpha Wolves of Yellowstone series, Rick McIntyre, Greystone Books, 2020–2024

A Society of Wolves: National Parks and the Battle over the Wolf, Rick McIntyre, Voyageur Press, 1996

Never Cry Wolf, Farley Mowat, McClelland and Stewart, 1963

Wolfer: A Memoir, Carter Niemeyer, Bottlefly Press, 2012

Wolves and the Wolf Myth in American Literature, S. K. Robisch, University of Nevada Press, 2009

Wolf Totem, Jiang Rong, Penguin, 2008

Wild Animals I Have Known, Ernest Thompson Seton, Scribner's, 1898

Lone Wolf: Walking the Line Between Civilization and Wildness, Adam Weymouth, Crown, 2025

ABOUT THE AUTHOR

Tristan "Bam" Argo

Taylor Brown is the recipient of the Southern Book Prize, Montana Prize in Fiction, and the Ron Rash Award. His novels include *Fallen Land, The River of Kings, Gods of Howl Mountain, Pride of Eden, Wingwalkers,* and *Rednecks.* An Eagle scout and avid motorcyclist, Taylor lives in Savannah, Georgia, and has traveled extensively in the American West.